MR
01/22

THE PRICE YOU PAY FOR LOVE 3

Lock Down Publications and Ca$h
Presents

The Price You Pay for Love 3

A Novel by *Destiny Skai*

Lock Down Publications
P.O. Box 944
Stockbridge, Ga 30281

Visit our site at
www.lockdownpublications.com

Copyright 2021 by Destiny Skai
The Price You Pay for Love 3

All rights reserved. No part of this book may be reproduced in any form or by electronic or mechanical means, including information storage and retrieval systems without permission in writing from the publisher, except by a reviewer who may quote brief passages in review. Printed in the United States of America

This is a work of fiction. Names, characters, places, and incidents either are products of the author's imagination or are used fictitiously. Any similarity to actual events or locales or persons, living or dead, is entirely coincidental.

Lock Down Publications
Like our page on Facebook: Lock Down Publications @
www.facebook.com/lockdownpublications.ldp

Book interior design by: **Shawn Walker**
Edited by: **Nuel Uyi**

Stay Connected with Us!

Text **LOCKDOWN** to 22828 to stay up-to-date with new releases, sneak peaks, contests and more…
Thank you!

Submission Guideline.

Submit the first three chapters of your completed manuscript to ldpsubmissions@gmail.com, subject line: Your book's title. The manuscript must be in a .doc file and sent as an attachment. Document should be in Times New Roman, double spaced and in size 12 font. Also, provide your synopsis and full contact information. If sending multiple submissions, they must each be in a separate email.

Have a story but no way to send it electronically? You can still submit to LDP/Ca$h Presents. Send in the first three chapters, written or typed, of your completed manuscript to:

LDP: Submissions Dept
P.O. Box 944
Stockbridge, Ga 30281

DO NOT send original manuscript. Must be a duplicate.

Provide your synopsis and a cover letter containing your full contact information.

Thanks for considering LDP and Ca$h Presents.

Previously...

After being cooped up in the room for hours, it was time for me to get out of the house. Domestic had a few errands, so I made it my business to find something to do. I ended up going to my house. It was no longer home because Aaron wasn't there. No matter how much pain he'd caused me over the years, I missed him terribly.

The eerie silence in the house was crazy. It was funny how I could hear his laughter. When I looked up at the staircase, it reminded me of the time I threw objects at him during one of our spats. That made me laugh. We had a lot of good memories. Those were the ones I held on to the most.

Walking throughout the house, I ended up in the kitchen. The refrigerator was filled with old food. "I guess I can clean up while I'm here."

For an hour, I emptied the fridge and filled two trash bags. With both bags occupying my hands, I took them to the side of the house and dumped them in the large garbage pail. Walking to the front yard, I spotted the mailman approaching the door.

"Hey, Mrs. Young. How are you?"

"I'm good, Matt. How about you?"

"Just earning a living. I haven't seen you in a while."

"Yeah. It's hard to sleep in this empty house by myself."

Matt nodded. "I'm so sorry for your loss. I can only imagine the pain you're going through."

"It's been rough. I'm just taking it one day at a time."

"That's all you can do. I'll be sure to keep you in my prayers."

"I would appreciate that." It was hard to smile, but I'd managed to keep my tears at bay.

Matt handed me the mail, along with a small package. "Have a good day, Mrs. Young."

"Thanks, Matt, you do the same."

Matt had been our mailman for years. I could remember the first time he met Aaron, he was so excited. Tampa Bay was his favorite NFL team.

Flopping down on the sofa, I opened the package first. It didn't have a return address on it, so it made me wonder if it was another scandal. "God, please do not let this be another scandal for money. My heart can't take any more drama."

Inside the box were pictures from Aaron's accident. Tears fell from my eyes instantly. I had never seen the damage up close and personal. Then there was a USB. I plugged it into the smart TV and let it play. A woman was sitting on a sofa. That woman was none other than Emilia. Someone I hated with a passion.

"By the time you get this video, I'll be long gone. I know I'm the last person that you want to hear from, but there's something that I must get off my chest before it's too late. Domestic is not the man you think he is. When the two of you met, it was by some string of luck on his behalf. See, Domestic and I had a meeting. I told him to get close to you so that I could be with Aaron. He and I met when y'all were having problems after your miscarriage. We were together for a month and I fell deeply in love with him. But he didn't want to be with me. You're the only woman he wanted a future with. It hurt me because I felt like he used me." Emilia wiped her tears away and continued to tell her story.

"I purposely got pregnant by his teammate and tried to convince him that it was his baby. That didn't work either. Instead of giving up, I took another avenue and enlisted Domestic for his help. His job was to make you fall in love with him so that you would leave Aaron. Things still didn't go as planned. No matter what I did, Aaron still didn't want me. I'm telling you this so that you can get away from Domestic. He's dangerous and possessive. A while back Domestic beat and raped me at the car wash one night. All because he thought I was wearing a wire. Get away from him before he kills you. That man killed Aaron so that the two of you could be together, and I have proof of that. If I end up dead, just know that it was by the hands of Domestic. I know you hate me. Hell, I would hate me too. But I'm telling the truth. If you don't believe me, check inside Domestic's wallet and you'll see a picture of you. I gave him that so he could find and seduce you. Be careful, Foreign, and I'm sorry for everything I've done to ruin your marriage and lose your husband."

When the video came to an end, I was bawling. My heart broke all over again. Then I thought back to that photo I found in his wallet. Emilia had to be telling the truth. It made me wonder: *Was our relationship a sham all of this time?* Whatever the case may be, I was now convinced that Domestic was responsible for my husband's murder. My only question was *how?*

The news was so painful. It made me feel like I was somehow responsible for Aaron's death. Revenge led me into the arms and bed of another man. Now, I was a widow because of my irrational thinking. If I could go back in time, I would've never slept with Domestic. As I laid in our bed, I cuddled with Aaron's pillow and wept. "I'm so sorry, Aaron. All of this is my fault. I brought that man into our lives and now you're gone."

Alexis was right all along. I didn't know what to do with this information. And if Emilia knew that Domestic was guilty, why didn't she have him arrested? If Emilia loved Aaron the way she claimed she did, her ass should want justice.

Unable to fall asleep, I removed myself from the bed and left the house in a hurry. For thirty minutes, I drove around aimlessly. There was only one person that I cared to see, and that was where I went. Maurice opened the door and, as always, he was smiling.

"Wow! I'm surprised to see you here."

"I'm sorry for just dropping by unannounced, but I had no place else to go." My voice was shaky.

"It's okay. Come on in."

Maurice escorted me to the sofa. The first thing I noticed was a travel bag. "Are you going somewhere?"

"I am. I'm investigating a high profile case and I need to interview a witness. He's locked up in the Broward County Jail, so that's where I'm headed."

"Oh yeah, I forgot you're some sort of agent or detective. How long will you be away?"

"Not long. Just a day."

I didn't want to be a burden, so I stood to my feet. "I should leave. I'm not trying to be in your way."

Maurice grabbed my hand. "What if I want you in the way? Sort of like a good distraction."

This felt like déjà vu from when I first met Domestic. Repeating the cycle was negative. I was not going back down that road again. Before I moved on, I needed to close the door on Domestic. It was clear that he would kill for what he wanted.

"I'm flattered, but I'm pregnant and my life is a mess."

"I like a little mess sometimes," he laughed. "We're not perfect. My life tends to get a little messy at times, but it's nothing I can't handle."

My phone rang. The sound of the ringtone sent frightening chills all over my body. I closed my eyes and took a deep breath. He was the last person I wanted to talk to. Strangely, my legs started to feel like noodles.

Maurice grabbed me at the waist. "Are you okay?"

"Yes. I'm fine."

"Is that him calling?" During my first visit with Maurice, I gave him a little intel on my relationship with Domestic.

"Yes."

"Did he do something to you?"

"No." I paused.

Maurice looked me in my eyes, and I could see the concern in them. "Are you telling me the truth?"

"I am. He hasn't touched me."

"Okay," he exhaled deeply. Maurice hugged me and I allowed it. After all of the shit I just witnessed, I needed a damn hug.

"I just don't understand why all of this is happening to me." Out of the blue, I became an emotional mess.

"What's going on with you?"

Unable to contain my true feelings, I admitted the unthinkable out loud. "I think he killed my husband."

"What?" he seemed surprised. "Why do you think that? Has he said something to you?"

"He hasn't admitted it to me if that's what you're asking. He's just so insensitive and never has a good thing to say about Aaron. It's like he hates him, but he doesn't have a reason."

"He may not have a reason in your eyes, but in his case Domestic hates Aaron because of the things you told him. The fact that the two of you were married made it worse."

"I'm afraid of him," I sobbed. "What if I'm right?"

"How about this? Why don't you come with me? You can visit your family, while I interview my witness."

I agreed.

We arrived in Fort Lauderdale a little after nine o'clock that night. Throughout the drive, I dozed off here and there. When I was awake, we shared deep conversations about life. As we drove through the city, it brought back a lot of old memories. Once I left for college, I never returned. Now, I was back and unhappy.

"Are you nervous?" Maurice glanced at me once we stopped at a red light.

"A little. I still don't know how you were able to get her address for me."

"That's easy," he smiled. "I work for the federal government. No one can hide from me."

"Okay."

We pulled up to an immaculate mini-mansion in Plantation Acres. My nerves were all over the place, and I became sweaty underneath my breasts. "Whew! Calm down, girl. It's going to be okay."

Maurice opened the door and helped me out. "Come on, big girl."

"Gee, thanks."

"It's okay. You still look as good as the day we met."

"Flattery will get you everywhere." The way he dropped compliments made me smile. Maurice was an absolute gentleman and very sweet.

"I hope so."

"Can you stay right here until I come back? I don't want to show up on her steps with an extra guest."

"Sure."

I took a deep breath and walked up to the house. From the door, I could hear children playing. That was the way I wanted my house to sound. My hands shook as I pressed down on the doorbell. A moment later the door swung open. Needless to say, this woman was not happy to see me.

"I know damn well you not on my porch." Blacque Barbee stood there with her hands on her hips. "You might as well take whatever fourteen-carat gold horse and carriage you rode on and get the fuck off my property?"

"Please, I need your help."

"No, the hell you don't," she snapped.

Corey must've heard the commotion. He hit the corner with a gun in his hand. "Bae, who you talking to?"

"Nobody. She was just leaving." Blacque Barbee folded her arms and huffed.

"Foreign?" Corey squinted. "Is that you?"

"Yes."

"Bae, why won't you let her in?" Corey slipped his gun into his pocket.

"Miss Sadity is not welcomed here. That's why."

Putting my pride to the side, I pleaded my case. "Please B, don't do this to me. I have no one else to turn to and if I go back home, I'm going to die."

"Not my problem, goodbye." Blacque Barbee pushed the door, but Corey caught it.

"Bae, stop. This is your family."

"I don't know her."

"What's going on?" Corey asked. I could see a great deal of genuine concern in his eyes.

"He's going to kill me," I cried.

Chapter 1

Domestic

The news of becoming a grandfather was finally starting to settle in. It wasn't what I was expecting. The life I laid out for my son was greater than him being a teenage father. That was my reality, and I wanted so much more for DP. When I became a young father, I didn't have any goals of going to college. I was raised amongst drug dealers and killers. And once my mother met Hugo, we instantly became a part of a mob boss family. It was a major play in my book.

After the birth of DP, I did everything to make sure he was taken care of. It didn't matter what type of crimes I committed. But I promised myself that his life would be easier than mine. As a father, I kept my promise and provided DP with all of his wants and needs. My goal was to get him into an Ivy League college. I wanted him to have the life I dreamed of at his age.

Walking out of my room, I stopped in front of DP's door. "Y'all ready?"

DP seemed like he was off in la-la land. "Yeah," he replied softly.

"Let's go."

The ride to Cheyenne's house was quiet. It was fine by me because I needed time to think. I didn't know how the meeting with her mom was going to go, but I was damn sure about to find out.

Cheyenne lived in the neighborhood I grew up in. The second I pulled in, all of my childhood memories bombarded my thinking. My chest tightened when I drove past our old house. It was the spot where I suffered a lot of ass whoopings from my mother. That was the most traumatic time of my life, and I hate every moment of it. I couldn't wait until I was old enough to get away from Veronica.

Cheyenne unlocked the door and let us in. Her mother was laid out across the living room, talking loud and laughing. I walked in and made myself comfortable on the sofa. Teresa smiled when she saw me.

"Girl, let me call you back. A fine piece of male specimen just walked up in here," she giggled and hung up the phone. "Well, how are you doing, tall and sexy?"

"I'm good," I chuckled. Teresa was the flirty type and quite hilarious. "How are you doing?"

Teresa sat up and crossed her legs. She made sure to show a little thigh. "Better now that I see you."

"Oh my God! Ma, stop. You are so embarrassing," Cheyenne screeched.

"Girl, hush. Ain't nobody embarrassing you." Teresa looked at DP and smiled. "Hey, son. How are you doing?"

"I'm good, ma." DP and Cheyenne sat down beside each other.

"So, what is this meeting all about, Mr. Payne?"

"The kids have something they want to tell you." I wanted Cheyenne to be the one to reveal her condition to her mother.

Teresa huffed and rolled her eyes. "What is it, Cheyenne? What have you gotten yourself into? You knocked up?"

Cheyenne's right leg started to shake. DP put his arm over her shoulder to calm her down. She held her head down. "Yes," she mumbled.

"Girl, speak up. I can't hear you through the mumbles," Teresa shouted.

Cheyenne held her head up. "I'm pregnant."

Teresa leaned back against the sofa. "Great! Just what I wanted to hear. You being pregnant. Another damn mouth to feed. Didn't I tell your ass to take those birth control pills? And what happened to condoms, DP? Y'all scared of condoms?"

"It wasn't like that," he replied.

"Do y'all know what y'all just did?"

Now, it was time for me to intervene. "Take it easy, Teresa. The damage is already done. At this point, we just need to figure out what's next."

"I don't know what's next. I'm a single parent taking care of her ass already and now she trying to bring in another mouth to feed. This is bull-shit." Teresa's reaction was exactly what I thought it would be.

Leaning forward in my seat, I folded my hands. "So, what is it that you would like for them to do? Have an abortion?"

"That's not a bad idea."

"Why don't we ask them what they want to do?" I insisted.

"Why? They ain't got no damn money."

"It's their life and future. Casey had DP at sixteen and I was nineteen. We weren't ready to be parents, but we made it work. And I don't want to be the reason they live life with regrets. So, in my honest opinion, it's their decision. At the end of the day, I don't believe in abortions and apparently, your mother didn't either."

"That was then. This is now." Teresa stood up with an attitude. "I need a drink. Do you want one?"

"No, thanks." After Teresa left the room, I focused on the kids and their opinions. "What is it that y'all want to do?"

"We want to keep it," DP spoke for both of them.

I looked from him to Cheyenne. She nodded. I looked at DP again. "Son, are you really sure about this?"

"Yeah, dad. We talked about it last night and decided that we'll get jobs after school. I know it won't be easy, but I promise I won't slip in my studies."

Teresa came back sipping on a beer. "I don't hear your plan, Cheyenne. Do you have a plan? Or do you expect DP to do everything?"

"I have a plan." Cheyenne rolled her eyes. "I'm going to finish school and go to college."

"Well, I would love to see that." Teresa flopped down on the sofa, and turned up the can of that cheap ass two-eleven beer.

"Teresa, I know you're upset, but we have to be their biggest supporters. They're kids. They can't do this by themselves."

Teresa held her hand up and surrendered. "Okay, okay, fine. We'll get through this together as a family."

"Thank you," I said sincerely. Somehow I knew that I would be responsible financially, but I left it alone. Time would tell.

"So much for me and you getting together." Teresa laughed hysterically. "Thanks, Cheyenne."

I couldn't help but laugh at her humor. "Teresa, your ass is crazy. We're in-laws now."

"Yeah, I see." Teresa giggled. "Does this mean y'all getting married too?"

"We will eventually," DP replied.

"Okay. I guess we'll just prepare for this baby." Teresa was finally calm.

Now that the family meeting was over, I took my ass home for the rest of the day. When I pulled up in the driveway, Foreign's car wasn't there, so I called her. The phone went to voicemail. Just as I was calling her back, she called me.

"What's up, baby? Where are you?"

"I'm at my parents' house."

"When are you coming home?"

"I'm not," she replied.

"What? What do you mean you're not coming home?" I needed answers because I was two seconds from going the fuck off. My dick was hard, and I wanted some pussy.

"Did you have something to do with Aaron's death?"

Her question hit me in the chest like a defibrillator. "Is that a serious question? Why the fuck are you asking me a question like this?"

Foreign grunted loudly through the receiver and screamed. "Just answer my damn question."

"No. I didn't have shit to do with his accident and you know that." The lie rolled smoothly off my tongue, like water off a duck's ass.

"Why are you lying? I know you had something to do with him dying."

"No. I didn't."

Foreign was sobbing. "Yes, you did and I know it."

Someone had been talking to her, and I needed to know who the fuck was in her ear. "Who have you been talking to?"

"Emilia. She told me everything, Domestic. So you can stop lying now."

"You gon' believe that lying ass bitch? Isn't she the same bitch that was fucking your husband?"

"I guess she's lying about the deal to seduce me. You know, make me fall in love with you so that she could get with Aaron."

"That bitch is fucking lying, babe. I swear!"

"So tell me this, Domestic. Why do you have a photo of me in your wallet? Explain that to me."

Damn, that bitch did talk to my lady. See, that's why Emilia's ass is in the dirt with worms now because she greedy and talks too damn much. "Foreign, baby, just come home please and we can talk about it."

"Talk! Talk about what, Domestic? How you've been manipulating me this whole time? You've never loved me. All of this shit was just a sham."

"Please baby, I'm begging you. Just come home and we can talk about this."

"No. I'm not coming there until you tell me the truth."

"I'm telling you the truth!" The fact that she didn't trust me was making me crazy. There wasn't any proof I did anything. "And you need to come home now."

"Bye, Domestic."

"I'm not playing with you, Foreign. Come home now before you regret it!"

"I already do. Goodbye!"

Foreign hung up the phone. I tried to call her back, but she sent me to the damn voicemail.

Foreign…

"Was that him?" Maurice put his hand on my shoulder.

"Yes," I nodded and wiped my tears. "What am I going to do?"

"We have to figure out a plan to get you out of this situation."

Corey walked into the kitchen. Blacque Barbee was right behind him. "Is everything okay in here?"

"No. She needs to stay here for a while. At least until I can get her out of this situation."

"Stay where?" Barbee folded her arms across her chest. She hated me with a passion, and I didn't understand why. True enough, my father didn't want me to hang around her, but I was a child. What the hell was I supposed to do, disobey my father?

"B, stop it. She's your cousin. Don't do that." Corey tried to reason with her.

"Whatever!"

"Her life is in danger. Won't you feel bad if something happened to your blood relative?"

"Nope. My sister was killed and I don't remember Miss. Sadity being by my side." Barbee snapped on him and left.

Corey shook his head. "I'm sorry. She can be a bit stubborn at times."

"It's okay. You don't have to apologize. She has a right to be upset," I sadly admitted.

"How so?" Corey asked.

"When we were younger, B and I used to be so close. When she turned to the streets, my father didn't want me around her. At that age, I didn't have a choice. So, I did what my father wanted me to do, and that was to stay away from my favorite cousin." My confession allowed me to become emotional. "I admired her. I always wanted to be strong and opinionated like her, but my father stopped me in my tracks. He threatened to leave me desolate, so I had no choice but to separate myself. I was only a child."

"I get it. Believe me, I do. She still shouldn't treat you like that. You can stay here tonight. I'll talk to her."

I was so relieved to know that he was willing to help me. "Thank you."

"You're welcome."

"I can leave her here?" Maurice asked.

"Of course."

"Thanks." They dapped each other up, and Maurice hugged me tightly before he left.

"Come on. Let me show you to the guest bedroom."

The guest bedroom was absolutely beautiful. It was filled with lilac colors. One of my favorites. "Thank you, Corey. I really appreciate your help."

"Any relatives of my baby, are relatives of mine."

He had a beautiful smile and perfect white teeth. "I appreciate you so much. You have no idea about the things I've gone through."

"I can only imagine, but get some sleep. Don't worry about B. I'll take care of her."

"Thanks, Corey. I appreciate your help."

The moment I was alone, I cried like a baby. If the truth came out that Aaron's death was not an accident, the backlash was going to destroy me. In no way, shape or form was I involved, but the media was going to have a field day with this one.

Blacque Barbee...

Foreign's presence had me vexed. Out of all people why in the fuck would she come to my house. Secondly, how the fuck did she know where I lived? I didn't give two fucks about who she was running from. The bottom line was, I didn't want any of the bullshit around me.

Corey walked into the bedroom and closed the door. He came over to the bed and sat down beside me. "Bae, why you so damn mean?"

I rolled my neck in his direction. "Trust me, that was not mean. Her ass was lucky that's all she got from me."

Corey sighed and grabbed my hand. "In this world, all we have is family. She told me what happened between the two of you."

Sucking my teeth, I pulled my hand away. "Whose side are you on?"

"It's not about sides. All I'm saying is that she's in deep with some dude and needs to hide out for a while." Corey grabbed my hand again. "B, I know you better than you know yourself. You have a heart of gold. And you know first-hand about being abused by a man."

It was just like him to bring up my past with Rich. That happened so long ago, and I wanted that shit to stay in the past. The shit with Rich was the reason I almost lost Corey and my freedom.

"You're right. I do know first-hand, but that's not my problem. Whatever mess she got herself into, she needs to get herself out of. Foreign has been a mess since that boy started cheating on her, and I don't want any parts of that bad publicity."

Corey sighed and stroked his jaw bone. "Just stop 'cause that's ridiculous. You bringing up old shit from when y'all were kids. At the end of the day, she's your family."

"That's easy for you to say since it's not about you and your family." This nigga was supposed to be on my side, right or wrong, so I snapped. "Well, damn, whose side you on? 'Cause I could've sworn you was fucking me at night."

"You're right." Corey sat down beside me, grabbed my hand, and kissed it. "All I'm saying is, it doesn't hurt to help. Be the bigger person for me, please."

Swinging my legs, I pouted. "Why I gotta be the bigger person? I don't want to."

Corey laughed and shook his head. "Look at my big baby acting like our kids."

No matter how mad I was with Corey, he could always make me laugh. "They had to get it from somewhere," I agreed.

"I'm glad you know." Corey stood up. "I'm going to shower. Are you joining me?"

"Sure," I smirked with nasty thoughts on my mind. Shower sex would be a great way to blow off steam and the hostility I was feeling.

Chapter 2

Veronica

My heels click-clacked against the concrete, as I sashayed to the front door. Hugo opened the door, and we stepped inside. There weren't too many people present. Just the ones who lived at the residence. Thank God for that! I was not in the mood to be bothered with the ghetto folks. Margo was sitting on the sofa, crying and holding a picture frame.

"I came as soon as I heard the news. I'm so sorry for your loss." I took a seat beside Margo and hugged her tight. "I'm here for you."

"They killed my baby," she sobbed.

"Who?" I questioned while glancing up at Hugo.

"I don't know. They didn't say."

"What happened?" Hugo asked.

"They beat my baby so bad and shot him. I don't think I can have an open casket because of the bastard responsible for it." Margo sniffled. "They found his body on the side of the highway. They discarded him like trash." She looked at Teddy's photo that she was holding, and put her hand on his face. "I won't rest until they find out who's responsible for killing you."

I wore a doleful look as I said: "I'm so sorry, Margo. I am. Whatever you need, we're here for you. After all, we're family at the end of the day."

Margo was visibly shaken by the ordeal. "I'm so lost. How will I find the strength to handle his arrangements. Why me, God? Why my family?" she screamed.

"Hey. Hey." I rubbed her shoulders. "You have me, and I'll make sure everything is handled."

Margo rocked back and forth. "I didn't have any life insurance on him."

"Don't you worry about that. Hugo and I will pay for everything. You just stay strong. When you're ready, we can go down to the funeral home to pick out a casket and plan the services."

Margo wiped her eyes. "You'll do that for me?"

I smiled and nodded. "Of course I will. Teddy was like a nephew to me."

"Thank you, Veronica. I don't know how I'll ever repay you."

"You don't have to thank me. Like I said," I paused, mustering up the fakest empathetic smile, "we're family."

Teddy stole from me and threatened our organization by talking to the law. He had to be dealt with. I didn't feel an ounce of sympathy on the matter at hand. If Margo would've raised him right in the first place, I wouldn't have had to kill him in the second place and I wouldn't be paying for a funeral in the third place. How I saw it, we were even.

After sitting with Margo for two agonizing hours, the husband and I said our goodbyes, and went back to our residence. Hugo looked at me and chuckled. "Just when I thought you couldn't be any more wicked than you already are."

"You know me. I'm full of surprises." I removed my coat and tossed it onto the bed. "That's one of the reasons you married me."

"Of course it is, darling. There's no room for a weak woman on my arm. Not with the type of business I'm into."

There was a knock on the bedroom door. "Who is it?"

"Demetri."

"I'm about to take a shower." Hugo walked towards the master bathroom.

"Come in," I shouted.

Demetri walked in and closed the door behind him. "Pops home?"

"He's in the shower."

Demetri's eyes bounced around the room. "How did everything go at Margo's house?"

"There was a lot of hooting and hollering. I could've sworn I heard the violins playing."

Demetri folded his hands. "Well, she did just lose her son. Have a little compassion for your friend."

"Well, if my friend's son wasn't a thief or a snitch, none of this would've happened. He knew the consequences of his actions and disregarded it."

"I know that, but you don't have to be so cold-hearted." I could tell Demetri was agitated by the way he aggressively rubbed his face.

"Darling, I've been cold-hearted all my life. Why should I stop now?"

"Mother, it's an ugly trait. You're too beautiful for that. Besides, not all change is bad."

"Son, I'm too old for change." I placed my hand on the side of his face. "This is who I am and I'm going to be this way until the day I die."

"I guess you don't believe in a higher power?"

Moving my hand from his cheek, I smiled. "The way I see it all saints aren't going to heaven, and all sinners aren't going to hell. Wherever I go after this life really doesn't matter to me. I've done too much bad shit to look forward to going to heaven."

Demetri shook his head from side to side. "I love you, mama. Goodnight."

"I love you too, son. Goodnight."

Foreign...

"Stop! Stop!" I fought back as if my life depended on it. "Domestic, please don't kill me." I clawed at his face. My breathing was hazy. Domestic's grip on my neck grew tighter by the second.

"If I can't have you no one will," he shouted with tears in his eyes.

"What about the baby?" I managed to muffle through shallow breaths.

"There's no family without you in it. You think I want to co-parent with you?"

By any means necessary I was determined to get free. "Domestic, I love you. I do. Please stop," I begged.

Surprisingly, he released me. My lungs were happy to finally receive fresh air. Domestic cried and walked to the dresser. I rolled on my side to catch my breath. When I looked up, Domestic was holding a gun. It was pointed in my direction. Suddenly, I held my breath.

"Domestic, please don't do this," I cried.

"I have to do this." He wiped the tears from his eyes. The gun remained clutched tightly in his hand. "There's no me without you."

"Please," I sat up so he could see my stomach. Gently rubbing it, I looked into his eyes. "Think of our baby."

"I'm sorry." Domestic squeezed the trigger, and all I heard was a loud pop. When I looked down, my stomach was covered in blood. Then I screamed to the top of my lungs.

"Foreign, Foreign." I felt someone shaking me. When I opened my eyes, Blacque Barbee was sitting on the bed beside me. "Wake up. You were having a bad dream."

Sweat rolled down my face. I used my hand to wipe it away.

"That was some dream you were having." Blacque Barbee rubbed my stomach. "Are the two of you okay?"

"Yes," I nodded.

Blacque Barbee smiled at me for the first time since I arrived on her doorstep like a runaway teen. "I made breakfast. You should come down and have some."

"I will," I smiled back.

Barbee patted my leg and stood up. "There are extra toothbrushes, towels, and washcloths in the bathroom closet. Hurry up and come down before it gets cold."

"Hey B."

"What's up?"

Swinging my legs around, I placed my feet on the floor. "Thanks for your hospitality. I know this was hard for you. For what it's worth, I never wanted to sever the bond we shared when we were younger. That was all on my father. I just wish I had the backbone to speak my truth and tell him the way I truly felt." A few tears dropped from my eyes. "I used to envy the way you made your own decisions. You did whatever you wanted to do and didn't care what anyone thought. Not even your father. If I was more like you, I wouldn't be in this situation right now. No one would be able to take advantage of me, or treat me like shit."

"There's one thing I learned in life. People will only do what you allow them to get away with. With that being said, it's never too late to take your power back. Stand on your own two feet. Don't let a motherfucker use you or treat you any kind of way."

"I wish it was that simple for me," I sighed with shame.

Barbee snickered. "Girl, you from Lauderdale. The hood. Stop acting like you from Beverly Hills."

"See, that's what I'm saying. I wish I was more like you. How did you get that way?" I desperately wanted to know.

"Get dressed and come downstairs, and I'll tell you all about it."

"Okay."

The steam from the shower fogged the bathroom and mirrors. Using my left hand, I wiped away the dew and stared at myself. The woman looking back at me was not who I wanted to become. She was damaged and broken beyond repair. I could remember standing in the mirror at home, crying about Aaron's infidelity. It all felt like a badass recurring dream. For the life of me, I couldn't fathom how my beautiful life turned out to be so ugly.

Tears flooded my cheeks. Domestic was supposed to be my savior. The new man I wanted to marry and have my child with. Within a matter of months, he'd managed to do a complete three hundred and sixty-degree turn. Domestic started as prince charming. Slowly, he revealed his true colors. The real-life definition of a wolf in sheep's clothing.

Sadly, I still loved Domestic.

Finally sucking up my emotions, I pulled myself together, got dressed, and headed downstairs to see what was on the menu. The kitchen table was loaded with a variety of foods and fresh fruit. In particular, the omelets and strawberries caught my eye. Barbee and Corey were seated at the table, eating with the kids.

"Good morning," I smiled cheerfully.

"Good morning. How did you sleep?" Corey inquired while slicing his omelet with a knife.

"I slept well. That mattress felt like a little piece of heaven." Once I grabbed a plate from the granite counter, I sat down and fixed my plate.

Breakfast was fairly quiet. Here and there Corey and Barbee would converse. When they weren't talking, the happy couple spent a lot of time making googly eyes at each other. Any fool with eyes could see they were truly in love. It made me slightly jealous. The way Corey looked at Barbee was confirmation that he didn't have eyes for anyone but her. Who could blame him? She was beautiful, and her Hershey skin was flawless. That was the type of love I desperately craved.

I married the love of my life, and I couldn't remember the last time Aaron looked at me that way. Now there was Domestic. I couldn't recall a time that he didn't look at me that way. The way he cared for me was a straight obsession. It made me question if he truly loved me, or if I was only his prized possession. Someone Domestic could control, being that he was much older than me.

Corey set his fork down and wiped his mouth with the cloth napkin. Then he looked at his watch. I could tell it was expensive, by the way it sparkled from a distance. "Bae, breakfast was all that as usual."

"Thanks, baby," Barbee smiled.

"CJ and Charli, let's go. It's time for school."

"I don't wanna go," CJ pouted and kicked his feet. He was so handsome, looking just like his daddy.

"Stop being a baby, CJ and come on," Charli shouted with sass, as she hopped from her seat and grabbed him by the arm. "Let's go, boy!"

All I could do was laugh.

"Charli, don't be so rough with him," Barbee pleaded while standing up.

"Stop, stupid girl," CJ screamed. Then he slapped Charli across the face. Charli screamed and pushed him on the floor.

Corey quickly jumped in and grabbed CJ's arm before he could reach his sister. "That's enough. Stop hitting your sister."

"She hit me first," CJ huffed. His chest rose up and down.

"She's a girl. Remember what I told you about hitting girls?"

CJ nodded.

"No. Use your words. Tell me what I said." Corey kneeled to meet him at eye level.

CJ was bashful when he responded. "I'm not supposed to hit girls and umm," he paused and played with his fingers, "I have a mama and sister."

"And what else?"

"I have to be my sister's protector."

"Very good. Now give me a fist bump." Corey then pulled Charli close to him. "Babygirl, this is your big brother and I don't want the two of you fighting."

Innocently, she nodded. "Okay, daddy."

"Now, give each other a hug." Corey was such a good father, from what I could see.

There wasn't a doubt in my mind that Domestic wouldn't be a great father. The problem was, he was a terrible boyfriend and I was certain he would be an awful husband. Barbee kissed the kids and Corey before they walked out the door. It was just she and I.

Barbee sat and watched me for a few seconds before parting her lips. "So, what's going on with you and this man you running from? And how did you find me?"

Slowly, I exhaled before spilling my guts for thirty minutes. I shared every detail of my life with my first cousin. Honestly, it felt good to relieve some of that pinned-up anger and frustration that consumed my mind and soul. Shaking my head, I wiped away my tears. "I just don't know what to do."

"Well, the first thing you need to do after you beat his ass is, move back into your own house." Barbee took a sip of her orange juice, and set the glass back on the table. "That relationship is toxic as hell. If you don't leave him now your ass is going to end up on Fatal Attraction."

"That's not funny," I replied.

"Who's laughing? Not I." Barbee leaned back in her seat. "I'm so serious. You better watch that show. You'll see what I'm talking about."

"What should I do?"

"I just told you to leave him. You're acting like you have to be with him just because you having his baby. There is a thing called co-parenting."

"I know that, but he keeps saying he refuses to let me go." This situation was new to me, and I didn't have a clue about what to do.

"Well, if he won't leave you alone voluntarily, then you need to get a restraining order on his ass."

"What is a piece of paper supposed to do? Tell him not to come around?"

Barbee shook her head slowly. A slight grin graced her full lips. "No, sis. You're missing the purpose of the restraining order."

Barbee had me confused. I was certain I knew the purpose. My main concern was Domestic ignoring the terms of the order. Domestic wasn't the type of man to back down from a challenge. Therefore, I knew I would have a major issue on my hands if I took this route. If I wanted a clean escape, I would need an army behind me.

"Well, please enlighten me. Apparently, I'm missing something." I frowned.

"Little cousin, let me explain something to you," she smiled.

"Please do," I giggled for the first time.

"Oh, I got you." B laughed and placed her elbows on the table. "Now that piece of paper is to inform law enforcement that your significant other is abusive towards you. With that being a known factor, that gives you the right to defend yourself by any means necessary."

My eyes never left her lips.

"This is where the fun comes in at." A devious smile crept across her face. "Do you have a gun?"

"No." I didn't know the first thing about a gun, let alone owning a gun.

Barbee's eyebrow slanted downwards. "So you mean to tell me that this man was a millionaire, living in a big ass mansion, his face was plastered on damn near every sports channel and y'all didn't own a damn gun for protection?"

"Stuff like that doesn't happen in our neighborhood," I stated with conviction.

"See, that's that crazy white folks shit. Everybody think they safe until sweet little Peter from boyscouts, who sold the cookies once a year, starts killing animals and then the neighbors because he has to fund his meth habit."

"Oh my God! Really, B?" I laughed loud and heartily. A few tears pricked my eyes. "Why are you like this?"

"No. The question is, why aren't you like this?" Blacque Barbee pointed her finger at me. "See, this is what happens when you shield your kids from their very own neighborhood. If your parents didn't keep you away from us, you wouldn't be going through none of this bullshit right now. That nigga would know not to play with you."

Blacque Barbee was right. All the facts she stated were things I had been thinking all along. "So what should I do? I can't face him."

"You have to face him. I mean you are pregnant with his child," she said while bringing me back to reality.

The depressing sigh from my lungs were heavy. "I don't want to," I pouted. "Why does my life have to be so complicated?" That was the question that played throughout my mind on a daily basis.

"Sorry, cuz, but there's no way around it. You have to find your voice. Stop letting the men in your life dictate your actions." Blacque Barbee paused for a few seconds. "That includes your father too."

Once again she was right. When it boiled down to men, I was soft. I allowed them to strip me of my truth as an independent woman. Today, all of that was going to stop and Blacque Barbee was going to help me with my transition.

"You're right," I agreed. "I'm ready to take control of my life. Can you help me with that?"

"Of course I can. Now finish your breakfast. We have a lot to do." Blacque Barbee's smirk had me skeptical. There was no telling what she was about to have me doing.

Chapter 3

Domestic

Sliding soft in the Maserati, I played slow jams all the way to work. R. Kelly's song—"For You"—had me thinking about Foreign and the way I've been treating her. That shit wasn't right. Nor did she deserve it. The fucked up part about the situation is her being pregnant with my child. All of that flew out the window when anger boiled deep in my soul.

Nodding, I thought back to when I spent my Saturdays in an anger management class. Somehow, it appeared that I needed to return and tackle my anger head on. My cellphone wasn't far from reach. I grabbed it and called Foreign.

"Come on, baby, pick up for me. Please!" The phone rang constantly until the voicemail spoke to me.

Normally, I would blow her up, but I decided to take a more subtle approach. The goal was to bring Foreign back, not push her away. So, I left her a message.

"Foreign baby, I know I'm the last person you want to hear from, but I need to talk to you. First, I want to apologize from the bottom of my heart for the way I've been treating you. What I did to you was wrong. You deserve more than what I've been giving you. Just come back to me, baby, and I promise that things will go back to the way things were. I'm nothing without you and my unborn child. Foreign, if you don't come back to me, you might as well put a gun to my head and pull the trigger. I can't live without you. I love you, Foreign. Give me another chance to make things right."

After pouring my heart out to a damn recording, it made me feel a little bit better. All I had to do was, sit back and hope Foreign felt enough love in her heart to forgive me. Allow me to right my wrongs. A king was nothing without his queen. And this king was hurting.

My exit crept up quickly. Minutes later, I was at my establishment with a smile on my face. It was going to be a good day, and I could feel that shit. The amount of customers present early in the morning was an added bonus. That equaled more money. As usual, Tracy was sitting behind the counter, sucking on a lollipop and doing nothing. The way she flicked her tongue around the candy made my dick jump.

"That blowpop making me jealous right now," I smirked.

Tracy grinned. She twirled the lollipop in a circular motion before popping it out of her mouth. "I bet it is, but for a small fee all of that could change."

The offer was tempting, but I had high hopes that Foreign's lips would be wrapped around it soon. "How about you do the job that I'm already paying you for!"

"Ha ha! That's cute." Tracy rolled her eyes and put the blowpop back into her mouth.

"Yeah, I know. Are we low on supplies?"

"I'm not sure, but I can check the closet."

"That would be nice."

Tracy cut her eyes. "Where is Foreign? She normally handles that."

"She's been sick a lot lately, so it will be a while before she returns." That was another wish of mine.

"Well, tell her that I asked about her." Tracy smiled.

"Yeah, I'll do that. In the meantime go do what I asked you to do."

"Yes sir. Boss, I'm on it."

"Don't be facetious. And hold my calls."

"Will do."

Backing away from the counter, I headed to my office. I had a shitload of work to do, and I didn't need any interruptions. Foreign left me in a small jam when I made her stay home. She had me accustomed to the extra help around the office. One hour passed before there was a knock on the door. Almost immediately, the door opened without me saying a word. Carlos walked in with Tracy on his heels.

"I'm sorry, Domestic. I told him you were busy."

"It's okay, Tracy. Go back to work." I stood up and fixed my jacket. "Close the door behind you."

When Tracy left the room, I eyed Carlos. He had a strange look in his eyes. I knew whatever it was couldn't be good. "What's the problem? And why are you barging into my office?"

"We have a problem?" he blurted out.

"And what would that be?"

"Emilia's missing."

"That was her plan, right? To go away and start fresh." I leaned against my desk and folded my arms. "So, how is that a *we* problem?"

"No. It's been days and our father hasn't heard from her. That's not like Emilia at all."

"Have you tried calling her?" I quizzed, knowing the whole truth.

"Of course I did. You think I'm stupid or something? Her phone is going straight to the voicemail."

"Let me try. Maybe she blocked your number." I grabbed my phone and called. It went straight to the voicemail.

"She has no reason to block me."

"You're right. It's going straight to the voicemail."

"I told you that." Carlos seemed agitated.

"Have you tried to contact the airlines to see if she boarded the flight?"

"No. I haven't tried that."

"Well, call them. If she boarded, then that means she doesn't want to be bothered. You of all people should know how your sister is."

Carlos exhaled and grabbed the bridge of his nose. "And if she didn't?"

"Then we need to see where the hell she disappeared to."

Carlos looked at me with a blank stare for several seconds before parting his lips. "Domestic, did you do something to my sister? The two of you were not on the best of terms a week ago."

It took everything in me to keep from snapping, but I kept my composure. True enough, he hit the nail on the head, but that didn't give him the right to accuse me. "Despite the fact your sister can be a true bitch, I wouldn't hurt her. Me and you are like brothers. I wouldn't do that to you."

"You right, man. My bad, bro. Pops got me tripping."

"It's all good, bro." We G-hugged.

"Thanks, bro. I'm about to go look into this. I'll keep you updated on what I find out."

"I'm here for you. Come on. I'll walk you out." Carlos and I made our way to the Mustang. Judging by the look on his face, I could tell he still had his doubts. That wasn't good on my end. I had to remove all doubt. "Listen, a friend of mine works in the precinct I'll have him track Emilia's phone to see if we could get a hit. You're not in this alone. I'm going to help you find your sister."

"I appreciate." Carlos froze as he stared towards the road. I turned my head to see what he was looking at.

Shawn…

On our way through the city, we made it our business to slide by Domestic's carwash. I still had it out for that nigga because of the way he did

Casey. That shit ate me up inside, knowing that I hadn't protected her to the best of my ability.

Just as we approached the building, Tim sat up with a questionable look on his face. "That's the muthafucka that killed Craig."

"What? Are you sure?" I questioned, just to be sure.

"Hell yeah. I'll never forget that car." Tim pulled his gun from underneath the seat and sat it on his lap. "Creep through the parking lot. I'm'about to let this nigga have it. And he out here with Casey's fuck ass baby daddy. You can't tell me that nigga ain't set this shit up for that stunt we pulled."

That was all I needed to hear to get me on board for a one eighty-seven. "Kill that muthafucka and that fifty cent-looking ass nigga," I shouted while cruising through the parking lot unnoticed. "He took our brother. Now he gotta pay."

"Fuck yeah, lil' bro. Get close to these clown ass niggas." Tim lowered the window, and pointed his burner out the window. That was when all hell broke loose. Squeezing the trigger, Tim busted multiple rounds. Domestic and the Spanish nigga that killed our brother ran and ducked beside the Mustang. The door to the Mustang opened, and Tim fired more shots. Not even a second later, an exchange of bullets came our way. It was like everything moved in slow motion from that point on.

The only person on my mind was my brother Craig. His life was taken by the nigga Domestic was talking to. He was responsible, and that nigga had to die for that shit. DP was gon' have to live life without his father. That nigga had to go.

Tim fired shots until his clip was empty. He dropped the gun on the floor. "Hit it, bruh. Get us out of here."

"Say less." My foot smashed down hard on the pedal, and the tires screeched as we fled the scene.

For the next minute or so, I kept my eyes on the rearview mirror. I needed to be sure that we weren't being followed.

"You think the nigga dead?" I asked.

"Shit! Ion know, bruh, but we'll find out soon enough. I do know for a fact I hit them niggas though. One thing about me is that I barely miss. If those niggas still alive, an angel was standing there with 'em."

"I know one thing—If these niggas ain't dead, we gotta hit 'em again. After that we gotta get the fuck outta Tampa."

"I'm with that, bruh. A nigga ain't trying to go to prison. Fuck all that."

"You have another place that we can lay low? The house too hot right now."

"Hell yeah. Hit the highway."

I had a feeling that I knew exactly where we were going.

Domestic…

The vehicle was all too familiar to me. I knew right off the bat that it was Casey's punk ass boyfriend and his brother. Sitting up, I put my back against the car. Blood gushed from my shoulder.

"That fuck nigga got me." When I looked up, Carlos was standing over me.

"Come on, bruh. Let me help you inside 'cause I gotta go. I can't be here when the law arrives."

"Yeah, I know." I huffed in pain.

"You know who that was, right?"

"One of the niggas I hired you to hit." Scrambling to my feet, I held my shoulder blade. Blood covered my hands. "Go 'head and get out of here. I'll hit you up later."

"A'ight, bruh. Take it easy. Call me if you need me."

"Gotchu."

Slowly, I limped to the entrance. Tracy was crying and screaming. My customers and other employees stood by in utter shock.

Tracy grabbed me by the waist. "Domestic, are you okay? I called the police."

I draped my arm across her shoulder. "Good. I'm fine. Just get me inside so I can sit down."

Once inside, Tracy escorted me to a chair. Then she grabbed a few towels and pressed them against my open wound. It felt like I was about to pass out. Apparently, I did because the next time I opened my eyes, I was lying on a stretcher in the ambulance. All I could hear was a bunch of medical terminology and the words, "He's awake."

"Sir, can you tell me who did this to you?" the paramedic asked.

"Nah. It all happened so fast."

Where I came from we didn't believe in snitching. My code of honor belonged to the streets. I believed in street justice. Not justice handed down by a racist judge that didn't feel my life was valuable enough for a death sentence. I shook my head by way of saying *no*, and closed my eyes. Case closed. Those niggas would feel my wrath as soon as my shoulder was straight.

Chapter 4

Foreign

One Hour Ago

"Where are we going?" I asked as Blacque Barbee drove us through the streets of Broward County.

"You'll see when we get there." That was all she said during the thirty-minute drive.

"Is that all you're going to say until we arrive?" She had me anxious as hell.

"Yep. All you need to know is that you and your baby will be safe. That's all that matters."

It wasn't that I didn't trust her or that I was afraid. I just didn't like surprises, but I didn't have a say in the situation. "You're right. I'll just be quiet until we get there."

"Thank you. That's what passengers normally do anyway."

Nodding, I agreed. Out of boredom, I decided to check my messages. It wasn't a surprise that one of them was from Domestic.

"Foreign baby, I know I'm the last person you want to hear from, but I need to talk to you. First, I want to apologize from the bottom of my heart for the way I've been treating you. What I did to you was wrong. You deserve more than what I've been giving you. Just come back to me, baby, and I promise that things will go back to the way things were. I'm nothing without you and my unborn child. Foreign, if you don't come back to me, you might as well put a gun to my head and pull the trigger. I can't live without you. I love you, Foreign. Give me another chance to make things right."

He sounded like a lovesick puppy. Too bad he didn't know how to treat me; therefore, I didn't feel bad.

Blacque Barbee pulled up to a warehouse east of the city. Seeing that area brought back so many memories from when I was a teenager. That was before my father decided I should be nowhere near the hood. Boy, was he wrong.

"We're here. Come on." Blacque Barbee shut off the engine and got out of the car. I unbuckled my seatbelt and did the same.

My mind was racing. I was totally confused about us being at a damn warehouse. The shit looked abandoned to me. "So, what's in here?" I checked my surroundings. If I didn't remember anything else about being in the hood, I remembered that important lesson.

"You're about to find out. Just keep walking." Barbee led us to a door that had a doorbell.

A big, buff black dude dressed in all black opened the door. He smiled widely the moment he saw my cousin. "Hey B, what's up, girl?"

Blacque Barbee hugged him. "Hey Merlin, how are you?"

"I'm good, baby. I can't complain."

"That wouldn't do any good."

"I know that's right."

"So, what brings you by?"

Blacque Barbee turned towards me. "Merlin, this is my cousin Foreign, and she needs your help."

"Hey Foreign, nice name."

"Thank you," I smiled. "It's nice to meet you."

"The pleasure is all mine." Merlin stepped to the side to let us in. "Come on in, ladies."

Merlin secured the lock on the door as we entered. That caused me to panic slightly. My heart rate increased, and I could feel a small knot form in my stomach. Every movie I've ever watched where a warehouse was involved, someone always ended up dead. Of course, I trusted B, but this Merlin character was suspect. And exactly what did she mean by, *I needed help*?

My curiosity was taking fear to the next level. Doing my best to calm down, I took a few deep breaths to level out the air in my lungs.

Blacque Barbee glanced in my direction. "Are you okay?" She placed her hand on my shoulder.

The warehouse was meat locker-cold. I guess that was their way of killing the germs or keeping dead bodies from rotting in unbearable heat. Either way, my ass was ready to go.

"Um. Yeah. I'm fine." I rubbed my stomach to make it seem as if the baby made me uncomfortable versus me being scared. My eyes bounced throughout the four corners of the room. Granted I wasn't street smart, I knew that I needed to watch my damn surroundings.

"It doesn't seem that way. Just relax. You'll be just fine," Blacque Barbee promised.

Merlin stepped behind the wooden desk and proceeded to open the drawer. When he raised his arm, I observed a small, black handgun clutched in his hand. Panic was an understatement. I took a deep breath, and swallowed the saliva that formed in my mouth.

"Please. I don't need that type of help. I don't need anyone getting killed behind this," I blurted out.

The room was still as Merlin looked at Barbee, who in turn looked at me and chuckled. "Nobody is getting killed. Merlin is going to teach you how to properly shoot a pistol." She then looked back at the burly man. "Forgive my cousin. She was shielded as a teen and knows nothing about the streets."

Merlin chuckled too. "It's all good. We all have one in the family."

That supplied me with great relief. "Yeah, forgive me 'cause I thought you were about to put a hit out on my child's father."

"No, girl." Blacque Barbee could no longer hold in her laughter. It was loud too. "I swear you grew up on the wrong side of the tracks."

"Tell me about it," I sighed. "I have a question. Isn't shooting a gun harmful to the baby?"

"No. The baby will be fine," Melvin jumped in. "I've helped lots of pregnant women in my day. So, trust me when I say you have nothing to worry about."

My eyes were on Merlin. "Well, that's a relief."

"I'm sure it is." Merlin took out a pair of black latex gloves and handed them to me. "I need you to put these on. This will prevent lead from getting into your bloodstream."

"Interesting," I nodded. That was new info to me.

"Are you ready to start?" Merlin asked.

"As ready as I'm going to be."

Merlin led the way to an isolated room. Barbee stood off to the side. "Foreign, go in the room with Merlin. I'll be sitting right here watching."

"Okay."

Merlin spent the next two hours teaching me about gun safety, how to load, shoot and take it apart. Once I had that memorized, Merlin pointed to me the booth.

"You ready to pull that trigger?" Merlin asked.

"Yes."

"Pick the gun up and hold it the way I showed you. Remember, do not rest your finger on the trigger. Keep it on the outside."

I followed every instruction.

"Very good. Now, straighten your back and relax your shoulders. Make sure your feet are planted firmly on the ground. Good. Good. Very good."

I felt like I was about to be a whole pro. Anxiously, I stood there waiting on him to tell me to pull the trigger.

"Ease your finger onto the trigger."

I was focused.

"Take a deep breath and squeeze the trigger."

Closing my eyes, I squeezed down on the trigger. *Boc!* My body jerked and I screamed. When the noise stopped, all I could hear was Merlin and Blacque Barbee cracking the fuck up.

"What the hell was that?" Blacque Barbee asked.

"I don't know, but it scared me."

"Give it here. Let me show you how to shoot." Blacque Barbee took the gun from my shaky hand and stood in my place.

"Do you need these goggles?" I asked.

"Nah. You keep those." Barbee aimed at the target and let loose.

Boc! Boc! Boc! Boc!

She handled that bitch like a pro. I stood there with my mouth wide open. "Damn," I whispered.

Barbee sat the gun down and showed me the target paper. She showed off her headshots. "That's how you shoot. Now come on and try again."

"I'll never be that good."

"Not as good as me, but all you need are the basics."

"Okay. I'll try again."

"That's the spirit," she shrieked. "But this time keep your eyes open. You need to see who you're shooting."

Merlin guided my hands the first few times and after that, I was on my own.

By the time we arrived back at Barbee's house, Maurice was sitting in the driveway waiting on me. My cousin and I hugged and said our goodbyes. "Thanks for everything, B. I know this wasn't easy for you."

"It's all good. Just don't be a stranger now and if you need me to come and pay that crazy-ass baby daddy of yours, call me. And remember everything I told you to do."

"I will."

"Be safe." Barbee went into the house, and I got in the car with Maurice.

"I see you and your cousin are getting along just fine." Maurice put the car in reverse and pulled off.

"Yes. We had a heart-to-heart this morning. Everything is good between us now."

"That's good. Family is important."

"Yes indeed," I agreed while yawning and getting comfortable in the passenger seat.

"Are you hungry?" Maurice asked sweetly.

"No. I'm sleepy." I yawned once more.

"Well, let the seat back down and get some rest. We have just about a four-hour drive."

The last song I heard was a slow jam by Keith Sweat, and that knocked me out. The next time I woke up, the sun was going down.

"Sleeping beauty, how was your nap?"

"Not long enough. I need my bed to get the full effect."

"While you were sleeping, someone was blowing up your phone."

In my gut, I already knew it was Domestic. He was so damn extra. All he had to do was treat me good and we wouldn't have any problems. After a long, much-needed talk with Barbee, I knew what I had to do. I had thirteen missed calls. Some were from a random number, and two were from DP. Now it all made sense. His ass was using his son's phone in hopes that I would call. However, the text message that came through stated otherwise. I called DP immediately.

"Hello."

"I just received your text, what's wrong?"

"Somebody shot my daddy."

Instantly, I grew frantic. "What? Is he okay?"

The sadness in his voice was heartbreaking. "I don't know. He's in the hospital and I can't go up there alone."

"Just sit tight and I'll be right there."

"Okay."

Just because Domestic and I were not on the best of terms didn't mean I wanted something bad to happen to him, or death for that matter. We had a child on the way, and both of his kids needed him. Tears started to fall from my eyes.

Maurice grabbed my hand. "What's wrong?"

Through the tears I sobbed. "Somebody shot him."

"Damn! I'm sorry to hear that. Is he going to be okay?"

"I don't know."

"Is there anything I could do? Do you need me to take you to the hospital?"

"No. Just take me to my car. I have to pick his son up."

"Okay. We're about thirty minutes away."

In a slump, I stared out the window and prayed that he would be okay. God couldn't be this cruel to me. I've already suffered one traumatic event. I couldn't handle another one.

DP and I were able to go upstairs and see Domestic. If it wasn't for my celebrity wife status, we would still be sitting in the waiting room. We walked in silence down the long empty hallway. The closer we got to the room, we could hear loud shouting. That made me put a little pep in my step.

Upon entering the room, I could hear Domestic cursing. "Give me my damn discharge papers so I can go home. I am not staying in here overnight. I'm fine."

"Sir, the doctor has to release you. He hasn't done that yet."

"Well, go and get him now." Domestic's eyes widened when he saw my face. A faint grin appeared. "I'm surprised to see you."

DP rushed towards his father. "Dad! I was scared you weren't going to make it."

Domestic used his left arm to hug his son. "I'm not leaving you that easy."

While the two shared a sentimental moment, I pulled the nurse to the side. "May I speak to you for a moment?"

"Sure," she replied softly.

"I would like to speak with the doctor about releasing him into my care tonight. He seems fine to me."

"He has a gunshot wound and we need to keep him for observation. Just in case he has any internal bleeding."

"I'm no doctor or nurse, but I would like to think that if he had internal bleeding we would know that by now. Did he or did he not undergo surgery?"

"Yes. He did, but ma'am—we still need to keep him overnight."

"Listen, um." I looked at her badge to see her name. "Marcy, I understand that, but I would hate to contact the CEO of this hospital while he's at home sleeping. You don't want that, right?"

Now I had Marcy's attention. "No. No. That's not necessary," she stumbled over her words. "I'll get the doctor right away."

"Thank you." Marcy scurried out of the room like a roach when the lights turned on.

It wasn't what you know, but who you know. Before I gave up my career as a real estate agent, I had the pleasure of selling a million-dollar mansion to the CEO and his wife.

Now that the nurse was handled, I turned my attention towards Domestic. He was sitting there, staring me up and down. "What happened to you? You had me worried sick about you," I confessed truthfully.

"Is that the only reason you came back?" Domestic chuckled, but it sounded sinister for some damn reason. "A nigga had to get shot for you to come back, huh?"

"You know why I left." I stopped and looked at DP. Just that fast I forgot he was in the room. "Can we talk about this later? I want to make sure you're okay."

"The hospital staff had been calling you since my arrival, but they couldn't get an answer."

"Yeah, I know. I was asleep." Moving closer to him, I placed my hand on his heart. "How are you feeling?"

"Better now that I see you," he winced and placed his hand over the bandage. It was obvious that he was in pain.

"No, seriously. Are you okay?"

"I'm in pain and I want to go home," he huffed. "And this bitch handling me like I'm a fucking kid or some shit."

"Domestic, you have to relax. You can't be rude to the staff and expect them to jump through hoops for you."

"Well, you talk to her then," he stated with pure irritation. "Because if I have to say another word to her, she gon' feel me and that's on God," he threatened.

DP sat in the corner and texted away on his phone, ignoring his father's temper tantrum. Hell, I didn't blame him. Domestic was a loose cannon, and he had no problem letting it be known.

The doctor walked into the room with the nurse on his heels. Needless to say, he looked less than pleased. That all changed when he saw my face. A smile appeared. "Mrs. Young, how are you doing?"

I smiled in return. "I'm doing pretty good."

"That's good to hear." His tone was a bit more serious. "I heard about the tragic accident involving your husband. That had to be devastating. I'm so sorry for your loss."

"Thank you. I'm just taking it one day at a time."

"That's all you can do."

Domestic cleared his throat and rose from the bed. "I hate to interrupt your reunion, but I am in pain and I would like to go home and recover in my own bed."

The doctor pushed his glasses off the bridge of his nose. "If you want to sign yourself out, I will allow you to do so. I'm not going to force you to stay."

"In that case I'm ready."

Quickly, I interjected. "Before you do that, does he have any internal bleeding or injuries that we should be concerned about?"

"No. He's going to be just fine." On a sly, I side-eyed the nurse. That heffa didn't know what the hell she was talking about. "I'm going to prescribe him some pain medication and an antibiotic. It doesn't have to be filled tonight. I'll provide a dosage that will help him sleep tonight."

"Thank you so much."

"It's my pleasure. I'll be right back with the discharge papers." The doctor left the room, and Marcy was right behind him.

Domestic was silent during the ride. He would doze for a few minutes then open his eyes. This man had to have the devil in him. Here he was suffering from a gunshot wound that could've been fatal, and he still had an attitude. To me, he should've been grateful that he's still alive. I just hoped when we made it to the house, he better be on his best behavior. All that crazy shit needed to be left outside. The second he raised his voice, I was going home. And that was a promise.

When I pulled up into the driveway and shut off the car, Domestic tried to open the door with his left hand. "Shit," he shouted.

"Wait and let me open the door for you." He sat back without a single word. I raised the backseat so DP could get out. Immediately, he headed over to help his dad. That was my cue to open the front door.

Domestic and I went into the bedroom and closed the door. He sat down on the bed and removed the sling that cradled his arm. Domestic frowned and threw it on the nightstand.

As I walked towards him, I placed my keys on the dresser. "Let me help you out this shirt." Domestic raised his left arm. Gently, I pulled the shirt off of his right arm and then the left. "Stand up and let me take off your pants." For the first time, he followed every command. Pain had a way of making the toughest man bow down.

"I want to take a shower."

"The doctor said no contact with water tonight. You can take a bath in the morning."

"Okay. I guess I'll just go to bed." Domestic laid down so I could tuck him in. Once he was covered, I sat down beside him. We just stared at each other for a few seconds. "Thank you for coming. I didn't think you would after that last conversation we had."

There he goes opening up that wound and jogging my memory with reasons I wanted to leave him. "About that," I paused. "We have a lot to discuss and I have plenty of questions."

Domestic sighed and avoided all eye contact. "I know, but can we talk about it tomorrow? This medicine is kicking in."

"Okay, goodnight," I stood up.

"Don't leave. I want you to stay." That nigga sounded nice and sweet.

"Okay, I can stay." I planned to stay all along, but I wasn't about to tell him that.

Fully clothed, I crawled into bed and laid on my side. Domestic did the same. We stayed that way until his eyelids grew lazy and fell hard.

Chapter 5

Domestic

Foreign was the epitome of beauty. A rare angel on earth and in the flesh. Despite everything, Foreign has been strong through it all. No matter how badly I've treated her, she remained at my side. Many would call it *stupidity*, I called it *loyalty*. Therefore, she should be rewarded.

Any man would be lucky to have her on his arm. Here I was the luckiest man on earth and treated her like shit at times. How ironic! However, Foreign wasn't too fortunate since I had a hard time controlling my anger.

Daily, I fought my demons and often took it out on Foreign. She was an innocent bystander. It was a struggle, and it affected the most important people in my life. My awful childhood reflected the man I had become. All of the pain I endured was now being inflicted on any woman that was in my life. It had to stop. I couldn't lose her or the ability to raise my child. Foreign was a runner, and I knew I would have to move mountains to find her if she were to slip through my grip.

Foreign cradled her stomach as she slept so peacefully. To me, that demonstrated her maternal instincts of protection. That was something my mother didn't possess. Quietly, I watched her sleep. I loved the fact that she didn't snore. One thing I couldn't handle was a woman that sounded like a grizzly bear.

It was hard not to touch her. So, I quit fighting my urges and stroked the side of her cheek. Her skin was so soft and smooth. Moving my hand, I made my way towards her belly. The temperature in the room was cold as a meat locker, but her body was warm to the touch. I rubbed it in a slow, circular motion.

A little time passed before Foreign finally opened her eyes and yawned. "Good morning, beautiful," I greeted her cheerfully.

"Good morning," she replied in between a second yawn.

"Tired, huh?"

"Yes. The baby is draining all of my energy."

"Get all the rest you need. I can fend for myself."

There was something on her mind. I could tell by the way she avoided eye contact. "Domestic, we—"

"We need to talk. I know." I finished her sentence before she could get it all out.

"Well, I'm listening." Foreign's eyes were now on me.

"Hmm. Where do I start?"

Foreign sat upright in the bed and folded her arms. "How about you start on the part where all of this was one big set-up from the jump. Why I found my picture in your wallet? And most importantly, did you have anything to do with Aaron's death?"

Under any other circumstances, I would be angry seeing her cry over Aaron's weak ass. Today was different. I saw all of the pain that I caused. It was time for me to fix it with the truth. "Foreign baby, I love you and that's the God's honest truth. There's no doubt about that."

Foreign shook her head. "Domestic, just tell me, please."

"Before we met, Emilia came to me about doing a job for her. At first, I didn't want to do it, but since I owed her a favor I agreed. The job was to seduce you and make you fall in love with me. When I looked at your picture, I was attracted to you instantly."

"What was the purpose in getting me to fall in love with you?"

"So that you would leave your husband for me, and Emilia could have Aaron all to herself."

Foreign sat there with a blank stare. I could only imagine how this information made her feel.

"The night we met was by fate. There was nothing scripted or planned behind that. We are meant to be together. Can't you see that?"

Foreign had heavy tears rolling down her cheeks. I knelt in front of her and wiped them away. "Baby, I know this hurts and I'm sorry that it had to come out this way. Trust me when I say that you are the best thing that has happened to me since my son was born."

"How can I believe that? This was all a part of a sick and twisted plan by an unstable, obsessed bitch."

"And that's what I'm telling you. Why would you believe anything she said?"

"Unstable or obsessed, she's no liar. Everything she told me has been proven to be true according to you." Foreign inched backward on the bed.

"Why are you backing away from me?"

Foreign stood up with her head slightly tilted. Her bottom lip trembled. "I need an answer from you and I need it now. Did you kill my husband so you could have me to yourself?"

"Baby, no! I swear I didn't kill him." Technically, I didn't. That was executed by Carlos.

"And why should I believe you?"

"I didn't have a reason to. Baby," I pleaded while easing towards her and ignoring the pain in my shoulder. "I already had your heart and you were pregnant at the time. My presence in your life wasn't going to be affected."

"How can I be sure you're telling the truth?" she sobbed uncontrollably.

"Think about it, baby, you're a smart woman." I tapped my temple with my finger. Foreign needed to feel where I was coming from, even if it was a lie. If I spilled the truth to her, Foreign was leaving me without a doubt and—most importantly—she was telling the police. It didn't matter what I had to say or do, I was determined to convince her that I was not responsible.

"Emilia's whole plan was to take Aaron away from you. She was in love with him. There wasn't a line she wouldn't cross to make that happen. I'm her scapegoat. Why can't you see that?"

Foreign shook her head. "This is too much."

"Don't you think that if I killed Aaron, Emilia would've locked me up herself? Can you honestly sit here and say that she would let me get away with taking away the man she loved?"

"I don't know."

"Come on, baby. Make it make sense."

"I'm trying to," she cried.

My words were getting to her. Grabbing her hand, I stood in front of her and looked into her eyes. "You know deep down inside that I'm right. That woman was crazy. I wouldn't be standing here if I was guilty. Locking me up would be her number one priority."

Gently, I wiped her face. Tilting her head up, I placed my lips on hers and kissed her softly. There was a little resistance, but I kept going until I could feel her body relax. That was confirmation that I fully had her heart and she wasn't going anywhere.

Lexi...

Sprawled out flat on my stomach, my hands clenched the sheets as my body rocked against the mattress. Lots of heavy moaning filled the room. Calvin was deep in a bitch guts, rattling my damn ovaries. That was the main reason I fucked him for so long. His ass knew his way around a pussy.

"Move your leg up."

Calvin pushed my left cheek up and long-stroked me fast. A throbbing sensation filled the lower part of my stomach. "Fuck! I'ma fuck around and get you pregnant."

This nigga was trying to mess up my orgasm. "No, you not."

"Yeah, a'ight. Watch I put a baby in ya ass."

The sex was so good I didn't have time to argue with him. "Boy, hush and fuck me."

Calvin did just that when he put me on all fours and pressed my chest into the bed. Relentlessly, he banged my box until the shit was sore and I was out of breath. The hard grip of my hair made me speechless. *What the fuck was he trying to do? Snatch a bitch bald or some shit!*

"Unt, Unt!" I gasped. "Let go of my hair."

"I'm cummin', shut up." He grunted, applying more pressure.

Calvin slammed into me harder and a whole lot deeper. Biting into the pillow, I closed my eyes and waited on him to finish. Seconds later, I could feel my entire wig slip off my head. Just when I thought he was going to stop, I was wrong. This energetic nigga lasted a few more minutes. When he was done, he laid on his back, laughing hard as fuck.

"Bae, what the fuck happened to your hair?"

"That shit ain't funny. I told you to let my shit go." My tone was snappy, but I was laughing too. Reaching down beside the bed, I picked up my lace front. "Yo' ass paying for me another install."

"You ain't saying shit. I'll pay for all of them."

"Good," I pouted and laid up under him.

Calvin rubbed the top of my head. "Thank God you ain't bald-headed."

"Why? You like bald-headed hoes anyway."

"Bullshit!"

"You must've forgotten that I've seen most of the hoes you smashed." Calvin didn't respond. He just laughed it off. His ass knew I was telling the truth.

My phone vibrated against the nightstand. Leaning over, I picked it up to see who was calling. I exhaled when I saw our house number flash on the screen. It better not be my mother starting shit today 'cause I was hanging up on her. Against my better judgment, I picked up.

"Hello."

"Hey, baby. How are you doing?"

"Hey, daddy. I'm good and you?"

"I'm doing fine."

I knew my father better than anyone. The sound of his voice told me that everything wasn't fine. There was certainly something going on, and I was about to find out. "What's going on, dad? I can tell that something is wrong?"

"Have you seen the news?"

"No. Why? What happened?" The last thing I wanted to hear was another scandal that had my brother's name attached to it. I cleared his name to save his reputation and I'll be damned if someone else tries to fuck it up. This time I was going to jail. Fuck all that extra shit.

"Last night somebody set Aaron's grave on fire."

"What? Are you fucking serious?" I shouted.

"Alexis Young, watch your mouth," he stated sternly.

"I'm sorry, daddy, but this has me pissed off. Like why can't my brother rest in fucking peace? This makes no sense whatsoever." I was so furious that I started crying. That shit hurt heart my heart. Who could be so heartless and inconsiderate?

"I understand, baby, but it's okay. His stone will be replaced."

"No!" I screamed. "Daddy, it will not be okay. That's disrespectful. Ughh, I'm telling you I better not find out who did it."

"Alexis, stop it. The police are going down to the cemetery to see if the cameras picked up anybody. Let them handle this. Whoever did it will be dealt with accordingly."

"Okay."

"I mean it. Alexis, I don't want you calling me from the precinct because you were arrested again."

"Oh my God! I get arrested one time and suddenly I'm a criminal."

"I didn't say that, but I had to pull some strings and get that assault charge taken care of." My father sighed heavily into the phone. "Listen, baby, just don't go out and get yourself in any trouble, okay?"

"I won't."

"Okay. I'll talk to you later."

"Okay."

"I love you."

"I love you too, dad."

After we hung up, I sat the phone on the bed. Covering my face with my hands, I let out a gut-wrenching scream. "I fucking hate people."

"What's wrong? What did your father say?"

"Someone set Aaron's grave on fire last night. It's all over the fucking news. Like who the fuck does some shit like that?"

"Damn, that's fucked up and mad disrespectful."

"Aaron didn't fuck with nobody, so this is just crazy to me." I stared at the walls for a few. "It probably was Foreign's boyfriend."

"Come on, Lexi. You don't see how crazy that sounds."

"I'm the crazy one, but none this shit started happening until Foreign started fucking buff daddy. Our lives were perfect until one day it wasn't." The disrespect towards my brother had me on go. There was no way I could just sit back and not do anything. I was determined to get answers.

Completely naked, I jumped out of bed and headed for the bathroom. "Where are you going?"

"Down to the precinct. That captain is about to reopen my brother's case. His death was no accident and I'm going to prove it."

"Are you sure you want to do that without any proof?"

Stopping in my tracks, I turned to face him with a mean mug on my face. "Really, Calvin? This is my brother we're talking about, so you damn right I want answers."

"Fine. I'm going with you." He surrendered to my request like I knew he would.

"Thank you. All I need is a little support."

Chapter 6

Foreign

Eight o'clock rolled around pretty fast. Sluggishly, I crawled from the bed and went into the bathroom. All I wanted to do was lie in bed all day. However, I'd agreed the night before to go into the wash so that Domestic could get some rest. The blast to his shoulder had him in a lot of pain.

Standing in the mirror, I thought back to the awful news. My mind was just spinning. I've been trying to wrap my head around someone setting Aaron's grave on fire. It was downright disturbing. The world we lived in was crazy and cruel. *Who in the hell would do some shit like that?* To me, it took a special type of crazy to lurk in the cemetery on a late night and disturb the dead. I hope they catch the weirdo and commit his ass to a mental facility.

A small part of me wondered if Domestic was behind the fire. It seemed like something he would do considering the fact he despised Aaron so much. Pushing that thought out of my head, I brushed my teeth, washed my face, and took a shower. The water hit my face and washed away the sleep in my eyes. It was certainly refreshing and much needed.

When I walked back into the bedroom, Domestic was pacing the floor, while talking on the phone. From the sound of things, I knew it was Tracy.

"Don't worry about the supplies, Foreign will be there to do the inventory and place the order. Just write down the items that you need and give them to her." Seconds later, he ended the call and looked over at me. "Good morning, baby. How are you feeling this morning?"

"I'm good," I yawned.

Domestic walked up to me and placed his big hands on my belly. They were almost able to cover my belly. Over the weeks my stomach grew bigger, and it was becoming more noticeable.

"And how is my baby doing?" Domestic was close enough to speak directly with his unborn child. "Is mommy feeding you right? Daddy is so happy about your arrival, and I cannot wait to meet you. I'm going to spoil you and give you the world."

Hearing those words made my heart smile. With confidence, I could honestly say that Domestic was going to be an amazing father to our child. There wasn't a doubt in my mind that would make me feel otherwise.

"Those are some extravagant promises that you're making," I added.

"Those are promises that I plan on keeping. As long as I have breath in my body, he or she will never want or need anything. And that's a promise."

"Well, I hope that you keep that same mindset when it comes down to me."

Domestic and I stood face to face. The intensity in our stare was high, but there was a soft, empathetic look in his eyes. When he opened his mouth to speak, I could feel that a slick remark was coming. "You're absolutely right, baby. After everything I've taken you through, you deserve that much from me."

Nodding, I smiled. "I agree and I'm holding you to that promise."

Domestic placed his hand on the back of my neck. His touch sent a chill down my spine and a slight tremble over my body. Those were clear indicators of abuse. Instant replays of his harsh treatment played out in my mind. I was still traumatized from being locked in that damn closet.

"Are you cold? You're shivering."

"A little," I lied.

Domestic placed fear in my heart. He let me know off the top that he was in control from the day we met. However, I shrugged it off as arrogance. Now, it all made sense. I just didn't pay attention. Casey tried to warn me, but I didn't listen. The love I have for him kept me in my place. Now with the baby on the way, I had no choice but to stick it out. Family ties were important to me, and I wanted my child to grow up in a two-parent household. That made a great impact on my life. That was always a goal of mine. Not co-parenting.

"Foreign, I want to spend the rest of my life making you happy. Just don't give up on me. I'm making progress. Allow me the chance to give you the world."

Abruptly, I interrupted his speech. "Domestic, I don't need the world. Just be the man that you were in the beginning. Find patience and let go of all that anger you have housed in here." I placed my hand over his heart. "When you get angry, you take it out on me. I'm not a punching bag, and I will no longer allow you to treat me as such. If you can't love me and keep your hands off me, I will leave you and that's my promise to you."

Domestic acknowledged my feelings with a slight nod. "I'm going to do whatever it takes to make this work."

"That's all I ask."

Domestic kissed me. I kissed him back. My hormones were raging. I could feel the wetness between my legs circulate. Domestic eased me onto the bed and removed my towel. Anxiously, I waited on him to remove his pajama pants and boxers. That thick one-eyed monster was hard and demanded my attention. Leaning down, Domestic tongue-kissed my pussy with his fat ass tongue. It moved rapidly in a circular motion. He slurped hard and loud like he was eating watermelon.

"Sss. Ouu," I put my hand on top of his head and pushed him further into it. He sucked, slurped, and popped his lips. Damn, he knew just what to do to me. "Ah! Ah!" The moaning never stopped. I could feel his fingers penetrating me. He stroked my kitty fast. Juices ran down the crack of my ass.

"Cum on this tongue," he demanded.

There was more fingering, sucking, and slurping for what felt like forever. He had me weak and at his mercy. I was squirming like a fish out of water. Domestic could ask for anything right now and I would say yes at that moment. A strong bolt of what felt like electricity shot through me. My juices gushed out into his mouth. Fluids were all in his beard. He wiped it away with his hand.

Domestic lowered his body onto mine. The tip of his head pressed firmly against my lips until he parted my shit like the red sea, stretching me open. Exhaling, I planted my feet on his waist and clenched my cheeks together. Domestic's dick slid in and out of me slowly. An immense amount of pleasure flooded my body. My pussy purred like a baby kitten.

Out of all the positions Domestic placed me in, I loved when he made love to me missionary style. It allowed me to look into his eyes and see the pleasure he received when we connected sexually. Some of his facial expressions were serious. Especially when he was concentrating on reaching his climax. That was next-level intimacy.

Domestic bit down on his bottom lip and arched his back. He released a loud grunt. "Shit!" The slow stroking suddenly stopped, killing my satisfaction.

"What's wrong?"

"It's my shoulder. You have to get on top," he winced in pain.

We switched positions.

Straddling his lap, I relaxed my muscles as his piece filled me up inch by inch. Careful not to touch his shoulder, I placed both hands on the mattress and bounced on his soldier. Domestic utilized his left hand to play with my erect nipples.

"Shit, girl!" He grunted.

"Mmm," I bit down on my lip from the pleasure and increased the speed.

My pussy was wet as the ocean and caused his dick to slip out. Pushing it back inside, I rode him a little slower with my hands now resting on his stomach. Moving up and down, I threw my head back and closed my eyes. His frisky fingers were now on my clit, stroking it intensely.

"Ahh! Ahh!" I moaned. "Make me cum! Make me cum!"

I was about to lose it. That move was hot to me, and I loved every second of it. This was what I missed. Sex was what put us together in the first place.

Lifting my feet, I slid them onto his thighs and rode him like it would be the last time. Another tingling sensation came into play. Before I could shake it off, I came for the second time. I was satisfied, but Domestic hadn't come yet. His dick glistened with my wetness. It was still hard. I wrapped my lips around his rod and sucked him up. His hand rested on the top of my head.

Domestic controlled my head while thrusting into my mouth. Those facial expressions made me want to laugh so bad. He had his eyes closed, so I knew I was doing a good job. There was a knock on the door.

"Pops!"

Domestic didn't open his mouth. He was caught in the moment.

"Pops!" DP shouted his name louder that time.

"Yeah," he finally answered. The sound of his voice had less bass than it normally did.

"Can I use your car?"

"Yeah."

Normally, he would ask questions about where he was going. My deep-throating skills prevented that from happening. Domestic cleared his throat. "Eat that dick just like that. This yo' dick. Make yo' dick bust."

Minutes later, I did just that. When it was all over, I laid down on the bed and looked up at the ceiling. "Now I have to take another shower."

"It's all good. It's plenty water in there," he grinned.

"Ha! Ha! You know what I mean."

Domestic leaned over and put his hand between my legs. "I guess you telling me I can't get a second round in of this good shit?"

"You forgot that fast that I have to go in and do the inventory and order more products."

"Nah, I didn't forget."

"We can finish this later."

"I need it now." Domestic ignored everything I said.

Two hours later, I took my second shower for the day and got dressed. When I made it to the wash, it was pretty quiet. The afternoon rush must not have come in just yet. Simple sex in the morning was a good way to start the day. Not all that freaky, strenuous sex and multiple rounds when you had to leave the house. At times I swear he could be a sex-crazed maniac. Domestic had me tired and sore. Hell, my jaws were even tired. The plan was to be out of there in two hours or less.

"Hey, Boss Lady." Tracy greeted me with a big smile.

"Hey, Tracy."

"Girl, where you been? Did your man tell you that I was looking for you?"

"He told me." I leaned against the counter. "I had to take a little break from this. This pregnancy has me super tired." She didn't need the real details behind my absence. We were cool, but not like that.

"Tell me about it. I've had enough kids to know." She giggled. "You'll see when y'all have more."

"Yeah. I don't know about all that."

"Girl, please, that man gon' blow you up again. I know y'all nasty. You give me private school and church girl nasty vibes." Tracy busted out into a fit of laughter.

It was funny. The girl was hilarious.

"Tracy, I am not playing around with you today."

Tracy smacked her lips. "Boss Lady, you know I'm telling the truth. It's written all over your face. Just admit that you have that old nigga wrapped around your finger."

"I'm with you when you right," I giggled.

Tracy snapped her fingers. "See, that's what the fuck I'm talking about."

"Unt! Unt! I have things to do. Where's the list of your supplies? You're not about to have me out here playing for hours."

"That's how I get my overtime." Tracy winked. "Don't tell the boss though."

"I like to mind my own business, but I'm almost certain that he knows that already.

The sticky note she passed me had a minimal list. That was a surprise. Tracy always felt the need to order extra shit for no apparent reason whatsoever.

"I guess I'll get to work now."

Sluggishly, I walked to Domestic's office and closed the door. Behind his desk, I sat down and turned on the computer. The room was silent. All I could hear was the tapping of my nails against the keyboard. If I was going to make it through my short shift, I was going to need some music. Pandora was my option, and Mary J. Blige was my alternative. Now, I was in my zone.

By the time I completed the orders for both car washes and printed out the invoices, one hour had passed just that fast. My work ethic surprised me. Normally, it took a little longer, but my motivation was to go back home and get in bed. Once my job was done, I filed the invoice and shut down everything.

On my way out of the office, I could hear faint whispers, as I walked down the hallway. Only a few feet away, I observed Tracy talking to a detective. His badge confirmed his identity. The moment Tracy saw me, she said something to the detective and he walked away. Out of curiosity, I stopped at her desk.

"What's going on?" My eyes burned holes in his back by the way I was staring.

"Huh?"

Tracy acted as if her ass didn't hear me the first time. So, I repeated my question. "What happened? Why was that detective here?"

"Oh. Um. He was here asking questions about the shooting with Domestic."

"Did they find out who's responsible?"

"Not yet. He just wanted to ask me a second round of questions to make sure I didn't leave anything out."

"Well, I'm headed out."

"Okay. Enjoy the rest of your day."

"You too." There was something off about Tracy's response and the way the detective walked off so fast. Then again it could be nothing. Therefore, I just brushed it off.

Domestic was in bed watching the sports channel when I made it back to the house. "You made it back fast. I wasn't expecting you for at least another hour."

"Yeah. I know. I'm surprised myself that it didn't take that long."

"You did the orders for both washes, right?"

"Yes."

"What was the total amount?"

"Twenty-five hundred."

"That's surprising," he stroked his chin.

"Well, that's a plus."

"Indeed," he agreed.

Flopping down on the bed, I kicked my shoes off and got comfortable. "Oh, while I was there some detective showed up."

Domestic muted the television and looked at me. "What did he want?"

"I don't know. He was talking to Tracy when I walked out of the office. By the time I made it to where they were, he left. I asked her what he wanted, and she said he had more questions about the shooting. I will say that her demeanor was a little off."

"What do you mean by that?"

"I can't say, but to me, I felt like she was probably hiding something. It could've been nothing."

"I'll ask her about it." Domestic nodded and unmuted the television.

Chapter 7

Marshall

Darkness lurked in the sky. The moon shone brightly, sending sparkly rays through my windshield. A dark silhouette walked into view and stopped at the passenger side. With no hesitation, I unlocked the door.

"Why did you come to my job? Are you trying to get me killed?" Tracy barked.

"I was in the area and decided to stop by and ask a few questions."

Tracy spoke with her hand in the air. "You don't get it. This man is crazy and he will kill me if he found out you are investigating him." Then she rubbed her temple. "I can't do this."

Placing my hand on her shoulder, I tried to ease her mind. "Stop worrying about that. He's not going to find out you've been speaking with me. I promise you that."

"You can't promise me my life." Tracy was on the verge of tears. "His girlfriend saw you and I know she's going to tell him."

"What did you tell her?"

"I told her that you were questioning me about the shooting."

Finally, I moved my hand. "That was good. He should buy into that without a problem. See, you know what to say and do."

"I hope so." Tracy stopped looking at the floor and into my eyes. "Listen, I have kids that need me. I need you to promise me that you will get me into witness protection," she pleaded.

"I'm working on that as we speak. We will keep you and your kids protected."

"Well, I need that done sooner than later."

"I need you to look at this photo." Grabbing the folder from the dashboard, I removed the still image. "Take a look at this photo and tell me if this vehicle looks familiar."

Tracy stared aimlessly until she handed it back to me. "I don't know. What does this have to do with Domestic? I thought we were going to discuss the murder of that boy."

"I have reason to believe that it's a possibility Mr. Payne was involved in the car crash that took the life of Aaron Young, Foreign Young's husband."

With squinted eyes, Tracy tilted her head to the side. "Wait. So, you think Domestic had something to do with her husband's death?"

"It has not been confirmed, but I believe so. The two are currently dating."

"They are," she agreed.

"So, let me ask you this. Have you ever seen a sports car at the car wash?"

"On several occasions. I mean hello, it is a car wash," she replied sarcastically.

To push the envelope a little further, I switched up my line of questioning. "No. What I mean is, has Domestic had personal visitors that drive a sports car?"

"Um. No." Tracy glanced out the window. Her keys jingled. "Wait, there is a guy that comes in to see him from time to time. His name is Carlos."

"Do you know his last name?"

"No."

"Would you recognize him if I showed you a photo lineup?"

"Yes. He's Spanish or Mexican."

"Okay. And lastly, I know you've spoken to Emilia about the murder of Keith. I just need to confirm that you are absolutely sure he stole forty thousand dollars from Mr. Payne?"

"That's correct."

"And how do you know that?"

"He told me when it happened. Keith didn't show up for work after that. Domestic left the office that day and when he returned, he told me not to mention anything to the police."

"Thanks for that." I glanced at the clock. "I'm not going to keep you much longer. If I have more questions, I'll give you a call instead of popping up at your job."

"Thank you. I would appreciate that." Tracy opened the door and got out.

Lexi…

Las Vegas, NV

"We're in Vegas, baby, get up!" Full of energy at eight in the morning, I was hooting and hollering like a plum fool. I opened the curtains to allow the bright sun to fill the room.

"Bae!" He whined like a sleepy toddler while punching the mattress. "What you doing?"

"Boy, getcha ass up. We came here to turn the fuck up, not sleep."

"But we just went to bed." Calvin covered his head with the pillow. "I just need a few more hours to recoup from last night."

"Nobody told you to buy all those bottles at the club. You need to learn how to handle your liquor. How you let me out-drink you?"

Calvin rolled onto his side and opened his eyes. "It ain't my fault you have a cast-iron man stomach like a mechanic."

That was the one thing we had in common. We loved to crack jokes on each other. He had me cracking up. "Boy, shut up!" I laughed. "You just mad because I can hold my liquor."

Diving onto the bed, I landed directly on top of him. "Come on Calvin, get up. I'm ready to get out of this room."

"Alright!" He grunted. "Get your heavy ass off of me."

"Ain't shit fat on me, but this pussy." I slapped him in the back of the head.

"Yeah. That lil' pussy is fat." Calvin flipped me off of him. I landed right on my back.

"Use that energy you have to go shower and brush that stank ass mouth," I giggled.

"My breath does not stank."

"It really does. It smells like you been eating ass all night."

"That's because I was. But it was your stank ass that I was licking.

"Go shower and hush."

Calvin grabbed a pillow and hit me with it, as he walked towards the bathroom. "I am."

"You have ten minutes."

While I waited on Calvin to get ready, I laid in the bed and took some cute ass selfies. My outfit for the day was a two-piece Fendi bathing suit and black see-through cover-up pants. The custom Fendi floppy hat made it complete. I was cute, and not a soul could tell me otherwise.

After a filling breakfast, Calvin and I walked hand in hand through the Aria Resort and Casino, looking like the celebrities that we were. The hotel was absolutely stunning. I only stayed at five-star hotels. Nothing less.

When we stepped out into the pool area, it was beyond lit. The DJ was playing that good down south Florida music. A bitch couldn't tell me I wasn't back home at a pool party. Calvin reserved us a private section. I was grateful for that. It was a pretty good crowd. Thankfully, no one spotted Calvin as of yet. I just hoped it stayed that way. I wasn't in the mood for photo ops and autographs. I wanted to enjoy our time together.

No sooner had that thought crossed my mind than I spotted two dudes smiling and walking in our direction. We were only steps from entering our section.

The light-skinned dude was nice. He had a six-pack and a body drenched in tattoos. "Yooo, CB. You and Aaron did y'all thang in the Superbowl."

The bodyguard stood in between us. CB was the name Calvin received in the NFL because of his speed on the field. That name fits him perfectly.

"It's cool, fam. They're fans." The bodyguard stepped aside.

Calvin was all smiles as he dapped the two dudes. "Thanks, man. I appreciate that."

"Sorry for your loss too. I know you and Aaron been best friends for years."

"Thanks, bro," he replied.

The dude looked at me like he was trying to figure out who I was. "You're Alexis, right? Aaron's sister."

"Yeah," I smiled.

"Sorry for your loss. I know how you feel. I lost my brother a few months ago."

"Thank you."

"Keep your head up."

"I will and you do the same."

Now his attention was back on Calvin. "Do you mind if we take a pic for the gram? My followers would love this shit."

"Yeah. That's cool." Calvin looked at me with uncertainty in his eyes. "Bae, can you take the pic for us?"

Instead of showing out, I smiled and agreed. They better be lucky they were fine. Light-skin passed me his phone and took three photos. His friend then took pics of us with his boy."

"Y'all enjoy the party."

"Will do."

Calvin popped the top of the bottle and turned it up to his lips. He took a big ass swig of the liquor. "Alright, you gon' be fucked up again."

"That's the plan." Calvin handed me the bottle.

"Nah! Pass me a cup. I'm not drinking out no damn bottle."

"Scary ass."
"I have class, thank you."
"Not in the bedroom, you don't," he said with a sly grin.
"I'm not supposed to." I stood in front of him. "And you like it."
"Nah, slim, I love it."
"You better or the next man will," I smirked.

After a few drinks in, the music had me hyped, and the liquor had me buzzing. Calvin was sitting down, drinking and rapping, while I danced in his lap. A few people watched us, and that was when they realized who Calvin was. Before we knew it, there was a stampede of people standing around, snapping pictures. The females were screaming his name, asking for autographs and pictures. Since I was in a good mood, I decided to let him take a few.

We spent three hours outside at the pool, and I was ready to go back to the room. Not to mention I was hungry as fuck, so room service sounded good to me. There was light movement through the hallway. Once we made it to the elevator, a nicely dressed couple was waiting. The doors opened, and we all stepped on.

Calvin looked at the woman who was wearing a sash that said: *Just married.* "Congratulations on your marriage."

The woman and her husband replied, "Thank you."

Her husband took a second look. "Hey, you CB?"

Calvin smiled, "That's me."

They took a pic and spoke a few words until we made it the thirteenth floor. "I'm rooting for y'all next season. I'm a real Tampa Bay fan, brother."

"We going back to the Superbowl next season."

"I'll be watching," he said before stepping off the elevator.

Inside the room, I ordered us some expensive ass gourmet food. It took them roughly thirty minutes to bring it, but it was good and worth the money. Calvin smacked on his food loudly. That shit was so annoying.

"Eww! Why do you have to eat like a horse?" I laughed.

"I'm hungry, shit. What. So I'm supposed to eat all cute and shit!"

"Just close your mouth. You are not on a farm."

"Fuck you," he replied with a mouthful of food.

"We gon' fuck later," I winked. "I'm eating right now."

"You damn right. We fucking on the balcony too," he smirked.

"Aye, you know I'm with that."

One thing about us: our sex life was good as fuck. The chemistry was amazing, and I couldn't have asked for a better sex partner. God knows that if the sex was whack, there would be no us.

My tray was empty, and I was satisfied. Now it was time to raid our bar. I opened up a bottle, and fixed myself and Calvin a shot. Passing him the glass, I held it in the air. Calvin did the same.

"Bottoms up, baby."

We downed our shots.

"Aye, let me talk to you." Calvin grabbed my hand and pulled me close to him.

In my spirit, I could feel a heavy conversation about to transpire. The seriousness in his voice was evident. However, I couldn't pinpoint it. "What's up?"

"How do you feel about me?"

"You know how I feel about you. Aren't we in a relationship?" I hated discussing feelings.

The way I've operated over the years steered me clear of heartbreak. When it came to being involved with dudes, I called the shots. No one was about to have the upper hand on me, period! Then Calvin came along. Now I was in a committed relationship. I'm not sure if I latched onto him because of Aaron's death. All I knew was, I loved what we shared and I didn't have any regrets.

"We are in a relationship. I get that. My concern is, how do you truly feel about me? Am I someone you can see a future with?" Calvin released my hand, and looked into my eyes. "When I look at you, I can see all of that. I can see you giving me my children."

Children, I thought. Honestly, I never thought of being anyone's mother. My face felt flustered, and the room suddenly appeared hot for some strange reason.

"Do you not see that when you look at me?"

"I think of a lot of things when I see you. We have an amazing connection, and I love what we have going on. It's been so long since I've been in a relationship that I'm not sure how to feel."

"Lexi, I get it. You've been hurt in the past. I was there for you when Cameron broke your heart. It was my shoulder you cried on."

"I know that and I don't want to talk about that." Reliving that painful moment was something I buried a long time ago. In a daze, I sat down on the sofa.

"I know you better than anybody and probably better than you know yourself. Daily you display that I-don't-give-a-fuck attitude, but I know you do. I've watched you go from athlete to athlete to suppress that hurt. You'll do anything to prevent yourself from catching feelings."

Calvin knelt in front of me. I wasn't an emotional person. Not anymore. The break-up turned me cold as ice. No one's feelings mattered to me. Fool me once, shame on you. Fool me twice, shame on me.

"I love you. I've loved you for years." Calvin admitted something I always knew.

I nodded in agreement.

"Patiently, I sat around and waited on you to stop wasting your time with men you cared nothing about. Allowing you to get all of that anger and hurt out of your system, so that you'll realize that what you needed was in your face all along. Do you understand that?"

"I do."

"I'm letting you know that you can let your guard down with me. It's okay to let me love you the way you deserve to be loved."

Using my thumbs, I wiped the tears from his eyes. "I have let my guard down with you. I feel safe when I'm with you. Since the day Aaron left this earth, you've never left my side. Not even for a day."

"Do you love me?" he asked sincerely.

"I do love you."

Calvin's smile was bright. I could see all thirty-two of his pearly white teeth. "Seeing that couple in that elevator made me realize what's important. Aaron's death told me that we don't have forever. We could be here today and gone tomorrow."

"That's true."

"So, with that being said, I think we should get married. We're already in Vegas, so let's do it."

"Calvin, don't you think that's a little sudden?"

"No. If we love each other, what's the problem?"

"It's just sudden, that's all. I wasn't expecting this. Normally, there's a proposal and after some time has passed, a wedding follows."

"I don't want to wait. I'm ready to change your last name."

Silently, I just sat there staring into space. I could see him clearly, but I wasn't looking directly into his face. His proposition had a bitch speechless.

Calvin grabbed the bag beside me and dug through it. Seconds later, he produced a teal box. "I planned to propose to you on this trip. Then I figured if you truly loved me you would say yes."

My mouth hit the floor. *Surprised* was an understatement. This was not what I was expecting. True enough, we've known each other for years, but we just started dating. On the other hand, we were living together and we had plenty of time to get married.

To me, the ring would solidify the seriousness of our relationship. So, I didn't understand why he couldn't just propose to me without us having to get married right away. Calvin acted as if he knew he was about to leave this earth.

"If you would've proposed to me, my answer would've been yes. I just feel like you're acting on impulse and alcohol."

"Wow," he nodded and bit down on his lip. "That's how you think of me. Then I guess you don't know me at all."

"That's not what I mean."

Calvin cut his eyes at me. They were dark like a snake's eyes. The snarl on his face was mean. He clutched the box tightly in his hand. "You know that I love you and that's not the alcohol talking."

Calvin threw the box onto the bed and headed towards the door.

"Calvin, where are you going?"

He ignored me and let the door slam behind him.

Chapter 8

Lexi

All night I tossed and turned. Sleep was not an option for me. It was two in the morning, and Calvin still hadn't returned. Multiple times I called his phone and not once did he answer. With each passing minute, I worried about his safety and his state of mind. The way I hurt him with my words. This would be the time I called Foreign to get her advice; but since I wasn't talking to her, I was on my own. Honestly, it hurt to have no one right now.

Fear kept me from being happy. Calvin called me out on my shit. I couldn't deny that. My first and last heartbreak destroyed me. It turned me into a certified, cold-blooded bitch. Caring about a man's feelings was the furthest thing on my list. Cameron did a number on me in college, and I never loved anyone again. It was his fault.

Bethune Cookman College

"So where are you going today?" Foreign asked while sitting on the sofa, eating ice cream.

"Cameron is in town to pick me up. We're going away for the weekend. It's going to be just me and my man," I giggled and danced in slow motion.

"Don't get pregnant, sis. 'Cause I'm not babysitting. That's gon' be you missing all the college parties."

"That's what our parents are for." Sitting down next to Foreign, I sat upright on my feet. "Do you think he's going to propose to me? We've been talking about our futures a lot."

"I mean it's possible. He does love you, I can say that."

"He does, doesn't he?" I played with the necklace Cameron bought me for Valentine's Day. A huge smile was stuck on my face. Cameron had my heart and soul. There was no other man that I wanted. Not even the fine ass dudes on the football team.

"Girl, you are crazy as hell," Foreign laughed. "I wish you could see your face right now. You all giddy and shit."

"Now don't nobody say shit to you about Aaron and the way you be all over him. Both of y'all nasty asses get on my nerves. I just want to throw up." I stuck my finger in my mouth.

"That's my husband. We're getting married after graduation and we are going to have a house full of babies for you to keep."

"Sis, you know I'm going to keep my badass nieces and nephews. That's a given. You know you having twins, right?"

"Yeah, I know y'all carrying around those twin genes."

There was a knock on the door.

"Ouuu, that's my baby right there." I jumped up and ran to the door like a kid at Christmas. When I opened the door, Cameron was standing at the door looking like a sad puppy. That dampened my mood instantly. "Hey, baby, what's wrong?"

"We need to talk."

"Come inside." I stepped back, giving him room to enter.

"Hey, Foreign."

"Hey, Cameron."

We went into my bedroom and closed the door for some privacy. Cameron sat down on the bed. The room was eerily quiet, and it made me nervous.

"Cameron, what's wrong with you?"

He sat quietly for a little longer. When he finally looked at me, there were tears in his eyes. "We can't go away for the weekend."

That caused me to panic. "What happened? Is it your parents? Are they okay?"

"They're fine."

Now I was confused. "Well, why do you look like you just lost your best friend?"

"I did."

"Who?"

"You."

"Okay, I'm really confused. What are you trying to tell me?" I stood firmly in front of him with my arms folded.

"Do you remember when you had finals and couldn't come to see me?"

"Yeah."

Cameron sighed and hung his head. "I cheated on you with my ex-girlfriend and got her pregnant."

Hearing that news was like a punch to the gut. Tears streamed down my face, and I fell to my knees. "How could you do this to me?"

Cameron eased on the floor and held me. "I'm sorry, Lexi. I really am. I never meant to hurt you."

"Well, you did," I screamed.

"It was a mistake."

"You cheated because I had to study for my finals?" Pulling myself off the floor, I snatched away from him. "Please don't touch me. I hate you so much right now."

"Not as much you're going to hate me when I tell you this." Cameron leaned against my dresser.

"What else could you possibly say to hurt me more than you have already?"

"We're getting married."

"What?" That was the straw that broke the camel's back. I held my stomach and rocked. "What did you just say?"

"My parents want us to get married and raise the baby together. I came here to tell you face to face. I owed you that much."

My eyes were filled with water, and my vision was blurry. In a matter of seconds, my entire life and future had been destroyed. Cameron was supposed to be my husband. I was supposed to have his kids.

"Get out!" I screamed.

"Alexis, I'm sorry. You know how much I love you. I don't love her. It was just sex. It's my parents. With my dad being a pastor of our church, he's worried about the image."

"Well, it looks like you've made up your mind. You can get out now. I never want to see you again."

Cameron tried to console me, but I fought him off. "Get your hands off of me." I kicked and punched until he released me."

"I'm sorry, Lexi and for what it's worth I still love you." After that weak-ass confession, he left.

Cradling my pillow, I laid in bed and cried my eyes out. It didn't take Foreign long to come inside. "Lexi, what happened? Are you okay?" Her voice was soft and filled with concern. Foreign crawled into bed with me and wrapped her arms around me. "Talk to me."

"He left me," I sobbed.

"Why? What happened?" The shock in her voice was evident.

"He cheated with his ex and got her pregnant. Now he's going to marry her."

"Damn, Lexi. I'm so sorry to hear that." Foreign stayed in bed with me until I fell asleep. That was how Cameron broke up with me one day before his wedding.

When I woke up and looked at the clock, it was nine o'clock in the morning. Calvin still hadn't returned. I called his phone again, but I didn't get an answer. "Calvin, where are you?" I sent him a text.

While waiting on a reply, I went to use the bathroom. A hard knock on the door startled me. At the same time, I was relieved. He was probably drunk and lost his keys. There was so much I wanted to say to Calvin, and I needed him to understand where I was coming from. It wasn't like I didn't love him. I wanted to take my time and not rush into anything. Hell, we just started dating.

Filled with great anticipation, I opened the door slowly. I was ready to give him a piece of my mind for storming out of the room like that. On the opposite side of the door was the bodyguard Calvin hired, holding a black bag.

"Where is Calvin? Is he okay?"

"Relax, he's fine."

"Then where is he?" I stepped out and peeped down the hall. He wasn't out there.

"I was instructed to give you this." The bodyguard handed me the bag and walked away.

Immediately, I closed the door and rushed to the bed to see what was inside. Unzipping the bag, I was taken aback by what I was holding in my hand. It was a sparkly, silver evening gown with a split and a pair of heels. "What is he doing?" I mumbled.

Lifting the bag, a card fell out. I opened it and read the contents out loud.

"Lexi, the love I have for you is indescribable. Each day we spend together is better than the last, and I never want it to end. We aren't perfect people, but we are perfect together. I've had my share of women and I'm ready to settle down for good, and I want to spend the rest of my life with you. I said all of that to say this. I will be at the Love Story Wedding Chapel at noon. A car will be waiting downstairs at 11:45 a.m. to bring you here. If you don't show up, that will be the end of our relationship and I'm moving on. Life is too short to waste time. I'm ready for marriage. Love, Calvin."

Damn, I needed Foreign. She was always my voice of reason. I went to the bar and grabbed the bottle we started last night. "Aaron, I need you badly right now." The tears flowed heavily. "You would know what to say."

For the next few minutes, I sat in heavy thought, staring at the wall. A cool gust of wind hit my face, and I could've sworn I heard Aaron's voice.

"I know I'm not tripping." I looked at the ceiling to see if I was sitting underneath a vent. I wasn't. The voice told me what to do, but I was hesitant. Seconds later, I could hear it again. So, I complied.

The phone rang multiple times before it stopped. "Hello," Foreign answered.

In tears, I replied. "I need to talk to you."

After spending thirty minutes on the phone with Foreign, I felt better about my decision. It was refreshing to know that she wasn't holding a grudge towards me. I promised that we would do lunch when I returned so we could hash out our differences. At the end of the day, she was still my sister.

Time was slipping away, so I went and took a shower and slipped on a pair of joggers. Packing my suitcase, I dropped the room key on the dresser and left.

Downstairs, there was a car waiting as promised. The driver helped me with my luggage, and I climbed into the back seat. He looked over his shoulder. "We'll arrive at the chapel in fifteen minutes."

"No. Take me to the airport please."

"Are you sure? I was paid to drive you to the chapel."

"I'll double your pay if you just take me to the airport."

"Okay."

The Rolls Royce pulled off smoothly, and I put my AirPods in. Jagged Edge's "Goodbye" played, and I started to cry. On the way out, I just stared aimlessly out the window, unsure if I was about to make the biggest mistake of my life.

Calvin...

Nervously, I kept my eyes on my Rolex. Alexis was due to arrive at the chapel in fifteen minutes. I wasn't sure she would show up. After I bailed out on her last night, I went to the casino and gambled for hours. Once I was tired of that, my bodyguard drove me around to look at a few chapels. When we were done, I ended up crashing inside his room. There was no way I was going back to that room.

My bodyguard, Dave, sat on the opposite side of the bench. I looked over at him. "Did she seem upset when you arrived?"

"No. She seemed worried."

"What did she say?"

"Nothing really. She just asked me where you were and if you were okay."

In the beginning, Aaron was a little concerned about me and Lexi having dealings. He never told Lexi how he truly felt, but he kept it real with me at all times. We were brothers, and that's what brothers do. Aaron didn't like her behavior, but he couldn't tell her what to do. Therefore, he just kept his opinions about her lifestyle to himself. We all knew that Cameron was the reason she acted out.

Before Aaron passed away, I told him that I wanted to be with her. He gave me his blessing and I ran with it. My thoughts consumed me heavily. All I could think about was Lexi. If she didn't want to commit to me, we were over. And there would be no second chance. When we made it back to Florida, she would have to move out. Of course, I wouldn't put her out. I would give her time to find a place, but she would have to stay in the guestroom.

Glancing down at my watch, I realized it was five minutes after twelve. Lexi wasn't there, and I had my answer. We were over. It hurt, but I would be okay in due time. Standing up, I adjusted my black coat.

"We can leave. She's not coming." Deep down I felt played.

We walked down the hall in silence. Then I decided to check my phone. It wasn't in my pocket. "Hold on. I left my phone."

"I'll grab it," Dave replied.

Frustrated, I leaned against the wall and waited on him to return. I guess my night would consist of gambling, drinking, and smashing a groupie or two. My relationship was over, and I no longer had to be faithful. It was crazy how I changed my life just to show her that I could be committed to one woman. My best wasn't good enough.

Dave returned with my phone in his hand. "Hey, before you leave, the pastor in the chapel needs to talk to you."

"Okay." On my way back, I walked with my head down. I'd never been rejected by a woman. It was a first time for everything.

Music was playing when I stepped back inside. Then I froze.

Lexi...

There I stood in the middle of the aisle, looking a hot mess and my face drenched in fresh tears. Over the speaker, *Stuck with U*—by Ariana Grande and Justin Bieber—played softly. I sang loudly, so he could feel how I felt.

So lock the door / And throw out the key / Can't fight this no more / It's just you and me / And there's nothing I, nothing I, I can do / I'm stuck with you, stuck with you, stuck with you / So go ahead and drive me insane / Baby, run your mouth / I still wouldn't change being stuck with you / Stuck with you, stuck with you / I'm stuck with you, stuck with you, stuck with you, baby—

Calvin was so handsome in his designer suit. The way he watched me made me want to just melt. Not once did he interrupt me. The song came to an end, and he was still standing in the same spot. Slowly, I walked to him and closed the space between us. He didn't seem too happy.

"Lexi, what do you want?" That wasn't the response I was expecting to hear, but I had to roll with it. What other choice did I have?

"Calvin, I want you," I admitted openly. "Last night I had time to sit and think, and I realized that I don't want to be without you. I don't want to spend another night without you in the bed to hold me or dry my tears when I think about my brother. You've been my rock, and I can't do this without you."

"Is that the only reason you want to be with me?" His tone was firm and unsettling.

"No." I wiped my eyes. "Calvin, I love you. I get butterflies when I see you. Daily you make me happy, and I'm not willing to give that up so easily. You treat me like a queen, and I know that you truly love me. And I kept thinking if I marry you would I be messing up your life? I don't know the first thing about being a married woman. That takes a lot of work. I'm scared, but I would rather be scared with you than be scared without you. You heard my song. I want nothing more than to be stuck with you and trying to make it work. That's how committed I am."

Calvin stroked my cheek with his finger. "I don't know the first thing about being a husband, but we can learn from each other. All we have to do is communicate with each other."

"I can do that."

"Alexis, what do you want from me?" He repeated his previous question.

I reached in my pocket and took out the ring. "Ask me again," I pleaded through my tears.

"Are you sure? I don't want to force this on you."

"I'm sure."

Calvin got down on one knee and took my hand. "Alexis Renee Young, would you marry me?"

"Yes. Yes. I will marry you."

"You just made me that happiest man alive." Calvin slipped that big-ass diamond on my ring finger. "Come on. Let's get married."

"Wait. I have to change my clothes and do my make-up."

"You don't need make-up, baby. I'll be waiting for you at the altar."

"Okay."

Rushing to the back of the chapel, I grabbed the black bag and found the bathroom. My college dream of getting married had finally become a reality. For that to happen, I finally accepted my past and let it go. That needed to happen so I could move on with my life once and for all.

Happily, I sashayed down the aisle. Calvin was the true definition of what a man was supposed to be. Today was the start of the rest of our lives and to new beginnings. Side by side we stood at the altar, and listened to the preacher read passages from the bible.

"After hearing the two of you exchange words not too long ago, I believe those were vows and there's nothing left to say. Are the two of you good with that?"

We both said yes.

"By the power invested in me, I now pronounce you Mr. and Mrs. Calvin Bailey. You may now kiss your bride."

Our kiss was soft, passionate, and long.

After the shotgun wedding, we went back to our room to celebrate our marriage. This trip turned out to be better than I'd imagined. I knew Aaron was in heaven smiling down on the both of us. As promised, we christened that balcony several times.

Chapter 9

Domestic

The Next Day

Ever since Foreign told me that Tracy was talking to a detective, I've felt uneasy. There was no telling what their conversation consisted of, but I was going to find out one way or another. I wasn't set to go back to work just yet, but I felt like I needed to go and do some digging.

Foreign was still asleep, so I decided to wake her up. "Bae." Careful not to startle her, I caressed her shoulder until she opened her eyes. "I'm about to go by the shop. I'll be right back."

"I don't think that's a good idea. You should be resting." She yawned and rubbed her eyes.

"I'm not doing any work. I just need to swing by there to see what's going on. I won't be gone for more than an hour."

"Okay, hurry back." Foreign adjusted her pillow and went back to bed.

For the past few days, I hadn't received a call from Carlos. My guess was they put the idea of Emilia being missing to rest. That was their best bet because that bitch was never coming back. Jumping in the car, I fired up the engine. The first thing I noticed was my gas tank. It was no longer full, and DP didn't bother to stop by a gas station.

"I need to talk to that boy," I mumbled. Before pulling off, I set the music and put on my shades.

Tracy was sitting at the desk with her head down. I could see her from the opposite side of the glass. The sound of the door automatically caught her attention. There wasn't a smile present. Tracy looked as if she was caught with her pants down.

"Good moming, Boss."

"Good morning." I leaned against the counter. "You don't look happy to see me."

"It's not that. I just wasn't expecting to see you that's all. Are you feeling better? How is your shoulder?"

"It's okay. I'm still in a little pain, but it feels better than it did a few days ago."

"That's good to hear. What are you doing here?"

"I was in the neighborhood and decided to drop by and see what was going on around here."

"Business is good as usual," she paused for a few seconds. "Oh, Detective Marshall stopped by."

"What did he want?" Emilia's partner was like a thirsty bloodhound. Birds of a feather flocked together. For him to visit was quite interesting. He wasn't present on the scene. That didn't mean it wasn't assigned. It just meant I needed to keep my ears and eyes open.

"He was asking questions about the shooting."

"Like what? Does he know who did it?"

"No. He wanted to see if I saw anything. I told him I didn't because it all happened so fast. After that, he left."

That wasn't enough information. I needed more than that. "Did he leave a card?"

"He did." Tracy handed me a business card.

"Thanks."

Detective Marshall was about to receive a call from me as soon as I made it to my office.

Lexi…

Tampa, FL

The paparazzi swarmed the airport once we landed on the private jet from our mini-vacation. Good news traveled fast. It hadn't been twenty-fours since we were hitched. Calvin and I were plastered on every news station, tabloid, and social media site. My father caught wind of it and called me right away. Surprisingly, he was quite happy. I know it had everything to do with my past and now my ability to finally move on with my life and be happy. They had the truck surrounded as we made our way through the crowd. But being who I was, I rolled down the window, so they could take a good photo of me.

Calvin laughed. "You have to give them something to look at, huh?"

"Of course. You know I welcome all the fans."

"You crazy."

"You knew that a long time ago." I rolled the window back up, and sat back against the leather seat. "Before we go home, can we go by the precinct? I need to speak with the detective."

"About what?"

"I need them to open Aaron's case. His death wasn't an accident, and I need to know who's behind it."

Calvin scratched his scalp and looked at me with a curious side eye. "What makes you think that?"

"The guy that Foreign is dating gives me a bad vibe. He's controlling and possessive. You heard the voicemail she left me."

"I did, but that doesn't make him a killer."

"Whose side are you on, Mr. Bailey?"

"Mrs. Bailey. Who else?"

"I know that's right." Feeling a bit shit, I clapped a hand over my mouth. It was surreal that I was officially off of the market.

"If you want to go and see the detective, we can do that."

"Thank you, baby. I appreciate that."

"You don't have to thank me. I love you and I got your back one-thousand percent." Calvin kissed me on the lips. "I'll always stand by you, right or wrong."

"I love you too."

"Hey, Taylor," he called out to the driver. "Take us down to the precinct."

"Got it," he replied.

The ride felt long as hell, and the jet lag was beating my ass. Every bump had me nauseated and dizzy as fuck. Slumping down in the back seat, I laid down in Calvin's lap.

"You trying to get freaky in the truck?" he grinned.

"Why you have to be so nasty all time? Get your mind out the gutter."

"I can't help that we both nasty."

"Not today. I don't feel good. Besides, you should be tired from our very long weekend."

"Hmm," his top lip curled. "Don't tell me you're pregnant already."

"And ruin this figure. I don't think so."

"Well, one day you will."

"No time soon."

"So, I can't get a baby from you?"

"Yeah, in like five years."

"I was thinking more like six months to a year."

"We can negotiate."

"Lexi, stop playing with me."

To divert the conversation, I rubbed his chest. "Don't you want us to enjoy each other before we start adding kids to the equation? You're in the prime of your career."

"Yeah. I do. But I'm not the one that has to carry it."

"My point exactly," I winked.

"Yeah, okay. I'ma let you have that for now."

"Good," I yawned.

It felt like I was sleeping forever when Calvin woke me up from my catnap. "We're here. Get up."

"Already?" I yawned once more. "I'm so tired."

"Well, let's get this over with so we can go home."

Calvin and I walked into the precinct. Several people were seated in the lobby. As soon as they spotted my NFL husband, they went crazy.

An older white man greeted him. "CB, man, I'm your biggest fan. Can I get a photo with you please?"

"Let the autographs begin," I mumbled.

"Stop that!"

"You handle that while I handle business." I walked up to the officer and rested my elbows on the counter. "I'm here to see the detective on my brother's case."

"What's your brother's name?"

"Aaron Young."

"The NFL player?"

"Yes."

"Give me one second." The woman tapped on the computer keyboard as I waited anxiously. "Um. It was Emilia that worked the case, but she's no longer here. I can let you speak with her partner— Detective Marshall."

"That's fine."

"Okay. Have a seat and I'll call him up for you."

"Thank you."

The fans were finally seated when I walked over and sat beside Calvin. "What did they say?"

"She's paging Detective Marshall. He took over once y'all thirst trap hoe got fired."

Calvin didn't reply. He just nodded. A few minutes passed before a gentleman came out and introduced himself. "I'm Detective Marshall."

"Hi. I'm Alexis Young and this is my husband—"

"Calvin Bailey, better known as CB," he finished my sentence before I could finish the introduction. "I'm a big fan."

"Thank you." Calvin shook his hand.

"What brings you by, Ms. Young?"

"I have some concerns about my brother's case and I would like to talk in private."

"No problem. We can go into my office." Detective Marshall escorted us down the hall and into a private room. "Come in and have a seat."

We did just that.

Detective Marshall sat down, folded his hands, and placed them on the desk. "So what concerns do you have about your brother's accident?"

"See, that's the thing. I don't believe it was an accident."

The detective's eyebrow slanted with curiosity. "And what makes you believe that?"

"Well," I swallowed my spit, trying to contain my emotions. Whenever I spoke about Aaron, it saddened me deeply. To lose someone you love was difficult enough, but to lose a twin was unbearable pain that I wouldn't wish on my worst enemy.

Calvin rubbed my back. "Take your time. You can do this."

"There are a lot of things that don't add up. For instance, no one knew that Aaron was taking classes. Just me and his wife, Foreign. No one knew where these classes were. And not to mention, Foreign has a boyfriend that despised my brother. I also think he's the one that set his headstone on fire."

"Is that right?" Detective Marshall scratched his chin and leaned back in his seat. "Are you implying that Mrs. Young had something to do with his death?"

"No. I'm not saying that at all. She loved Aaron and I knew that for a fact, but this new man she's with is jealous, controlling, and possessive."

"Hmm. That could be a formula for fatal attraction but doesn't necessarily make him a killer. We're currently looking into getting footage from the cemetery. Do you have any proof that he could be behind this?"

"Not really!" I shrugged in disappointment. "I do have a message that Foreign left on my voicemail. That's what heightened my suspicions."

"Okay. Let me hear it."

Pulling my phone from my purse, I went to the voicemail and hit *play*. That message was saved specifically for this reason. The room was silent, as the message played on the speaker.

"Lexi, I know you're upset with me and I'm sorry for the way things went down between us. You have to know that I loved Aaron. I still do and I miss him so much. Before he died, I took him back so we could work on our marriage. A few days later he was dead. Another thing you should know is that I didn't invite him to Aaron's funeral. I told him it was a bad idea for him to show up, but he didn't care. It's like he had this weird obsession with Aaron. Things are really bad and I need you. This man is crazy and abusive. He just burned Aaron's jersey right in my face. Lexi, you're my only friend. Please call me back."

When the message stopped, the detective had a blank stare on his face. It was hard to determine what he could be possibly thinking. I guess all that training came in handy. His poker face was on point, and he was quiet until he cleared his throat.

"That's some pretty interesting evidence, but again it's not enough to make an arrest. We need evidence that proves his guilt beyond a reasonable doubt."

"I know it's not the smoking gun that you need, but I do believe it's enough to take homicide into consideration." Frustrated with the words I didn't want to hear, I exhaled deeply. "Can you just please look into it and ask a few questions or check the surveillance cameras where he did his counseling?"

"Yes. I can ask around and see what I can find," he agreed.

Calvin leaned forward. "I'll be more than happy to know that you will take her accusations seriously. I'm sure I can arrange some playoff tickets and a skybox for your cooperation."

Detective Marshall's eyes lit up like a fiend getting a free eightball. "You have my word. I'll do all I can do to get to the bottom of this."

"Thank you." Calvin stood up and shook his hand. "We appreciate your effort."

"No problem. I'll be in touch."

Upon my feet, I shook his hand as well. "Thank you."

"You're welcome."

A huge weight had been lifted off of my shoulders. All I needed for him to do was, put one hundred and ten percent into finding my brother's killer. There wasn't a shadow of a doubt that Foreign's buff ass nigga was behind everything. My heart was dead set on him, and I knew I was right. No one could tell me any different. In the meantime, I would conduct my investigation as well.

Chapter 10

Domestic

It was one week later, and my shoulder was feeling much better. I felt like a new man. And now that my little setback was out of the way, I was ready to get back to the business. First on my list was bitch ass Shawn and his brother. Them niggas had to see me for blasting at me like I'm some weak ass fuck boy. Casey better get her tears and black dress ready because his time on earth was about to expire.

Carlos was already en route so we could chop it up. We had to switch up the location. Tracy was on my radar with that sneaky shit, and it was time to keep my grass cut. She was safe until I found out otherwise. The bar wasn't crowded, being that it was early in the afternoon, so that was guaranteed privacy.

As expected, Carlos was sitting in the back awaiting my arrival. When I sat down at the table, he was already drinking. He looked as if he hadn't slept in days. "My brother, what's going on? You look like shit."

Carlos downed his drink and aggressively sat the glass on the table. It was a surprise it didn't break. "That's how I feel."

"What's going on?"

"It's my pops. He's losing it since he hasn't heard from Emilia. She still hasn't called, and her phone still going straight to voicemail. Something is wrong and I know it."

"Have you reported it to the police?"

"Not yet." Carlos waved the waitress over. "Let me get a refill. You want a drink?"

"Nah." That was my first answer, but I quickly changed my mind. "On second thought, bring me a whiskey—neat."

"Be right back." The skinny waitress smiled, and skipped off in her itty bitty shorts and flat ass.

"When I leave here, I have to go down and file a missing person's report. I hope she's good because he's barely sleeping or eating."

Emilia was not the subject I wanted to discuss, but I needed to ease his mind so I could get to the point of the meeting. "I'm sure she's fine. You know how she gets. The last time I talked to her, she told me she wanted to just disappear and start over."

Carlos looked me in the eyes and nodded. "That's true."

The waitress approached us and sat our glasses down. "Enjoy!" She was so damn bubbly; somebody enjoyed their job.

Carlos sipped his new drink a little slower. So, what you called me here for?"

"The shooting. I wanna get back at them niggas for that shit they pulled at the wash." Taking a sip of my whiskey, I allowed him the chance to respond, but he didn't. It was like he was out of space. "Did you hear what I said?"

"Yeah. I hear you, but I'm not feeling that shit."

"Damn, why not?"

"It's too hot right now."

"These niggas shot at us, bro. What the fuck you mean?" I found myself getting a little too loud, so I had to calm myself down.

"I get that, but I killed their brother." He pointed back and forth between us. "We are still alive. You need to learn how to chill. Do you think I made it this far by being sloppy? Fuck no!"

In a way it made sense, but I wasn't trying to hear that. Them niggas had to see me expeditiously. "That's why I'm coming to you. It's why I hired you in the first place. You're the best at this shit."

"Exactly!" Carlos took the last shot. "I'm the best and I'm telling you to lay low. Just stay strapped and pay attention to your surroundings. I promised my girl that I'm out of the game for good. I'm retiring, bro. I need to be here to raise my kids."

"Damn bro! You just gon' back out when I need you the most? That's wild as fuck, man."

"Domestic, think logically for one second. Put that street shit to the back of your mind. You are supposed to be a legitimate businessman, right?"

"Right," I agreed.

"There was a driveby at your business establishment. Don't you think the law is watching you from a distance? That shit sounds like street beef." Carlos tapped his temple with his finger. "Think about it 'cause I know you ain't trying to go to prison."

"Hell nah!"

"Then think like a businessman and not a thug. I'm trying to keep you from dying or going to prison."

"A'ight. I'll chill." That was the furthest from the truth, but I wasn't about to keep going back and forth with Pastor Carlos. Now all of a sudden, he was a savior. It was all good. I'll just handle shit my way.

"Good! I thought you'll see it my way." Carlos stood up and dropped a hundred-dollar bill on the table. "I have to go, but I'll get up with you later, brother."

"A'ight, brother!"

After the meeting, I went back home. Upon my arrival, Foreign was walking out the door. I parked the car and got out, meeting her on the porch. "Hey, baby. Where are you going?" I grabbed her by the waist and kissed her soft, luscious lips.

"I'm about to go by my house to check the mailbox and grab a few things."

"Okay. I'll go with you."

"You sure? I'll be fine by myself."

"Yes. I'm sure. I don't need you lifting anything heavy while you carrying my child. That's what I'm here for."

"Okay." She agreed.

"We'll take my car," I suggested.

As we walked down the steps, an unmarked car pulled up. "Are you expecting someone?"

"No."

My instincts caused me to step directly in front of Foreign just in case some shit was about to pop off. "Stand behind me until I tell you to go in the house." I put my hand at the small of my back in case I needed to pull out my Glock. We stood in place until the door opened. The second I saw who it was, I dropped my hand at my side.

"We good."

The well-dressed man walked up with a straight face and his hands shoved down inside his pockets. "I'm Detective Marshall from the Tampa Bay precinct."

"You're Emilia's partner," I stated.

"Correct."

"Well, how can I help you?"

Corny ass Detective Pip Squeak looked straight past me and directly at my woman. "Actually, I'm here to see Mrs. Young." That muthafucka had some big nuts disrespecting me on my property.

"What is this about?" Foreign questioned.

"It's about your late husband, and I would like for you to come in and answer a few questions." Detective Marshall acted as if he didn't want to speak in front of me.

His punk ass wasn't about to stop me from speaking up. "Why can't you just tell her what it's about?"

"We can discuss this matter at the station," he insisted.

"Well, she's not coming down there until you tell her what it's about."

Foreign stepped up and placed her hand on my arm. "Domestic, relax, please." Then she stood directly beside me. "Please forgive my boyfriend. Can you just tell me what it's about and I'll come to answer the questions at a later date?"

Detective Marshall stood in silence for a moment, but his eyes never left mine. We had a stare-off for several seconds. Then he finally shifted his focus back to Foreign. "When there's a death and an insurance policy is involved, we have to interview the spouse. It's minor on your behalf since Aaron's death was an accident."

"I can do that."

"Okay. I'll leave my card with you. Just give me a call."

"I will do that."

Detective Marshall reached into his breast pocket and pulled out his card. When he passed it to Foreign, I tried to intercept it, but she was quicker than me. With a nasty snarl on my face, I glanced at Foreign.

"Come on, baby, let's go." The detective walked off, and I escorted her to the passenger seat.

Foreign snatched her seat beat and buckled up with an attitude. Ignoring her semantics for the moment, I got into the driver's seat and fired up the engine. Instead of me inciting the argument, I waited on her to kick it off. Looking at the lock on the dash, I decided to give her few minutes to herself and allowed the music to keep me entertained.

Foreign sat with her arms folded and bottom lip poked out. It looked juicy enough to suck. The woman just didn't understand that her actions were turning me on in a weird, kinky way. Deep into the song, while I was rapping about money and bitches, Foreign shut the stereo off completely.

Stricken with anger, she snapped. "Domestic, what is your problem? Do you have to embarrass me every chance you get? I mean damn, it's like every time Aaron's name is involved you lose your fucking marbles. The man is dead!" She screamed. "What are you competing with? He's never coming back. He can't take me away from you. Only you can do that and I'm two seconds from walking away from you. I'm tired of this shit."

This was a new woman. A bold woman that I didn't know existed inside of her. Yet, I had no idea who she was talking to. Foreign caught me off guard with her reaction. "You sure you want to talk to me like that?"

"I said what I said!" Foreign rolled her eyes and looked out the window.

"So you disrespecting me behind a lame, dead ass nigga?"

Foreign's head spun around swiftly. "See, that's the shit I'm talking about right there. You are so fucking disrespectful and sad. You don't respect me as a woman, but you quick to say you're a real man."

"I am a real man."

"Tuh!" Foreign huffed with a slight laugh. "I beg to differ. A real man wouldn't be upset behind a woman grieving her husband. You knew I was married, but you didn't care."

"It's obvious you didn't care either. Yo' ass wasn't worried about that nigga when I fucked you the first night, so stop acting like you was so in love with him."

"So fucking what! He cheated and so did I. You can't make me feel bad about a careless decision that I made."

"Now I'm a careless decision?" That shit had me hot under the collar. I wanted to knock her ass upside the head, but I changed my mind when I looked at her stomach. "You say that shit now, but don't forget that I'm the one that pulled you out of that depressing ass marriage by the bootstraps. I'm the best nigga you ever had."

"Yeah, okay. That explains why I'm in this depressing-ass relationship."

"I'm going to let that slide and kill this argument before we both say something that we'll regret."

"Too late for that." Foreign turned the stereo on and blasted the music, drowning out my thoughts.

Foreign…

As always, Domestic apologized for acting like a complete asshole that has no home training. But hey, who was I kidding? I met his mama. They were so dysfunctional and crazy. Domestic was seconds away from hearing me say that I regret the day we met. It was the truth. His actions had me questioning if I wanted to keep the baby. Abortion wasn't an option. I was too far along for that, and I desperately wanted to be a mother. Deep down my inner spirit told me to haul ass and don't look back.

To keep me from jumping off of the deep end, I reached out to Blacque Barbee for a much-needed pep talk. Domestic had me ready to do something crazy, and I was trying to keep my sanity. We had been on the phone for about fifteen minutes. My mouth was running fast like ninety going north. Barbee didn't say a word until I took a deep breath.

"Have you calmed down now?" She giggled.

"A little bit."

"Good. You don't want to stress your baby out. He or she does not want to be bald-headed when they enter this world."

That was my first laugh of the day. "I know right. My poor child has no idea what they about to get into."

"That's why you need to do what I told you."

"I am. I'm doing my best to stick it out and let things fall into place. He just makes me so mad." The more I expressed my feelings, the angrier I became. "I can't do this anymore."

Barbee sighed. "Girl, that's what men do. They ain't nothing but overgrown kids who want to be breastfed."

"You are crazy."

"We have to be crazy with these fools. You see what happened when you cursed his ass out. He didn't touch you at all, and you didn't have to pull that gun out on his ass."

"That's true. I just think he was more shocked than anything. Domestic is so used to me being timid when he raises his voice. I'm over that shit now. Today made me realize that I can't be weak. That's when he walks all over me."

For the little bit of time I spent with Barbee, she taught me some valuable lessons and so far so good, it felt good to get my voice and power back. Domestic was no different from Aaron, except in size, and I would never allow Aaron to talk to me crazy. Barbee gave me that gun, and now I felt like I could hold my own if it came down to things getting physical.

"See, you got this. This nightmare will be over before you know it."

"I hope so," I sighed with uncertainty.

"Just remember you are doing this for your baby and her future. That will make everything worth it in the end." Barbee spoke like a mother, and I listened as if I was her child. "Where is he anyway?"

"He went to go do pickups from the car washes. I'm here by myself. His son is at his girlfriend's house."

"Where is your friend—Maurice?"

"I haven't talked to him since we left you."

"It's probably best that you keep him at a distance. But you can call and let him know you're okay."

"I am. I've just been trying to focus on Domestic and make this shit work. He keeps bringing up the wedding, and you know that's not happening. Not with him anyway. I'm just over it."

"Well, I placed the order with my guy. Your new documents should be there in the next two weeks."

"Can you have him expedite it? I don't think I will make it another two weeks in this town."

"Yeah. I can ask him and see what he says."

"Thanks! I'm ready to move on with my life."

"Black girl, where you at?" The loud voice in the background was nobody but Corey.

"I'm in the kitchen," Barbee shouted. "Well, my man and rugrats are here so I have to tend to them."

"Thanks for listening to me vent with my craziness."

"That's what I'm here for. Just remember the reason you're doing this, and everything else will fall as planned. If you need me, just call no matter how late it is."

"Thanks, B. Talk to you later."

"Later."

After we hung up. I laid down on the bed and stared at the ceiling. Reality set in and in my heart, it was truly over. Our relationship would never work, and I refused to walk down the aisle with him. Springing to my feet, I went into DP's room and rambled through his desk. Quickly, I penned a brief letter to Domestic. The way he showed his natural black ass in front of the detective made me see the light. This man hated Aaron with a passion. Now, I was starting to take everything Emilia said as the truth.

When I returned home, I exhaled a sigh of relief. It felt good to be back in my house, but I wasn't happy. Aaron was no longer there, and God knows I missed his presence. The massive home that I built with my husband was supposed to be the place where we raised our children. Here I stood in a million-dollar mansion, with expensive furniture, and paintings, yet it was empty. There were no children and—unfortunately—no husband either. An eerie silence sent cold chills down my spine.

Before I did anything, I headed straight to the kitchen. There wasn't anything in there to eat, but spring water was always an option. First thing in the morning, I was going to the grocery store and get some food up in there. With my water bottle in my hand, I proceeded upstairs to my bedroom. After the long day I had, all I wanted was the bed. Stripping out of my clothes, I slipped on one of Aaron's shirts. His scent was still embedded into it.

Flashbacks of the good times in the bedroom made me smile. There were so many good memories beyond these walls, but also some bad ones. To make peace and carry on with my life, I decided to only hold onto the good ones. When I laid down, the mattress was extremely soft and cold. Over the years, Aaron's side of the bed was empty more times than I could count on my hands and toes. It hit different this time, knowing it would be forever.

Snuggling up with his pillow, I could still smell the scent of his body wash. The last time we were intimate played in my mind. It made me smile. Aaron's presence was definitely in the room that night. Maybe that was him letting me know he was watching over me. Being back in my home would allow me to grieve properly and in peace. Sleep came easy, as I drifted off into the clouds.

Chapter 11

Domestic

My rounds at the wash were complete, and I needed to go and relieve some pressure. It was time for me to drink, so I went by the liquor store. The way Foreign came at me earlier had me wanting to fight then fuck. She tried a real nigga hard as fuck. I wanted to smack her ass in the mouth, but I held it in. One thing I told myself was to try and keep my hands to myself. At least until after we were married. Foreign was about to learn the hard way about disrespecting me. After I got her down that aisle, I was about to show her who was the boss. It was a new sheriff in town, and she was going to see how I got the name *Domestic*.

Casey should've been the perfect example for her, but nah. Foreign thought she was exempt from these ass whoopings. That wasn't the case. I tried to go easy on her since she was carrying my child. In about six months all that shit was going to change. Foreign knew how I felt about a slick-tongued woman. I was liable to snatch that motherfucker clean out her mouth. So, before I went home, I made a pit stop to keep myself from slapping her down.

By the time I made it across town, I had consumed half of a bottle of Tequila. I hooked a left on South Manhattan Avenue, pulled directly in front of the building, and hopped out with my keys in my hand. Saint Patrick's Catholic Church. Dressed like the businessman I am, I slow-strolled through the double doors of the Cathedral in all-black slacks and a button-up shirt, dressed for the occasion. I was a little tipsy, but I felt good as fuck.

The chapel was silent as a church mouse, except for the clacking of my Tom Ford dress shoes. Slowly, I crept into the confession booth and sat down. The door slid open. Then I began.

"Forgive me, Father, for I have sinned. It has been months since my last confession."

Together, Father Abraham and I made a sign of the cross. "May the Lord be in your heart, that you may know your sins and be truly sorry."

"My fiancée made me so angry today. That bitch disrespected me in the worst way."

"Demerius!"

"I'm sorry, Father, but she did. You see how upset I am."

"I do," he replied. "And you haven't been here in a while now. Where have you been? How is Casey?"

"Sinning left and right. I'm no longer with Casey. Her name is Foreign." I took a deep breath and rubbed my head. "I've been trying to contain my anger, but I feel like I'm about to explode. I've also committed the most heinous sin that I can't talk about right now."

"You can't be forgiven for it if you don't confess it. You're not supposed to hold in your anger. You have to release it positively. Has she experienced the things you put Casey through?"

"A mild version. She hasn't seen how bad shit could get."

"Demerius!" Whenever he called my name, I knew a curse word slipped.

"Sorry, Father."

"You need to pray more and lay off the booze. That's a recipe for disaster and an overnight stay in the county jail. And you need to let go of your past with your mother. She's the reason you can't love properly."

"I know and that's why I'm here. I am sorry for all of my sins. Father, please help me understand."

"May the Lord, who sanctifies the repentant sinners, forgive your sins and make you worthy of eternal life. In the name of the Father and of the Son, and the Holy Spirit. Amen."

"Amen," I repeated.

Immediately after absolution, I got up and left the booth. It was dark when I made it back out to my car. Eight o'clock barely graced the clock, and it looked like it was midnight. Back in the car, I twisted the cap off the bottle and proceeded to drown my problems in alcohol. It was my coping mechanism, and it worked for the moment.

On my way home, I flew through the streets like I was in the batmobile. A little traffic was present, but I weaved in and out of lanes, trying to get home. Checking the dash, I easily hit eighty miles per hour. "Get the fuck out the way!"I shouted at the slow-ass station wagon in front of me.

Just as I got closer to crossing the intersection, the light went from yellow to red in a split second. Switching lanes in a hurry, I pushed through the light. Not even five seconds later, I could see the flashing of red and blue lights.

"Ain't this 'bout a bitch," I mumbled as I pulled alongside the road. "Here we go."

Prepared for the bullshit, I took my registration and insurance card from the glove box and removed my wallet from my pocket. In the side mirror, I could see the officer walking towards my vehicle. I waited until he tapped on the window before winding it down.

"License and registration."

Without hesitation, I handed it out the window. The cops and I were like oil and water. We didn't get along for shit, and I wanted to be on my way as quickly as possible. In my eyes, it was *fuck them boys in blue*.

"Do you know why I pulled you over?" The officer shined his light on my documents.

"Nope! But I'm sure I'm about to find out."

"You ran a red light doing eighty miles an hour. The speed limit is forty. Do you have any weapons in the car?"

"No."

"Any warrants?"

"No."

"Where are you going in a hurry?" Dickhead cops were the worst ones, and that's exactly what he was acting like. "You have a lick to bust?"

That was the reason I hated them motherfuckers. They talked all that shit behind that badge. But I guarantee if I caught his ass in plain clothes and off the clock, he wouldn't be so tough. "Why you need a better-paying job?"

He eyed me for a few seconds. Apparently, his comeback was too slow.

"Listen, just write me my ticket so I can go." The officer walked back to his patrol and got inside.

Anxiously, I sat in the car for minutes on end. This clown-ass cop had me sitting in the car like I had nothing else to do with my damn time. If I would've been on my back-in-the-day shit, that motherfucker would've had to catch me. The Maserati would have him eating dust with no problem.

By the time his pot belly ass returned, I had come up with a hundred ways to kill him. He passed my docs back through the window then proceeded to shine his flashlight into my car.

"Have you been drinking?"

"Man, can you just give me my ticket so I can go?" I was doing my best to keep from snapping.

"Sir, answer the question."

"Do I look drunk to you?"

"That's not what I asked. You have an open container in the car and I need to know if, in fact, you've been drinking." Silently, I sat in the driver's seat, considering my next move. Somehow, I knew what was about to transpire.

Bingo! I thought.

The officer rested his hand on his holster. "Sir, I need you to step out of the vehicle.

"For what? I haven't done anything wrong."

"Sir, please step out of the vehicle." When he repeated the command, his hand was no longer on his holster. This time his hand was clutching his service weapon. "Do it now!" he shouted aggressively.

Somebody had to be praying for this fool. My first mind wanted to lay his ass out on the road, but I knew I couldn't get away with it. He had already run my name in the system. If I killed a cop, they would have to settle for street justice. I was not going to prison.

The officer took a step back when I opened the door. Porky had that killer look in his eyes like he missed his quota on killing unarmed black men. Provoking him was not on my list of things to do, so I raised my hands into a surrendered state.

"Place your hands on the hood of the car."

He could wait to pat me down once I was in that position. By the time he was done, backup had arrived. Finally cuffed, they placed my black ass in the back seat of the patrol car. The scent wasn't welcoming at all. That shit smelled like onions, feet, and ass.

Down at the county jail, I was processed, booked, and placed in a holding cell. Straight out the gate, I called Foreign to pick me up. Her phone rang several times before going to voicemail. It was still early, so I knew she wasn't asleep just yet. I tried calling three more times to no avail.

DP was the last person I wanted to call, but I had no other choice. "Hello."

"DP!"

"Dad?" There was uncertainty in his voice. "Why are you calling me from jail?"

"They arrested for having an open container and running a red light. Are you home?"

"Yes."

"Where is Foreign? Is she asleep?"

"No. She's not here."

That couldn't be right. "Are you sure?"

"Yeah. When I got here, her car wasn't in the driveway."

"Okay. I'll be out in a few hours."

"Okay."

Foreign being MIA struck a mean nerve inside of me. The last time she pulled a Houdini, she told me she was leaving. All of those memories resurfaced, and my mind started to wonder. If Foreign cheated with me when she was married, she might have been cheating on me as well. Why else would she not answer the phone for me?

Someone had to bond me out, and I knew just the person to call. Foreign had some explaining to do when I saw her. There was no reason I should have to call upon another woman to handle business for me.

Foreign...

The following morning, I woke up energized and ready to conquer all of my problems. It was time to put all of this shit to bed. My life had been completely turned upside down, and I was ready to start fresh. I picked up my phone from the nightstand, and saw that I had multiple missed calls from a number I didn't know. There were also calls from Domestic. The voicemail message indicated that I received a call from the county jail. However, I didn't know anyone that was locked up.

"That had to be a mistake," I mumbled and dialed Maurice's number.

"Hey, stranger," he chuckled. "It's nice of you to call me."

"I know. I'm sorry about that."

"No apology needed. You're going through enough so you get a pass," he replied sweetly.

"Thank you." Maurice always made me feel flattered, and that was something that I needed.

"How are you and the baby doing?"

"We're good. I've been a little stressed out, but I've finally come up with a solution to end all of that," I replied with confidence.

"And what is that?"

"I'm leaving Domestic."

"Are you sure about that?" Maurice questioned with doubt. It was almost as if he didn't believe me. Hell, why should he? I said that weeks ago, and I still went back to him. Even after everything that Emilia revealed. At first, I didn't believe her, but now it all made sense.

"I'm positive this time."

"If you are for certain this time then good for you. That's not the type of relationship you or your baby should be in, or around. That child will feel every emotion he takes you through. I know you don't want to raise your child in a toxic environment."

"I don't and that's why I'm leaving. I'm also selling the house. Without Aaron, it's no longer a home."

"I can understand that."

The knock on the door immediately caught my attention, so I headed downstairs to answer it. Tip-toeing, I peeked through the peephole.

"Maurice, I'm going to call you back. Someone is at the door."

"Don't go missing on me again." I could hear his smile through the phone.

"This time I won't. I promise. Will you be home later? I would love to see you if that's okay."

"Of course."

"Okay. I'll call you later."

"I'll be waiting."

"Okay. Bye."

"Bye," he replied and hung up.

Behind the door, Lexi stood with a smile on her face. "About time you answered. You about to let all this caramel melt." Lexi walked in and hugged me tightly. "I missed you so much."

"I missed you too," I smiled. We let each other go, and went into the living room. "So, how is married life going for you?"

"Girl, we are still in the honeymoon stage."

"That's true," I agreed.

We both laughed.

"Honestly, it feels the same as when we were messing around. It's just a piece of paper."

"Yeah. It's just a piece of paper until you have to go to court and petition the right to your man's assets and money."

Lexi nodded. "I peep the shade, sis. I can't believe she is doing this to you. Especially after everything Aaron took you through. That lady is crazy. She's the reason I moved out in the first place."

"That was long overdue."

"Tell me about it," Lexi agreed and flipped her hair.

"Ouuu! Yes. Let me see that ring."

Lexi extended her arm so I could get a good look at the big-ass rock Calvin gave her. "This is so nice."

"I know right." We fell silent for a moment. Lexi sighed and then looked me directly in my eyes. "We need to address the elephant in the room."

Instinctively, I placed my hand on my belly. "I am the elephant in the room."

Lexi laughed. "You're not that big."

"Tell that to the scale. But go ahead, I'm listening."

"I'm sorry for the way things went down between us. When Aaron died, it was like I died with him. He was my twin and it hurt to lose him."

"Lexi, it hurt me too. I loved Aaron. I still do. None of that has changed. I will always love him. That man was my everything. Out of everyone you should know that."

"I know. It's just that I know how bad Aaron got when you started cheating on him. Aaron wanted to die, and it hurt me to know that you were the cause of his pain."

"But why? It was you who told me that I should cheat."

"I know. I wanted you to cheat back and hurt him, but not ask for a divorce."

"The straw that broke the camel's back was the sex tape, the underage girl, and then the affair with Emilia. That shit hurt me. You have no idea how embarrassed I was when all of his infidelities came to the light." Expressing my feelings had me very emotional. "Your brother made me feel like I wasn't enough woman for him. I was tired of being treated like a second option to his groupies."

"That I understand, but my question to you is why did you bring your boyfriend to his funeral? That was the ultimate disrespect. When I saw that, I ain't gone lie, I never wanted to be friends with you again."

"You have to believe me when I say that was not intentional. He knew what I was going through with the family, so he offered to drive me. He was supposed to stay in the car until the service was over. I begged him not to come in and then he got mad when I spoke about Aaron the way I did. He said it was disrespectful because he was my man."

"Is he crazy or what? He must've forgotten that he was a side nigga and you are married to my brother still to this day."

"He is crazy and that's why I left him." It felt good to say that.

"You left him?" Lexi's eyes widened.

"Yeah, I—" Then I paused. I had to think about what I was about to say before opening that door. Lexi was a sister to me, and she had the right to know.

"What?" She squinched her eyes.

"This is going to sound crazy, but I know it's true."

"What's that?"

"I think Domestic had something to do with Aaron's death. That wasn't an accident. Someone intentionally ran him off of that road."

Lexi's eyes grew into tiny slits. "I fucking knew it!" She screamed out while pointing her finger. "I've been saying that shit for the longest, and y'all thought I was crazy. Ouuu, I wanna kill him myself. I'll pay somebody to do it. He gonna pay for what he did to my fucking brother."

"Calm down, Lexi. Domestic is going to pay for what he did to Aaron. I promise you that. You don't need to be caught up in this. Getting justice for Aaron will be all we need."

"How can you be so certain that's going to happen? There's no evidence to tie him to the murder."

"Oh, I have evidence," I smiled.

"What evidence do you have?"

"I'll show you. Hold on."

On my feet, I walked over to the entertainment system and grabbed the remote. Lexi rocked nervously in her seat until the video started. As she listened to Emilia's confession, she bawled hard like a baby. When it was over, Lexi looked over at me. "You have to give this to the detective on Aaron's case. Detective Marshall said he could reopen and arrest Domestic, but he needs solid evidence that will tie him to the murder."

"That detective came to see me yesterday, and Domestic got so mad that he wanted to talk to me about Aaron."

"I bet he did." Lexi wiped her eyes. "I think I'm going to be sick." She darted from the sofa and ran into the guest bathroom.

I followed.

As I stood outside of the door, I could hear Lexi throwing up her guts and organs. I tapped lightly on the door. "Lexi, are you okay?"

"Yeah."

A few minutes later, she walked out dabbing her mouth with a paper towel. "Do you have a ginger ale?"

"I have nothing but water. I have to go grocery shopping today." Lexi went into the kitchen to get a bottle of water. Then she took her place back on the sofa next to me. "Are you pregnant?"

"Hell no!" she blurted out.

"Why you say it like that?"

"You sound like Calvin. I'm not ready to be anybody's mother."

"Well, I hope y'all using condoms?"

"Nope!"

"You'll be pregnant soon. I know y'all nasty asses like a book."

"Before I came here, I went by my doctor's office to get back on birth control. Calvin is not about to get me knocked up and make me lose my shape. Then I have to get lipo because he wants to cheat on me with every groupie that comes his way."

"And he's okay with you being on birth control?"

"No. I'm not telling him either."

"Lexi," I shouted in disbelief. "That's not right and you know that. Marriage is about compromise. You can't make a selfish decision like that."

Lexi rolled her eyes. "Chile please, I can and I did."

"Okay, if he leaves you for his side chick and baby, don't say nothing."

"I'll beat his and her ass that day."

"That's all more of a reason to give that man what he wants. Stop being so damn selfish. You sound just like your brother."

"That was my twin," she smirked.

"Don't I know it." The room was instantly quiet. Lexi and I were thinking about the same person. It was still fresh. "I miss him so much."

"Me too. I just want him back."

"I want him back too. But since that can't happen, we can send him some company."

By no means was I a hood chick, but I understood exactly what she was saying. "We cannot kill him, Lexi. We'll let Detective Marshall handle this."

"Okay." Lexi didn't sound too convincing.

"Alright, go to jail if you want to."

"Girl, you sound just like my daddy. A bitch go to jail one time and y'all won't let a bitch live."

All I could do was laugh. "I'll hold you down tho'."

"Who said I'm getting caught?"

"You right. Anyway, I'm dropping this. I need to go meet up with the detective and see what he wanted to talk to me about."

"Yeah. Let's do that."

"Okay. Let me go and grab my purse."

Chapter 12

Domestic

Finally free from the pissy-smelling holding cell, I grabbed my property and walked out the door. Fresh air was what I needed. That was no place for me to live. When I checked my phone, Foreign hadn't called me—not one time! "Oh yeah," I chewed on my bottom lip. "This bitch ain't called me all night or morning. She must be fucking somebody."

Tiffany was parked out front. I hopped in the car and closed the door. "Thanks for picking me up."

"No problem. You know I got you." Her smile was flirty and seductive.

"At least somebody does."

"Where's your girl?"

"The hell if I know. She hasn't answered any of my calls. That's why I called you."

Tiffany faced forward, but I could see her looking at me from the corner of her eye. "Damn, that's the only reason you called."

"Don't act like that. You know I fuck with you the long way." My mind was on Foreign heavy. All I could see playing out in my mind was her fucking another nigga while I was in jail.

Those good girls loved to play that innocent role, but deep down they legit be hoes. Now she had me questioning her behavior. Clenching down on my teeth, I waited anxiously to see if Foreign would answer the phone. She didn't. All I got was that funky ass voicemail. This broad was testing me badly. Aggravated, I sat my phone in my lap and spaced out.

Tiffany looked over at me. "You good?"

"Yeah."

"You sure about that?" Tiffany was a very nosey chick. She wasn't letting anything get past those ears.

"I'm good. I'm just ready to get home and shower."

"DP home with you?"

"Yeah." Now, my eyes were cut in her direction. "Why?"

"Just asking. How is my godson?"

"About to make me a granddaddy." There was no excitement in my voice.

"What?" Tiffany hit the steering wheel and started laughing. "Hell, no! I know damn well he doesn't have that girl pregnant." Tiffany was in disbelief.

"Dead ass!"

"Damn! That's you and Casey all over again. How many months is she?"

Slowly, I dragged my hand over my face. "Honestly, I don't know yet. We'll find out when she goes to the doctor. Her mother hasn't taken her yet."

"How did crazy-ass Teresa take the news?" Tiffany tapped her nails against the steering wheel as we sat at the red light.

"Teresa doesn't care about shit except herself."

"You know she raggedy as hell. After all, we did grow up together. I'm sure Teresa happy Cheyenne having a baby with DP because you have money and she knows that baby gonna be well taken care of."

"Exactly!"

"Teresa probably thinks she can get some dick now." Tiffany laughed hysterically until she had tears in her eyes.

"Check this out," I laughed. "She was like damn now we gonna be in-laws and our chance to be together is over."

"What you said?"

"I ain't say shit. Teresa know ain't nothing going on between us. If I didn't fuck her when we were younger, I'm not doing it as an adult. I'm good on that."

Tiffany smiled and popped her lips. "I know that's right."

"Is somebody jealous?"

"Jealous for what? I can still get that." Tiffany was so sure of herself, but she was right.

"You sure about that?"

"Of course, I'm sure. Am I lying?"

"Nah!" I chuckled. "You know I'll still take you up through there."

A few years back, Casey caught me cheating and decided to pay me back and fuck someone else. She moved out and went to stay with Tiffany for a couple of weeks. One day Tiffany came over to get some clothes and money for DP. We talked for a while, took a few shots, and smoked a blunt. The both of us were tipsy and feeling good. Tiffany got a little flirty, and my hands became frisky. She was wearing a tight skirt, and her thighs were looking good. Her breasts were perky, and those chocolate nipples poked through her shirt like Hershey kisses.

Tiffany caught a glimpse of my hard dick through my pants and licked her lips. From there, I knew we were on the same page. A little more flirting took place. Not long after that, I had Tiffany bent over on the sofa—screaming my name. We both knew what we did was wrong, but the sex didn't stop. Casey came back home so we could work on our relationship. However, Tiffany and I kept going with our affair. Three times a month we would have a sneaky link. But once she started dating, we stopped altogether. It had been at least a year since we stopped having sex. Tiffany had a little animosity towards Casey, and that's why she agreed to help me kidnap her.

Tiffany took me to the tow yard so I could pick up my car. That had me heated because that shit was a waste of money. She parked the car, and I opened the door. Tiffany placed her hand on my thigh. "Are you still coming over?"

"I have some shit to handle right now, but I'll come by when I'm done."

"I'm serious."

"I am too. You know I have to give you your money back. I'll call you when I'm done."

"Okay," she replied with disappointment in her voice.

"Thanks for bonding me out and picking me up. I appreciate that."

Tiffany grabbed my hand and placed it between her legs. I could feel the heat and the thumping of her pussy when she did that. Out of the blue, she moaned. "Well, when you come over, you can show me how much you appreciate me."

Flashbacks of us fucking replayed in my head, and I caught an instant erection. "Chill, Tiff, I'm coming. I promise."

"You better."

"Take that pussy home and put it on ice for me."

"Oh, I am," she hissed.

"Bye, witcha horny ass." Tiffany giggled and pulled off.

Those bastards at the tow yard charged me close to two-hundred dollars to get my shit back. That fat ass cop knew he didn't have to do all of that. Shrugging off that old problem, I took my ass home to see what the fuck was going on.

Foreign's car was nowhere in sight when I pulled up. Unlocking the door, I went inside and headed straight to the bedroom. It was obvious she hadn't slept there, since the bed was still made up. From what I could see, nothing was out of place. A sheet of paper on the dresser caught my attention. It was a letter addressed to me.

"Domestic, by the time you read this letter, I'll be gone. I thought that I could stay with you and work on our relationship for the sake of our child. Sadly, I was wrong. I can't do this anymore. The more I try to love you, the

harder it gets. You will never change! And I can't afford to have you tear me down in the process. Take some time to calm down and register what I'm telling you. This relationship is too toxic for me, and I can't help you with your past traumas. If you truly love me, get the help you need so we could healthily co-parent our child. Always, Foreign."

Rage filled my body, and I could feel the heat seeping from my pores. Foreign had me that mad. Crumbling the letter in my hand, I threw it against the wall. "Bitch, you gon' leave me? Okay," I nodded. "I got something for you."

Without hesitation, I called her again, and again.

Foreign…

"See, he keeps calling me. He won't stop." Domestic was blowing up my phone every damn minute. So, I sent him a quick text. *Stop calling me. We have nothing to talk about right now. You need to calm down first and seek professional help if you want to see your child.'*

"That bitch ass nigga crazy," Lex added.

"Answer the phone and put it on speaker," Detective Marshall said.

I put the phone on speaker. "Domestic, why do you keep calling me? We need space."

"No. We need to talk. Why would you just leave like that? You gon' break up wit' a nigga through a letter. What kinda shit is that?" Contrary to his language, Domestic was pretty calm.

"You have issues that I can't help you with. The disrespect, the abuse—It's too much for me. I can't do this with you."

"Baby, we getting married soon. We don't have time to be going through the motions. And I told you I was sorry for what I did to you."

"You locked me in the closet overnight."

"Foreign, I told you that I was sorry." Domestic was pleading like a teenage boy that was losing his first love. He was too calm for me, and I didn't like it. I needed him to be angry.

"I'm sorry, but I don't forgive you and that's why this will never work. And I'm not marrying you?"

"Why not? I thought we were past that."

"That's the problem. You're past it, but I'm not. I'll never forgive you for that. And I will never marry you."

"Listen," he cleared his throat. "I've already told you that I won't die if you leave me, but you will. And I meant every word I said. Now, come home."

"Domestic, I'm serious. I am not coming back to you."

"You have two choices."

"And what two choices are those?" I asked.

"You can come home voluntarily, or involuntarily. If I have to come and force you back into this house, you will regret it. I promise you that."

"Good luck with that."

"I won't need the luck. You will."

"Bye, Domestic. I'm not doing this with you."

"Bitch!" he shouted. Finally, he had officially flown off the handle. "Get your ass back here. How the fuck you gon' kidnap my fuckin' child and think I won't do shit about it? You got me fucked up. You better ask Casey what happened to her when she tried to take my son away from me."

"You know I should've listened to her. She tried to warn me, but I didn't listen. It's okay 'cause I'm listening now. So, once again, bye. I'm hanging up."

"When I catch you, I'm going to kill you. Mark my words!"

As bad as I wanted to hang up. I couldn't. There was so much more that needed to be said. "Never in a million years did I think you would treat me like this. When I decided to leave my husband, you promised you would never hurt me. Aaron was a lot of things, but an abuser wasn't one of them."

My comment instantly struck a fire underneath Domestic's ass. "Fuck Aaron! He didn't give a fuck about you."

"Aaron loved me. You're the one that don't give a fuck about me. All you want to do is, control me and abuse me the way your mama did you."

"Since you love that nigga so much, I'ma send you to be with that bitch ass nigga. That pussy got everything he deserved and you next!"

Quickly, I ended the call. Talking to Domestic was draining. He said a lot of crazy things, but I truly believed he would kill me. It was also confirmed that he killed Aaron. And if he didn't do it, he had someone to do it for him. That was the reason I had to get away from him.

"Did you get all of that?"

Detective Marshall stopped the recording. "Every single word."

"So, can you go and arrest him now?" Alexis asked.

"While it's clear that he hated Aaron and he has an anger problem, it's still not enough to charge him with murder. It's enough to bring him in for questioning. However, I'm almost certain that he won't talk to me."

"Well, it sounds like you need to get creative. That bastard killed my brother." Lexi snapped.

"I'm doing my best."

"And I appreciate that," I smiled. "Just work fast. He's crazy and I don't feel safe."

"Does he know where you live?" Detective Marshall asked.

"Yes," I nodded.

"Is there any place you can go for a while? At least until we can arrest him on one of these charges."

That piqued my interest. "What other charges?"

"We suspect that he killed someone. I can't go into detail, but it's someone that used to work with him."

"Okay. I'll be careful. Hopefully, that video from Emilia will be enough."

"Please do. I'll be in touch." He pushed his chair out and stood up. "I'm going to watch it and see."

"Okay."

Detective Marshall escorted Lexi and me back towards the lobby. Then we left. My plan to get rid of Domestic was going as planned. If it wasn't for Blacque Barbee, there was no way I would've gone through with it. We had a solid plan in place. Within the next few weeks, Domestic would be locked away forever in a six-by-nine cell until the day he died.

Upon leaving the precinct, I dropped Alexis off at her house. She wanted me to stay, but I had one more stop to make. The neighborhood was completely silent and ducked off. That was the main thing I loved about the area. After I parked my Bentley in the driveway, I knocked on the door and waited for an answer.

The baritone voice on the opposite side of the door was sexy as I could remember. Maurice opened the door, and he had the nerve to be shirtless. His athletic body looked like it had been dipped in chocolate. If I wasn't pregnant, I would've jumped right on his dick as soon as we got inside the house.

"Wow! She showed up," he smiled. Maurice had the perfect set of pearly white teeth.

It didn't matter what he said to me, I always felt like a shy school girl. "I told you I was coming."

"And I must say it's a pleasant surprise." Maurice stepped to the side. "Come in. I'm allowed to have company," he teased.

"It's nice to be missed." We walked over to the sofa and sat beside each other. For the next thirty seconds, I organized my words.

"How is everything going? Is your child's father okay?"

"I wish he wasn't," I huffed.

Maurice's eyebrow slanted. "Has something else happened?"

"Yes. And this time I need help getting away from him." I looked him in the eyes so he could see and hear the seriousness in my tone. "Can you help me?"

"Of course. What is it that you need me to do?"

The sincerity in his voice was loud and clear. That was all I needed to hear. If I could get him on board with my final plan, I would be home-free.

Domestic...

This bitch had me fucked all the way up. Foreign grew some big ass balls overnight. If she thought I was letting any of that slick rap slide, that bitch had another thing coming. Once she hung up on me, I took a shower. All of the cold water in Tampa couldn't get me to cool off. Foreign was about to live out a real episode of 'Fatal Attraction,' fucking with me. She thought Aaron made her famous. Meanwhile, I was about to make her go viral.

Unlike the previous night, I wasn't speeding on my way to Tiffany's house. Filled with different emotions, I wasn't cool with her bringing up my childhood issues and threatening to take my child. I loved her unconditionally, and she spits in my face like I mean nothing to her! All behind a nigga she would never get back. Foreign had a lot of nerves.

Yeah, I had some issues but it was nothing we couldn't work through. When Foreign needed me, I was there for her. Now, I couldn't get the same in return. It was all good because she was going to feel me sooner or later.

Tiffany's porch light was on when I pulled up. Killing the engine, I grabbed my bottle and walked up on the porch. To my surprise, I didn't have to knock. She greeted me with open arms, a smile, and some sexy, black lingerie.

"You ready for daddy, huh?" I chugged the bottle and grabbed a hand full of ass.

"We've been ready for daddy." Seductively, Tiffany licked her lips, and my dick jumped. She closed the door and locked it.

I was already tipsy, so the furthest I made it was to the couch. Flopping down, I leaned my head back and sighed.

"You good?" Tiffany asked out of concern.

"She left me."

"What you mean she left you?"

"Foreign left me a letter saying she couldn't be with me anymore."

"Why?" Tiffany removed my shoes one at a time.

Once more I turned the bottle up. "I hit her."

Tiffany sat down beside me. "Domestic, I know you better than that. And if she left you, I know you did more than that. Did you do her the same way you used to do Casey?"

"I didn't mean to."

"Well, I'm here for you." Tiffany unbuckled my pants. "The way I will always be. No matter what." Tiffany freed my dick and kneeled in front of me. "I'm going to make you forget all about her. Trust me. So, lay back and relax."

Chapter 13

Casey

My brain couldn't register what my eyes just witnessed. As I sat in the car across the street, I watched Domestic and Tiffany doing shit they had no business doing. Tears filled my eyes. She was our son's godparent. And based on what she was wearing, next to nothing, she had to know he was coming. It was the betrayal for me. It all made sense as to why she called him that night. Domestic didn't threaten her. That hoe volunteered and lied in my face.

For the roughest fifteen minutes in history, I sat in the car thinking about my next move. When I decided to stop by to see what Tiffany was up to, I never expected to see Domestic. I wanted to leave right then and there, but I needed confirmation to make sure my eyes weren't playing a nasty trick on me.

The suspense was killing me, so I got out of the car and crept across the street. Quietly, I snuck on the side of the house and squatted down by the window. In my heart, I didn't want to believe that the one person I considered a sister would cross me like this. This girl knew how I felt about Domestic, and how hard it was for me to leave him.

My heart was beating fast, and several knots formed in the pit of my stomach. I wanted to know, but at the same time, I was scared to face the truth. It was time to put on my big girl panties and face reality.

Slowly, I rose until I was face to face with the window. Squinting, I moved my head to the side until I had a clear view. My heart dropped to the pit of my stomach. In my view, I could see my baby daddy and my ex-best friend butt ass naked on the sofa, getting it in. Tiffany was on top, riding his dick and kissing him in the mouth. It hurt to watch, but I needed the proof. I pulled my cellphone from the back pocket of my jeans, opened the camera, and hit *video*.

The longer I watched, the angrier I became. I felt stupid, knowing they had been having sex all this time. This wasn't just a fuck for them. It was far too much chemistry and compassion. No one could tell me any different. Just as I thought I'd heard too much, Tiffany started to moan loudly. Then I could hear her pleading that she loved him. That hurt, and my heart couldn't take anymore. I just wanted to get out of there. Stepping away, I backed up and hit the garbage can. It hit the ground hard.

"Shit!" I looked around to make sure no one was around to hear. Most importantly, make sure they didn't hear me. When I peeked through the window again, they were still going at it. In a hurry, I rushed back to the car and pulled off.

Shawn and Tim were sitting in the living room, smoking a blunt and talking shit when I walked in. Despite how distraught I was, I still managed to hear Domestic's name.

"What's up bae, you okay?"

"Yeah. I'm just tired," I lied.

"You sure you good, sis?" Tim asked.

"I'm sure. What are y'all talking about?"

"Yo' punk-ass baby daddy," Tim answered.

"What about him?" I asked.

Shawn passed the blunt to Tim. "That nigga set my brother up to be killed."

Still standing, I folded my arms. "How do you know?"

"That nigga was with the dude that killed Craig and shot at us. We blasted at the nigga, but he didn't die." Shawn never told me that it was him that was responsible for the shooting. I found out that information from DP.

Tim exhaled the weed smoke. "I'm sorry, sis. I love you and all, but I'm not stopping until I kill him."

"I don't care. He's not my concern. Just make sure my baby isn't around him when you do it."

Afterward, I went into the room to clear my head as much as possible. That task was easier said than done. In the dark, I laid on my back and stared at the ceiling. Images of the two played in my mind like a movie. It was like watching a porn video. I cried like a baby, but I made sure I was quiet. The last thing I needed was Shawn coming in and questioning me. I had enough problems on my plate that I couldn't handle.

Life for DP would be hard at first without his dad, but he would get over it. Besides, he had no worries. Once Domestic died, he would inherit everything his father owned. My baby was going to be set for life. Since Domestic and Tiffany wanted to play a dirty-ass game, they were about to see there weren't any rules. Those two trifling bitches had been playing me behind my back and laughing in my face. Now, I was about to have the last laugh. Karma was a bald-head bitch, and they were about to get what was coming to them. I couldn't wait for their secret to get out in the open. Social media was going to help with that.

Foreign...

The following morning, I was awakened by the bright rays of the sun. My eyes fluttered until they were able to adjust. When I finally opened them completely, I was greeted by a set of brown eyes. Frightened, I jumped up and realized who they belonged to.

"I'm sorry. I didn't mean to scare you."

"It's okay," I yawned. "How long have you been sitting here watching me?" It was cute and scary at the same time.

"Not long. I'm just getting up myself. So, don't think of me as a creep," he chuckled. "I'm just admiring your beauty."

"Thank you." This man had me feeling flattered early in the morning, and before I brushed my teeth at that.

Maurice was shirtless once again, exposing that beautiful, grown man chest. Instinctively, I peeked underneath the blanket to see if I was naked. The clothes that I wore were gone, but I was dressed in an oversized t-shirt. Nervousness took over me. Our eyes locked.

"We didn't have sex. I wanted you to be comfortable, so I changed your clothes." Maurice caught on quickly.

"Are you sure about that?" I had to be certain, being that I could be a pretty hard sleeper when I was tired.

"Of course! I was the perfect gentleman."

My hormones screamed: *You didn't have to be*. But my mind said: *Take it slow, remember that's how you got stuck with Domestic*.

"How did you know what I was thinking?"

"I'm a grown man and I know a lot about women. I was raised by a single mother. My dad died when I was twelve, so she taught me everything I needed to know about women. Therefore, I know you were wondering if I had taken advantage of you while you were sleeping."

"She sounds like a wonderful woman."

"She truly is. That's my world."

"Where is she?"

"She lives in Kansas City, Missouri."

Maurice didn't strike me as the type to do that, but I needed to be certain nothing happened between us. I wanted to, but it didn't feel right to sleep with him while I was pregnant by someone else.

"It's not that I don't trust you," I exhaled. "It's obvious I do since I spent the night here. My life is a mess right now, and I don't know if I'm coming or going. And the last thing I need is sex to cloud my judgment."

Maurice grabbed my hand and kissed it. "Foreign, I like you. I like you a lot. Just having you here with me is enough. We can go as slow as you like, as long as you don't lead me on."

"I won't do that because I like you too." We locked eyes and I wanted to kiss him so bad, but I fought the urge to cross that line at that moment. The way Maurice stared at me, I was certain he was feeling the same thing. Quickly, I changed the subject but eased my hand from his grip. "Can I ask you a question?"

"Sure."

"Why does your mother live in Kansas and you live here?"

"Well, I moved here temporarily for work. I have a sister back home that takes care of my mother while I'm away. Once my assignment is over, I'll be going back."

"Permanently?"

"Yeah."

That gave me more of a reason to not sleep with him. "Oh wow, so you're just here for the moment?"

"Don't say it like that."

"Like what?"

"The way you're saying it."

"I'm just saying. Last night you expressed to me about wanting us to date once all of this is over."

"I meant everything I said."

Disappointed, I shook my head. "Listen, Maurice. I'm not like you. I don't know how to study a man and pick up on things that appear to be common sense. Aaron was my first in everything I did. Domestic was the second. What I don't need is another man playing on my intelligence or emotions. So, if you only trying to find a sex partner while you're here, I can't help you."

"Is that how you see me?"

"I'm just asking. You went from wanting to date me to you moving back to Kansas when your assignment is up." Maurice had dampened my mood in a matter of seconds. It was time to go. When I tried to get up, he grabbed my arm.

"Where are you going?"

"I should go."

"No." He ran his hand across his face. "You asked for my help and I promised to do that."

"And I appreciate that."

"That's not all. I know you and I don't know each other that well, but I want to pursue something serious with you. I also want you to come back with me to Kansas. You can start fresh and we can be together."

"I don't know about that."

"Why not? You said it yourself that you wanted to go away and start fresh with your baby."

"I do."

"Okay, so take a chance on me."

"I'll think about it."

"That's fair," he agreed. Maurice grabbed my hand once again. "It's something about you that I like so much. Can I kiss you?"

Butterflies flooded my stomach. It was just a kiss, but I knew it could lead to more than that. Despite my mixed feelings, I agreed with a nod. In slow motion, we leaned in halfway and our lips touched. Maurice placed his hand on the back of my neck and slipped his tongue into my mouth. His lips were soft as silk. The intensity of the kiss sent pleasant chills over my body. Desires of the flesh surfaced. I needed to stop him before we took things too far.

The warmth of Maurice's hand creeping up my thigh made me horny as hell. A tingling sensation from my clitoris was making it harder to avoid sex. My body wanted sex, but I wanted real love and loyalty. That wasn't too much to ask. Maurice's fingertips grazed my pussy lips, and I was ready to let him in. On my shoulder, the devil and angel battled each other. They had me confused as hell.

"Maurice, we can't do this," I uttered between seductive moans. With no hesitation, he stopped. "I'm sorry."

"Don't apologize. It's okay. I'm a grown, patient man. You'll let me know when you're ready." His voice was sincere and I knew he wasn't upset, judging by the way he licked his lips. "And when you do, you'll love it. Trust me."

Whew! This man had me clutching my pearls. Maurice didn't know how bad I wanted to get naked right then and there. Last night, while I was lying on his chest, I messed around and grazed his thick ass penis. All night long I thought about him penetrating this cat. He looked like the type that stared into your eyes while he stroked you slowly and kissed you in your mouth.

Jesus, please be a fence. I said a silent prayer in my mind: *'God, please give me the strength to sleep with this fine piece of man. Amen!'*

"I will," I nodded. "I'm about to shower and get dressed. I have court in a few hours."

"I'll go with you," he insisted.

"No. You don't have to."

"I know I don't." Maurice kissed me on the forehead. "I wasn't asking. You can use my shower. I'll use the one in the guest bathroom." Maurice left the room so I could get ready.

When he left the room, my smile instantly turned into a frown. I was not in the mood to deal with Aaron's conniving, weave-wearing ass mammy. It was hard to believe that she was dragging me through the mud for my husband's money. Something that I was entitled to. I earned every dollar he left behind. Aaron hurt me enough to owe me in the next life too. All of the pain and heartache I suffered at his hands was priceless. There was no price tag on mental health. One thing I knew for sure, though: that saddlebag bitch never had to worry about me ever again in life.

***

Hillsborough County Courthouse

Maurice and I arrived at the courthouse ten minutes before it was set to start. From a distance, I could see my parents sitting on the bench. Both of them stood and met us halfway.

"Hey, mom. Hey, dad." I hugged them both.

"How are you feeling, baby girl?" my father asked genuinely.

"I'm okay." Beside me, Maurice stood quietly until he was introduced. "Mom and dad, this is my friend—Maurice." Then I looked at Maurice. "These are my parents—Mr. and Mrs. Hamilton."

"It's nice to meet you both." Maurice shook hands with both of them.

"Friends, huh?" My father looked at Maurice with the side-eye.

"Yes, sir. We are just friends."

My father looked right at me. That man wasn't trying to hear that. "Daddy, we are just friends."

"Where is my grandchild's father?" He looked down at my stomach.

"Can we talk about this later, please? I can only deal with one dramatic situation at a time." I was not in the mood to discuss my relationship status with him.

"Yeah. You just make sure you come by the house."

"I will," I promised. "Now, let's go inside and get this over with."

The courtroom was quiet when we walked in. Mr. Young was seated on the left side, so my parents and Maurice sat on the right. Meanwhile, I took my place beside my attorney, Marcus Hall. Aaron's evil ass mammy kept glancing in my direction. We were once close, but—thanks to her—that was over. However, I didn't have a problem with his father. The only person missing was Lexi. She promised to be there, but I guess she was running late.

"Mrs. Young, how are you?"

"I'm good. Just ready to get this over with."

"I can only imagine what your experience has been like. The loss of a loved one is hard enough. To add legal trouble into the equation is brutal."

"Tell me about it."

"Well, today that will be over with and you can start your healing process."

As soon as he finished his sentence, the judge stepped out from her chambers. "All rise. The Honorable Judge Cynthia Campbell presiding."

"You may all be seated." Judge Campbell sat down and flipped through the folder. "We are here today for the case of Young vs. Young. Since you both share the same last name, I'm going to use your maiden name, Ms. Hamilton, so there's no confusion. Mrs. Young, you are petitioning the court on behalf of your son's estate. The late Aaron Young. I am going to allow both sides to present their case, evidence, and any witnesses you may have. Once that is finished, I will make my ruling."

The judge looked over at Aaron's mother's attorney. "Mr. Jacobs, you may begin."

This was about to be an exhausting morning. I could only imagine the things that battle-ax told her attorney. In a few minutes, I wouldn't have to wonder because everyone was about to hear it.

Chapter 14

Detective Marshall

All hell was about to break loose once I cracked the lid on this case with a sledgehammer. I've worked tirelessly trying to build a case against Demerius Payne. Day by day, things were getting better like fine wine. There was a lot of circumstantial evidence and witnesses to place reasonable doubt in the jury's mind. But the star witness of this case would be Emilia. With her involvement, she could be charged, but immunity could be offered in exchange for her testimony. Strangely, she was nowhere to be found. Once I solved this case, and I was definitely going to do that, the captain had no choice but to give me a promotion.

Sipping on my Cuban coffee, I watched the confessional video made by Emilia for the third time. There was something off with her demeanor and confession. It was as if she was in distress or some sort of trouble. The evidence was good. However, there was only a slight chance it would be admissible in court. That meant I still needed that smoking gun. Nevertheless, it was enough to raise a few eyebrows and suspicions.

To add to my concerns, her brother Carlos paid us a visit when they hadn't heard from Emilia. He filed a missing person's report. Based on what I knew as her partner, Emilia would never cut off communication with her father. She took care of him, so that didn't make any sense to me.

There was a knock on the door. "Come in," I shouted.

The door opened and in walked Katie from the records division, holding a folder. "Here's everything we found. There are some questionable things in there, so you'll find it quite interesting."

"Thanks, Katie."

"You're welcome. If you need anything else, let me know."

"Will do."

Katie exited my office quickly, and I jumped right into the folder, thumbing through papers. There were tons of questions, and we needed answers. Almost immediately, I spotted a few things that didn't sit too well with me. In a hurry, I left my office and ran down the hall to find the captain. His door was open, so I walked right in.

The captain looked up. "What can I do for you, Marshall?"

"As you know, Emilia's brother filed a missing person's report."

"I do," he nodded.

"Well, I had Emilia's phone and bank records pulled." I handed him the folder.

"Did you find her?"

"See, that's the odd thing. Emilia was moving to California to start fresh, but her phone has been off and there is no bank activity. If she truly left the state why hasn't she spent any money? You and I both know that something is wrong with this picture."

Captain Fuller leaned back in his seat and folded his hands. "Absolutely. What was the last cell tower her phone pinged from?"

"Um. Her last activity pinged off of a tower near Torreya State Park before her flight was scheduled to leave."

"And did you confirm that she did not board that plane?"

"Yes. I did."

"Okay. I'm going to set up a search party to check out the area. Scour the area and see if you can locate any evidence. It sounds like we're going to be looking for a body. Round up everyone and have them meet me in the conference room in ten minutes."

***

The meeting lasted thirty minutes. There were a total of twelve officers and detectives assigned to the search party. On our way out to the site, I paid a visit to public enemy number one, Demerius Payne. Our encounter placed a bad taste in my mouth. It made me feel as if I was barking up the right tree. He was guilty of something, I just didn't know what.

Tracy was sitting at the counter when I walked in. It was like she saw a ghost once she laid eyes on me. Before allowing her to blow our cover, I stated the nature of my business. "I'm here to see your boss. Can you call him for me?"

"Yes." Tracy picked up the phone. She informed him that I was present and hung up the phone. "You can go to his office."

Demerius was sitting behind his desk. He appeared to be busy.

"Mr. Payne." I stood in front of his desk with my hands behind my back.

"How can I help you?"

"Do you mind if I have a seat? I have a few questions that I need to ask you in regards to your relationship with Foreign."

"Sure." Demerius finally looked up at me. "What is it that you would like to know?"

"Were you and Foreign involved with each other before the death of Aaron Young?"

"Yes. They were having problems at the time we met."

"How so?"

Demerius folded his hands and placed them on his desk. "He was cheating on her, but the whole world knows that. You do too. What I will tell you is: Foreign wanted to leave him, but he wouldn't let her go."

"So, did you and Aaron ever get into a physical altercation?"

"I never saw him before."

"Did Foreign tell you that she was leaving her husband for you?"

"She did."

"What happened when she left him?"

"She didn't leave him," he sighed. "He died before she got the chance to leave."

It was time to get to the point of the interview. "I'm going to ask you straight up, did you kill Aaron?"

"No."

"Did you kill Keith?"

"Who?" Multiple wrinkles spread across his forehead. Demerius instantly tensed up. I knew he was guilty. I've interviewed many criminals that attempted to lie in my face. It didn't go well. I saw right through the bullshit.

"The young guy that used to work for you. His name is Keith, right?"

"Look, man, I didn't kill nobody." Demerius stood up and rubbed his hands together. "I'm done answering questions, so if you're not arresting me for something then you can leave my office now."

Standing up, I fixed my coat and smiled. "Thanks for talking to me." As I walked off, I stopped in my tracks and turned around. "When is the last time you spoke to Emilia?"

"A week ago. Now, bye. Have a good day."

"Before I go, I believe this belongs to you." I reached into my coat pocket and pulled out a white envelope. Domestic took it from my hand. "You've been served."

On the way out, I winked at Tracy. "Have a good day."

"Bye," Tracy responded with an attitude.

The sky was covered with grey clouds when I finally arrived at Torreya State Park. The team was parked alongside the road, scouring the grounds.

Pulling up behind the van, I parked the car and got out. It was a little too hot, so I removed the jacket I was wearing and tossed it in the front seat.

Several men were standing around in a circle when I joined them near the coordinates we received from the records. "Hey, Marshall. Nice of you to join us."

"Yeah, I know."

"Come over here. I need to show you something."

Uncertain about what I was about to see, I followed him a few feet away to find out.

Foreign...

"Your Honor, the plaintiff—Mrs. Young—is only petitioning the court because my client has moved on with her life. When Mr. Aaron Young was alive, they had a public, tumultuous marriage. There was a lot of cheating and scandals involving the deceased. However, they were still legally married at the time of his death." Attorney Marcus Hall paced the floor while taking occasional stares at the real witch of the south, better known as Aaron's mom.

"There was no indication that a divorce was taking place. Mrs. Young does not need the property. Nor does she want it. This is all a ploy to make my client's life a living hell because she is grieving the loss of her youngest son. Mr. Young purchased the home in question for my client, and her name is listed on the deed."

"She didn't want my son, so she shouldn't want his house either," Aaron's mother screamed to the top of her lungs.

That shit made me snap. "You don't know anything about what went on in my house, so you need to mind your damn business. I've kept quiet for too long and today is not the day. I am sick of you condemning me for what your son," I pointed in her direction, "did to me."

The judge intervened. "Mrs. Young, please refrain from having unnecessary outbursts in the courtroom. Your attorney had his chance to speak. Ms. Hamilton, calm down please."

"I'm sorry, Your Honor," she replied.

"Counselor, do you have the deed?"

"Yes. I do."

"Let me see that evidence."

Mr. Hall handed the deed to Judge Campbell.

"So, Your Honor, as you can see, my client's name is listed as the owner, and we have no reason to be here."

Judge Campbell pushed her glasses down to the bridge of her nose. "Mrs. Young, in this deed Ms. Hamilton is listed as the owner."

"That's a phony document." Aaron's mother became very belligerent. "She's a real estate agent and can forge documents."

"That is a lie and you know it. Aaron bought that house for us. Why are you sitting in this courtroom lying?"

The closing of the courtroom door interrupted the argument. Everyone's head was on a swivel. In walked Lexi wearing a pair of dark shades. "Your Honor, my name is Alexis Young-Bailey. I'm Aaron's twin sister and I'm the only person in this room, besides Mrs. Foreign Young, that knows what was happening in their marriage."

Lexi's appearance took me by surprise. Not once did she mention taking the witness stand for the hearing.

"Please come to the podium and remove your shades," Judge Campbell instructed.

Lexi took her seat beside the judge and removed her shades.

"Please, state your name for the courts."

"Alexis Young."

"And you are of what relation to the deceased?"

"I'm his twin sister."

"What can you tell me about the situation between Mr. Young and Ms. Hamilton?"

"Well, after my brother was drafted, he did purchase the house for himself and Ms. Hamilton."

"Now, was there a divorce in the works?"

"Yes."

"By who?"

"Ms. Hamilton."

"Thank you, Jesus," Mrs. Young shouted like she was in church and about to catch the Holy Ghost.

"Mrs. Young, what did I say about the outbursts?"

"Sorry, Your Honor." That bitch was getting on my last nerve.

"Please continue, Mrs. Bailey."

"Ms. Hamilton wanted to divorce my brother for his excessive cheating scandals."

"But wasn't that all speculation?"

"I was present on multiple occasions when Ms. Hamilton caught him. See, what no one knows is that my brother had a sex addiction. He was determined to make his marriage work, and Ms. Hamilton agreed to stay with him. The day he was killed—" Lexi dropped her head. Speaking about Aaron's death was extremely hard for her.

"Take your time, Mrs. Bailey." The bailiff handed Lexi some Kleenex.

Lexi regained her composure. "I'm sorry."

"You don't have to apologize. Losing a sibling is hard."

"On the day he was killed, Aaron had just left his final session. He was finally ready to be the husband that Ms. Hamilton wanted him to be. Ms. Hamilton loved my brother unconditionally, and everyone knows that." Lexi's stare was cold as ice when she looked at the woman that gave birth to her. "Including my mother. So, I don't know why she's doing all of this. Ms. Hamilton wasn't there for the money. She was there because he loved him."

A huge wave of relief came over my body. It almost felt like baptism was taking place.

"Thank you, Mrs. Bailey. You may step down."

Lexi left the podium and sat beside her dad. Mr. Young had a smile on his face when he winked at me. In return, I smiled back. One thing I could say was that he always remained neutral in the situation, and he treated me like a daughter from the day we first met.

"Well, I think I've heard enough testimony from both sides. We will take a thirty-minute recess. When we return, I will make my ruling." Judge Campbell banged her gavel, and the court was dismissed.

Throughout that first hour of court, the two attorneys argued both sides of the case and went over the evidence. Some were the truth, and the rest were lies. Of course, Mrs. Young told a bunch of lies and spoke about things she did not know of or barred witness to. If I wasn't worried about catching a charge and going to jail, I would smack the shit out of her in that courtroom. But I was happy that Lexi spoke on my behalf.

Outside of the courtroom, Lexi hugged me tightly. "I'm sorry you have to go through this. I swear she gets on my last nerve."

"Mine too." That was another thing we agreed on. "Um, Lexi, this is my friend—Maurice. Maurice this is my sister—Lexi."

"Nice to meet you," he smiled. They shook hands.

"I remember you," Lexi examined him from head to toe. "We saw you at the restaurant."

"Yeah. That's me." Maurice laughed.

"I never forget a face." Lexi reached into her purse. "My husband is calling me. I have to take this."

Maurice and I went to the cafeteria. I was hungry as hell. The irritation subsided a little bit, but not enough to forget about what was happening. It was still a lethal combination. "How are you feeling about everything that's taking place?"

"I'm still pissed off. That bitch sat right in that courtroom and lied about my character. She acts like I'm some groupie that's after his money."

The cafeteria wasn't serving anything I was interested in eating. To settle the hunger I felt, I grabbed a bagel with cream cheese and a bottle of orange juice. By the time we made it back down the hall, the hunger was gone and my belly was satisfied for the moment.

The hearing was back in session. I wasn't worried, not one bit. Aaron's mother wasn't entitled to anything outside of what he left for her in his will.

"Court is back in session. Now, I took a moment to go over the deed while we were on a brief recess. Mrs. Young, you made some very serious allegations toward Ms. Hamilton today in my courtroom. Upon my investigation, I did confirm that the deed to the house is legitimate. Therefore, I am going to dismiss your claim. There was no evidence to prove your case or allegations."

Mrs. Young was not happy.

"What I find interesting about this case is that you sat in my courtroom and threw stones at your daughter-in-law while hiding your hand. I don't know why you think I live under a rock because I don't. I'm a football fan, and I love your son's team. I am truly sorry for your loss, but your son was not perfect. And it's unfair that you expect his wife to be. You're condemning this woman for being tired of the scandals and in all honesty, you're no better than her. No one in this courtroom is."

The judge was laying her ass out.

"Now, for the life of me, I can't understand why you are so motivated to petition her to stay in a house that's rightfully hers. It's not about the money, and any fool with eyes can see that. As I did a little digging into financial records, I found a million-dollar policy for the defendant and you are the sole beneficiary of said policy."

That came as a surprise to everyone in attendance. Multiple gasps could be heard throughout the quiet room.

"I don't know anything about that."

"Mrs. Young, please don't sit in my courtroom and lie in my face. This policy has been paid from your checking account dating back to less than a year ago. Now, I don't know whose eyes you trying to pull the wool over, but I'm not the one."

Mr. Young was furious, and it showed.

"You also petitioned the court for a paternity test of Ms. Hamilton's unborn child. Is that correct?"

"Yes, Your Honor."

"I am going to grant that to you, so you can find out if the child Ms. Hamilton is carrying is, in fact, your grandchild." Judge Campbell looked me in the eyes. "Ms. Hamilton, I am ordering you to complete a Prenatal Paternity Test to establish paternity."

I agreed.

Judge Campbell banged her gavel. "Court is adjourned."

Chapter 15

Lexi

"Wow! You had a million-dollar policy on Aaron and didn't tell anyone?" My father shouted at my mother.

"Yes. I did. He was my son. What's the problem? It wasn't like Aaron didn't know this."

"Somehow, I don't believe that."

"You can believe what you want to. I don't care." Her attitude was so nonchalant.

"That's obvious." My father stood in the middle of the floor, massaging his temple. "I'm so tired of dealing with you. I want you out of this house. Take that million dollars and find you a place to stay."

That woman's entire attitude changed.

"What do you mean get out?"

"Exactly what I said. Get out and get out now. I've had enough of you." My mother wasn't moving fast enough, so he grabbed her by the arm and snatched her from the chair she was sitting in. The last time I saw him that angry, mom had cheated on him. It made me wonder if she was cheating again.

"Get your hands off of me," she screamed.

"You have ten minutes to gather what you can. After that, I'm throwing you out of here. So, please don't make this harder than it needs to be." With that being said, my mother left the room with her head hanging down.

"Dad," I called out just above a whisper. "Are you okay?"

"I will be."

"This may not be the right time to say this, but Aaron's death was no accident. Detective Marshall has re-opened the case and is doing a thorough investigation.

"What?" My father stumbled slightly at the news. I rushed over and helped him to the sofa. "Someone purposely killed my son?"

"That's what I believe."

"I don't understand," he sobbed. "Who would want to kill Aaron?" My father's eyes were fire-red as a heavy flow of tears flooded his face.

"I'm not sure, but I think Foreign's ex-boyfriend, Demerius Payne, is behind it. He's obsessed with her and when she tried to leave him, he threatened to kill her. I think he might do it. We went to the police and reported it. She also took out a restraining order on him."

"But, why?"

"I'm not sure. All I know is that—based on his phone call—he hated Aaron. I promise that I'm going to find out who did this to him. We will get justice for Aaron."

From the corner of my eye, I could see my mother standing in the cut. I couldn't stand the sight of her. She was my mother and I loved her, but she had some fucked up, controlling ways.

"I'm checking in at the Marriot on Westshore. I'll call you with the room number."

"Don't bother." He refused to give her eye contact.

As soon as she left, I decided to follow her. I was truly convinced that my mother was cheating, and it was my job to figure it out. If that was the case, she had a lot of explaining to do. That entire ordeal had my mind racing. From what I could see early on, I had a feeling that a divorce would probably be next. When it rained, it poured. Ever since Aaron left, our lives had been in shambles. My mother hasn't grieved properly because she was too upset with Foreign to do so. Once Aaron's killer was brought to justice, we could all move on as a family.

The first stop my mother made was to the Bank of Tampa on Henderson Blvd. I backed into a corner and put the car in park. Twenty minutes passed before she returned to her car. From there, I followed her to the hotel. There was a parking lot across the street. It was empty, but I was certain I wouldn't be seen. My mother's valet parked her car, and she went inside. Apart from me wanting to leave, I stayed because I needed answers. While I waited, I rolled up some exotic weed in a cigarillo.

One hour later, I was still in the same spot. That potent ass weed had my ass high as fuck. I was seeing unicorns, candy clouds, and gumdrops for raindrops. Everything looked sweet and lovely. My eyes bounced around, and it felt like I was floating on clouds. Since I hadn't seen anything, I decided it was time to go home. I was ready to get down and dirty with my husband. To refer to Calvin as my other half felt good.

Buzzed from the weed, my reflexes were slow as I put the car into drive. As I eased off the brake, I took another glance at the hotel. "I know that's not who I think that is." My eyes had to be playing tricks on me. I put the car in *park* and got out. Clear as day, I could see my mother approaching a man. On the inside, I was furious and I was about to demand answers.

Before I could take an extra step, I felt a strong, rugged hand cover my mouth and snatch me backward. Wildly, I kicked and clawed at my abductor. I tried to scream, but I was unsuccessful in doing so. The next thing I knew: I was being thrown into a dark, cold van. I was scared for my life and couldn't do a damn thing about it.

Domestic…

One Hour Ago

"This is Demerius speaking, how can I help you?"

"Hello, you don't know me but I know you. I'm a friend of Foreign, and I need to talk to you about something important."

The female on the phone had me curious. No one called my work line for personal matters. "And what is that?"

"I can't tell you over the phone. Can you meet me?"

"For what? I don't even know you. What's your name?"

"My name isn't important."

"If you want me to meet you, your name is very important. So, tell me what you want before I hang up."

"If you don't want to be in prison in the next seventy-two hours, I suggest you show up."

The phone call sounded very sketchy, but I wanted to know what information this mysterious woman had on me. Somehow, I knew it was in regards to Aaron's murder. Against my better judgment, I decided to ease my curiosity. "Give me the address."

One hour later I was sitting in a hotel room. Sitting across from me was an older woman wearing red lipstick on her devious lips. "Do you know who I am?" she asked.

"No. Should I?"

"I'm Mrs. Young. Aaron Young's mother. I believe you are dating my son's ex-wife, and you're the alleged father of her baby."

That was the last person I expected to be sitting across from. Her demeanor was calm. Too calm for my liking. "I am the father of her baby, but I'm confused as to why you called me here."

"Well," she crossed her legs and leaned her back against the headboard. "From my understanding, I've been told that you are the one responsible for the death of my son."

This woman was poking the bear, but I couldn't allow her to see me get defensive. The last thing she was about to get from me was a damn confession. She was better off recruiting another sucker. "And you would be incorrect. I had no reason to kill your son. But you know that already. And I know that his death was an accident."

"Oh really?" Mrs. Young grinned. "I'm sure I can think of a few good reasons you would have to get rid of him. You were dating his wife and got her pregnant. Aaron was a threat to you, so you had to get rid of him. The police would certainly believe that story. All they need is a motive."

"As I said before, I have no motive for any of that. Foreign belongs to me now. And no disrespect, she was mine before your son had that fatal accident. Nothing's changed since then."

Mrs. Young's laugh was wicked. "Is that what you really think?"

"It's what I know."

"And what is it that you think you know?"

"I know everything."

This bitch was crazy and talking in circles. I didn't have time for that, and it was time for me to leave that room. "I'm done with this."

I walked towards the door.

"We have a common alliance, Emilia Flores. And I know that she hired you to seduce Foreign and take her away from Aaron."

That made me stop dead in my tracks. A huge smile was on her face when I turned around to face her.

"I thought that would get your attention. Now, come back over and have a seat."

I did as I was told. Apparently, she knew more than she led on.

Mrs. Young placed a Newport cigarette in between her lips and lit it. Taking a long drag, she held it between her fingers. "I'm going to put you up on game and in return, I want something from you."

"Okay."

"You need to stay off the radar for now," she warned.

"Why?"

"Foreign has you on her radar, and she's been talking to that detective about reopening Aaron's case and treating it like a homicide."

Stroking my beard, I thought back to the questions Detective Marshall hit me with. No wonder he came to visit me today asking me questions about me and Foreign's relationship. "Why should I believe you?"

"My daughter said it."

"Who's your daughter?"

"That's not important. But think about it, why else would Foreign take out a restraining order on you?"

It made perfect sense. But why would Aaron's mother call me and provide me with crucial information? Something with this lady was not adding up.

"How do you think I know about the arrangement between you and Emilia?" Mrs. Young dumped her cigarette ashes onto the dresser and looked me dead in the eyes. "I'm the one that hired Emilia to seduce Aaron. As far as I'm concerned, you were probably behind his accident."

"Why would you do something like that? He was your son."

"I always thought he was too young for marriage. My son," she emphasized the word *son*, "had just been drafted and thought it was a good idea to get married and take himself off the market. I wanted him to explore his options, but he didn't listen to me." Mrs. Young took another drag from the cigarette before putting it out. "A few months ago Aaron had my name taken off of his insurance policies and his will. He left everything to her. I'm the one that gave birth to him. I believed in him and made sure every scout in the country wanted him. But, what did I get in return?" She paused for a few seconds. "I'll tell you what. I got nothing in return because they're legally married."

All this time I thought I had the worst mother in history. I learned quickly that my mother wasn't the only psychotic bitch on the planet. As much as I didn't want to believe her, I had no choice. It was obvious that she and Emilia were in cahoots.

"Why are you telling me all of this?"

"We have a common problem between us, and her name is Foreign. She has to go. That's the only way I can benefit from his death."

"So, you mean to tell me that you aren't well off?"

"No. I placed my trust in an accountant, and he's run off with my money. Now, he's nowhere to be found."

"I'm sorry. I can't help you with that."

Mrs. Young burst out into a fit of laughter. That bitch lost every marble in her head. "Oh, you thought I was asking? No. No. This is a demand. If you get rid of Foreign, you can stay out of prison and avoid sitting on death row. Because that's exactly what you're going to get if you go down for Aaron's umm, accident. I know a few prosecutors that are quite fond of me."

"You expect me to kill my unborn child?"

"Oh sweetie, that's not your baby. That's Aaron's baby. My grandchild."

"Nah. That's a lie." I couldn't believe what I was hearing.

"If you say so." Mrs. Young handed me a piece of paper from her purse. "Take a look at this."

The paper was a court document for a petition of Aaron's house and a paternity issue. My heart sunk into the pit of my stomach. Foreign lied to me about carrying my baby. I was furious.

"I'll do it," I agreed.

"Good," she smiled. "Then after that, you need to disappear."

"I can't believe I let Emilia pull me into this bullshit." Using both hands, I rubbed my face. "This is entirely too much, and I didn't sign up for this shit."

"I know you didn't, but this is your fault." Mrs. Young pointed her slender finger in my direction. "You had one job to do, and that was to make Foreign leave my son. Not kill him!"

"I did that, but Aaron refused to let her go. Foreign was confused after the meet-up between her father and Aaron. They convinced her to work through the marriage."

"Aaron was too stupid to see what he truly needed. So, the way I see it, he was a casualty of war. I don't know why he married her in the first place. We had a great relationship, and I was the center of his universe until he didn't need me anymore. Foreign didn't love him unconditionally. If she did, she would've never fallen for you." Mrs. Young hated Foreign with a passion. Her greed for Aaron's money caused her to do the unthinkable. Money was truly the root of all evil. Therefore, I trusted no one when big digits were involved.

The poster boy, Tampa's finest QB, was set up by his very own mother.

"How soon can you get this done?" she quizzed.

"I'm not sure, but it will be soon."

"Okay. How will I get in contact with you?"

"Give me your number."

Mrs. Young grabbed the notepad from the table and scribbled her number on it. After that, I left. The first thing I needed to do was, retrieve that video Emilia sent to Foreign.

Chapter 16

Lexi

"What the hell is wrong with you? Snatching me up like you crazy," I yelled. This fool blew my goddamn high. "I thought I was being kidnapped."

"You were about to ruin my investigation, and I can't have that," Detective Marshall replied as he sat across from me inside of the cold van. "What are you doing here anyway?"

"I was following my mother," I openly admitted.

"Why?"

"Today we went to court and found out my mother purchased a million-dollar policy on my brother several months ago."

Detective Marshall took a moment to think. He had a curious look on his face. Then he leaned forward with his hands folded. "So, are you suggesting that your mother is behind your brother's death?"

To think that my mother is responsible for the death of my twin killed me hurt on the inside. I didn't want to believe that she ruined our lives by taking away the most important person in my life. Tears of pain and anger streamed down my face, just thinking about it. I had to look at things that transpired. It all made sense to me.

"Honestly, I don't know. I'm hoping it's not true."

"Well," he scratched his nose, what are the chances that Mr. Payne is up there in the room with your mother?"

"At this point, I wouldn't doubt it. This coincidence is far too big for my liking."

"Does he know what you look like?"

"He saw me before but I don't think he would remember where he saw me at?"

"This is what I need you to do. See if you can get her room number and go on that floor to see if he's in there."

"I can do that. I'll be back."

"Try not to let him see you."

"Okay." My mind was focused on finding out what happened to my damn brother. If I had to take my mother down, so be it.

The hotel lobby was slightly empty when I walked through the automatic doors. A slender woman with glasses was at the front desk, talking on the phone when I walked up. She signaled me to wait, by raising her pointer finger. In a matter of seconds, she greeted me.

"Welcome to the Marriot. How may I help you?"

"My mother left me a key at the front desk. My name is Alexis Young. I have my driver's license if you need it."

"As a matter of fact, I do," she replied with a smile.

I passed her my license and provided my mother's first name. A short while later, she handed me a key with the number 502 written on the outside.

"Thank you."

With the key in my hand, I made my way to the elevator. Once inside, I hit the button for the fifth floor. Patiently, I waited until the elevator came to my stop. The doors opened, and I made my way out. Abruptly, I stopped in my tracks when I saw Domestic exit the room. It looked as if he was talking to someone. Quickly, I stuck my hand inside the doors to keep them from closing. Not even a second later, I could see my mother skinning and grinning with the man that was a suspect in my brother's supposedly *accidental* death.

"What the fuck is she doing meeting up with him?" I mumbled. This shit ultimately fucked up my day. As the elevator doors closed in front of me, I cried and screamed at the top of my lungs. The elevator came to a stop on the second floor. An elderly black couple joined me. I exchanged glances with the woman with salt-and-pepper hair and high cheekbones, when the door beeped for us to get off in the lobby. She looked at me with warm, loving, motherly eyes.

"Baby, whatever you going through has already been handled by God. Allow him to lead the way. You are blessed."

That melted my heart, and a faint smile spread across my dry lips. I could feel the texture when I licked them. It was exactly what I needed to hear. "Thank you."

"You're welcome, child." She smiled before we all exited the elevator.

Taking quick strides across the street to where the van was parked, I informed Detective Marshall about what I had seen. Soon after, I went home to drown myself in liquor.

Calvin wasn't home when I first arrived, but during my second glass of Jose Cuervo, I heard the door slam. When he walked in, I was downing the drink. He immediately saw my tears and rushed to my aid. "Baby, what's wrong?" He took the glass and sat it on the counter. "Lexi, talk to me, baby, please."

Through the tears and my sniffles, I managed to utter the words that were killing me softly. "I saw—" I heaved and cried. "My mother at the hotel with Domestic." Then I screamed out in pain. "Foreign's ex-boyfriend. I think she had something to do with his death."

"Baby, are you sure?" he asked sincerely.

I nodded. "Yes." Then I went on to tell him what unfolded play by play.

Foreign...

"Are you hungry," Maurice asked.

"I am."

"What do you want to eat?"

"Um. Let's go to Sonic. I'm craving a greasy burger and some fries."

Maurice chuckled. "Greasy food is not healthy for the baby." His smile was beautiful. I loved the way his chocolate skin glistened in the sun.

"I know, but he or she will be okay. I drink lots of water."

"I hear that." Maurice made a left turn at the intersection. "One greasy burger coming up."

While I sat back in anticipation, I decided to scroll through my Instagram to see if our court hearing was trending. As expected, it was. The Shaderoom stayed on top of all the dirt that happened in the lives of celebrities and regular people. If you had an interesting story, your ass was getting posted.

The headline read: *Deceased football star Aaron Young's mother battles wife in court for his mansion.* In the comment section, they were going ham on his mama and Aaron's cheating ways. A few people were not happy about me moving on so quickly. But I didn't take it to heart because none of those bitches knew me or my story.

My DM was flooded with messages. Out of curiosity, I opened it to see what people were messaging me. The first set of messages contained encouraging messages, but there was one name that took me by surprise. It was Casey, DP's mother. She sent me a video. When I opened it, I was stunned by what I was looking at. Clear as a sunny day, I was looking at Domestic dick down some girl I didn't recognize. This nigga was no better than Aaron. It was funny because he swore me up and down that he was a real man that didn't need to cheat. What I couldn't understand was why she sent it. To clear up any questions I had, I sent her a message.

Foreign_Young: Why did you send me this video?

PrettyGirl_Casey: Last night I caught him sleeping with my best friend Tiffany. I just thought you should see what Domestic was doing. Get out while you can. I warned you before, so please take heed to what I'm trying to tell you. I'm pretty sure you've seen his bad side already. Protect yourself and your baby.

Foreign_Young: I appreciate it, but I left Domestic. We're no longer together so he can fuck whoever he wants to. He's no longer my concern.

PrettyGirl_Casey: That's good. Take care

Foreign_Young: I will. Thanks

PrettyGirl_Casey: You're welcome

Seeing Domestic in that video didn't make me feel any type of way. We were over for good. Hopefully, he would leave me alone and pursue the woman he was fucking in the video. As far as I was concerned, he never had to worry about me or my baby ever again in life. I was going to make sure of that.

We pulled up to the Sonic on Fowler Ave. The tantalizing scent from the building made my stomach growl. My baby was hungry. It was easy to tell by the sudden movements.

Maurice rolled down the window. "Can you lean over and see what you want?"

"Yeah," I laughed. "I'm not that big."

"I'm joking. You know that I think you are very sexy." Maurice had the most seductive look in his eyes. *Damn*, me and this stupid ass no-sex rule was getting on my last nerve. My hormones were raging for sex, and I didn't think it was appropriate to sleep with another man while I was pregnant. My mind and vagina were on two separate pages, and I needed help. Against my better judgment, I decided to shoot Blacque Barbee a quick text. *'Is it wrong to sleep with someone while you pregnant with another man's baby? Don't judge me lol.'*

"I swear you know what to say to a woman. Because I feel fat as hell."

"Cut it out. You are not fat! Now, what would you like to eat?" Staring at the menu had my greedy mouth watering. "Um. Get me a double bacon cheeseburger meal with tater tots and a side of five-piece chicken tenders with a lemonade slushy."

"You and the baby want anything else?" He chuckled.

"No. That's it for us." Shit, I was hungry as hell.

Maurice placed the order. In the meantime, we made small talk until the waitress rolled out on her skates to collect the payment. That was what I loved about coming to the fast-food joint. It took me back to when I was a little girl. My father used to take me there on Friday nights. That was a part of our father-daughter outing.

"So, how are you feeling after doing the paternity test?"

"I'm glad that she will know that this isn't Aaron's child, so she could move on and leave me the hell alone." Rubbing my stomach, I reflected on all the fake she's shown me over the years. For her to act in this manner confirmed that she was never happy about our marriage. It's funny how quickly things could change when money is involved after the death of a loved one.

"How was the relationship with the two of you before Aaron passed away?"

"It was good. At least I thought it was. His dad never changed up on me. He's been good to me since we started dating. That man has always treated me like a daughter."

"It sounds like jealousy. Sometimes mothers become possessive with their sons."

"I'm learning that now." My phone beeped. It was a text message.

Blacque Barbee: BOFL! Girllll, who you trying to give that pregnant WAP to?

Foreign: Maurice Lol!

Blacque Barbee: If you want to sleep with that man, go 'head

Foreign: Seriously? Isn't that nasty?

Blacque Barbee: You not with the BD anymore, so oh well! Shit, pregnant women have needs too. I know how it is. I mean unless you want to use that rose. Lol! Do you, boo! You do like him, right?

Foreign: Yes. He's so sweet and sexy too

Blacque Barbee: Well, there is your answer. We have one life to live. Live it to the fullest. Hell, you've been through enough already. Fuck it! Be happy

Foreign: You are so right. I've been with two men in my life. I guess a third one won't hurt.

Blacque Barbee: Nope! Just hope that it's good.

Foreign: Oh, it will be. I felt his print last night lol. It's big too (Eggplant emoji)

Blacque Barbee: Well, find out shit!

Foreign: I am. Thanks, B!

Blacque Barbee: You're welcome. Call me tomorrow

Foreign: I will

"Here you go." Maurice handed me my food. I was so caught up in my conversation with Blacque Barbee that I didn't realize the waitress had returned with our food.

"Thanks." Consumed with hunger, I removed my food and got to work.

"You're welcome." For about thirty minutes we ate our food and listened to some old-school R 'n' B. It felt like I was on my first date back in high school. In all honesty, I could date Maurice. Hell, I was thinking about relocating to Kansas with him. There was nothing in Tampa for me. Aaron was dead, and Domestic was on his way to prison.

After we left Sonic, Maurice took me by the house to get some clothes. I was a pregnant widow with needs, and they needed to be handed. All that good girl shit was out the window. As Blacque Barbee stated, we only live once, and I wanted to enjoy my life to the fullest. How else would I establish a relationship with Maurice? We needed a connection beyond a conversation. Sex would put a stamp on our foundation. Especially, if the dick was great. But somehow, I felt I had nothing to worry about.

Back at Maurice's house, we showered together. At first, he was skeptical, but I reassured him that I was really ready. The man bathed every inch of me inside of his walk-in shower. It was his gentleness for me. Not once had I been caressed the way he did me. Aaron or Domestic never made me feel the way this man made me feel. The feelings I felt were a sense of being wanted and appreciated. If he kept this up, he could move me to the end of the earth.

In Aaron's defense, he was a young, handsome, million-dollar athlete. The world was at his fingertips, and the women were endless. Mentally, I wasn't prepared for that. Neither was he. Aaron cheated with any female that threw pussy in his direction. Domestic was a different story. He was handsome as well, but he was older. I expected him to know what a commitment was. Unbeknownst to me, he had mommy issues and didn't know how to love and care for a woman.

Maurice carried me into the bedroom, and laid me down on the bed. "Are you sure you want to do this? I'm not in a rush. We can wait until you're certain about this."

On our way to his house, I contemplated repeatedly on having sex with him. My mind and body battled constantly. I was ready, and there was no turning back. Seductively, I gazed into his welcoming eyes. "I'm ready for you to make love to me."

Maurice didn't respond. Instead of responding, he lowered himself between my legs. Erotic chills erupted within my body. I was comfortable as he nibbled gently on my pearl tongue. After my first orgasm by mouth, he pulled me to the edge of the bed and pushed every inch of his thickness inside of me. Aggressively, I dug my acrylic nails deep into his back, while moaning in his ear.

Chapter 17

Domestic

"Bitch, you out here riding around with some nigga. Just wait until I catch yo' ass." Anger filled my body as I punched the steering wheel of my fine automobile. Foreign had me ready to catch two bodies. Not because her mother-in-law demanded that I do so, but due to the fact she was disrespecting me.

Shortly after I left the hotel, I decided to go by Foreign's house to see if she was home. Upon my arrival, her car was not in the driveway. Therefore, I took it upon myself to sit and wait for her to get back. That was a mistake on my part. Forty-five minutes later, she pulled up with some nigga. My first mind said: *confront her*, but once I calmed down, I took a different approach. I followed them.

Now, here I was sitting outside this nigga house—knowing he was in there dropping dick in my pussy and feeding my alleged baby. After hearing what Aaron's mother had to say, I didn't know if the baby was mine or not. It was obvious the paternity was now in question. That news crushed me. Here I thought I was about to be a father for a second time, only to be told I might not be.

Foreign was playing a dirty-ass game, and she was about to meet the same fate as Emilia. Pulling away from the house, I put the radio on the quiet storm. Keith Sweat was whining through my speakers, but his tunes increased my pussy rate back in the day. In deep thought, I cruised the dark streets of the bay. The life I thought was perfect was everything but that. My cellphone started to ring. It was Carlos.

"What's up, bro?"

"Have you seen the news," he asked.

"Nah. Why?"

"They found Emilia's body a few hours ago."

"What? Her body. Wait, what the hell do you mean they found her body?" That was the last thing I expected to hear. I could've sworn I buried that bitch deep enough to not be found.

"She's dead. Somebody killed her."

"In California?" I had no problem playing dumb.

"She never made it to California."

"So where did they find her?"

"Somebody buried her at Torreya State Park," he sniffled.

"Damn bro! I'm sorry to hear that."

"Somebody killed my sister, bro. That shit killing my father, man. What the fuck I'm supposed to do?"

"I know this is hard. Where you at, bro? I'm about to pull up on you."

"I'm on my way to my dad's house."

"I'm on the way."

"A'ight." Carlos hung up the phone.

"Fuck!" That shit just added to my stress. Now wasn't the time to fuck around and slip up. I had to shake life real quick. For now, I had to meet up with Carlos and see what the cops were saying. After that, I was about to fall off the grid. I needed help, so I hit up my brother.

"Hello."

"Aye bro, I need you."

"What's up?"

"We can't discuss this over the phone. I need to talk to you in person."

"I'm at the house. Come by."

"Okay. I have somewhere to go right now, but I'll call you when I'm on the way."

"A'ight. Just hit me up."

"One."

"One," he repeated and hung up.

The visit with Carlos was informative. Roughly, I sat there for an hour giving my condolences to the family. So far, they had no leads in the investigation. That was good news, but I knew it wouldn't be long before they came to question me. No matter how hard they pushed, a confession wouldn't be something they would get from me.

Pulling up to my mother's house, I texted my brother Demetri to come outside. Seeing Veronica was not what I wanted, so I kept my ass outside. Demetri got into the car, and we did the handshake we created when we were teenagers.

"What's going on, brother? You done got yourself into some shit again and need my help, huh?" He smirked.

"That's the story of my life," I chuckled while shaking my head in disbelief of all the bullshit I was facing.

"A'ight. Whatchu need from me?"

"It's simple this time. I swear." Over the years I've had Demetri save my ass from a lot of heat I caused. "All I need for you to do is, stay at my house for a few weeks and run the car washes. The job is easy 'cause Tracy will make sure everything runs like clockwork."

"Trust me. I don't need help from her. I know what to do."

"Is that a yes?"

"Hell yeah! I need a break from this house. Veronica is crazy. She's not thinking logically right now." He admitted what I already knew.

"Bro, we knew that our whole lives."

"This is different."

"How so?" My curiosity was speaking.

"She killed Teddy."

"Why?"

"He stole some work and was talking to the police."

"He deserved to die. What's the problem?"

"The problem is: she killed him, offered to pay for the funeral arrangements, and is sitting around his mama like she ain't did shit. This too much for me, and I need a break."

"Bro, that's how the game goes, or did you forget about that?" Demetri must've forgotten the rules of the game. Veronica wasn't my favorite person, but I had to side with her on this one. "He fucked up when he did both. You know we don't talk to the police."

"I get all of that," he sighed. "I'm not gon' sit here and lie. I've been thinking about getting out the game for a while now."

"Do it, shit. You already know there are only two ways out, death or jail."

Demetri nodded in agreement. "Yeah. I know. That's why I'm going to do this for you. So, where are you going?"

"I don't know yet. I'm stuck between Virginia and New York."

"Go to New York and get a taste of that fast, city life."

"I'm leaning more towards the north." I passed him the spare keys to the house and the shop. "These are the extra keys."

"A'ight. I gotchu, bro."

"Thanks, bro, you just saved my life, again."

"Like always." Demetri and I did our handshake, and he got out of the car. "Be safe out there. When you get posted, hit me up 'cause ya' ass still didn't tell me what you running from." He grinned.

"My chick put out a restraining order on me and they trying to lock my ass up. I just need a break until the dust settles."

"Okay." Demetri closed the door, and I pulled off.

On my way home, I made a quick stop by the gas station. In the car, I made a Molotov Cocktail and sat it in the cupholder. Then I made the twenty-minute drive to Foreign's house. Of course, her car wasn't in the driveway. It was cool though because I was about to teach her ass a valuable lesson about fucking with me.

Circling the block two times, I made sure no nosey neighbors were sitting on the porch playing neighborhood watch. The coast was clear, so I pulled up into the driveway and got out with the mean concoction in my hand. Launching the cocktail like a missile through the front window, I watched as it went off and started the fire. That would teach that unfaithful bitch about playing with me. Then I pulled off slowly without bringing attention to myself.

Chapter 18

Foreign

Repeated sounds of my phone going off in my ear woke me up. "What the hell?" I uttered with sleep in my eyes. The time on the clock let me know that it was well after midnight. "Who's calling me this time of night?"

Honest to God, I didn't want to answer. I contemplated not answering a few times, but I figured it had to be an accident or—even worst—a death. Considering those possibilities, I answered with a sluggish voice.

"Hello."

"Foreign, is this you?" It was my neighbor from across the street.

"Yes," I yawned. "What's going on?"

"Your house is on fire," my neighbor stated in panic.

"What?" Now I was up and fully alert. "What do you mean my house is on fire?"

"*Your house in on fire*. The fire truck is out here now putting out the flames. You need to get here quick!"

"Okay. I'm on my way."

"Okay."

Maurice was looking directly at me when I turned to face him. "What's going on?"

"My neighbor just said that my house is on fire." Hopping from the bed, I threw on a pair of sweat pants and a sweater. "We need to get there now."

Maurice got up and got dressed quickly. "I'm ready."

When we pulled up on my block, it was flooded with red and blue lights. Smoke filled the air, and my heart raced at an unusual pace. The sight of our memories going up in smoke felt like I was receiving the news of Aaron's death all over again. That shit truly hurt my heart. Quickly, I got out of the car and approached the house. Maurice was right on my heels.

"Excuse me, ma'am, this scene is secured." The officer stopped me in my tracks.

"This is my house. What happened?"

"I'm afraid I'm not at liberty to say." The officer was too rude for my liking, and he was two seconds from getting cursed the fuck out.

Maurice stepped in. "This is her home, and she has the right to know what's going on."

"And who are you?"

"I'm CIA Agent Maurice Rawlings." Maurice showed his credentials.

The words that left his mouth took me by surprise. "CIA agent," I mumbled underneath my breath. We were going to discuss that as soon as this ordeal was over.

"My apologies," Officer Attitude nodded. It was funny how his demeanor changed so suddenly. "The officers were able to put out the fire and keep it from spreading. Right now there is only some damage to the living room area. A Molotov Cocktail was recovered inside the home."

"A what? I don't know what that is." I didn't know what the hell he was talking about.

"It's a glass bottle filled with a flammable substance."

"Okay, so what does that mean?"

"It means that this fire was started purposely. Do you have surveillance cameras in the home?"

"Yes."

"Detective Marshall is inside. He'll want to see those to see if the culprit is caught on camera."

"Okay," I agreed and walked away. The minute I stepped into my burned living room, the fumes tickled my nose. My cough was violent.

Maurice grabbed me by the arm. "You shouldn't be in here. The smoke isn't good for the baby."

"Mrs. Young," Detective Marshall approached me. "He's right. Let's talk outside." We stepped onto the porch. "Do you have cameras inside your home?"

"Yes."

"Where is the system located?"

"Inside the study room. It's down the hall on the left."

"Okay. I'm going to take the footage and watch it later. I need to see if it caught the person responsible for the fire."

"Please do," I sighed.

"I'll be in touch as soon as I find out something."

"Thanks, detective," Maurice and I replied simultaneously, and the two men shook hands.

Detective Marshall started to walk away, but then he stopped and turned around. "Do you think he did this?"

I knew exactly who *he* was. So, I nodded. "I wouldn't put it past him."

It took around roughly an hour for them to leave the scene. Once they were gone, I grabbed a few items from the house and left. One thing about life was certain: When it rained it poured.

Blacque Barbee…

The Next Day

"Girl, this is a cute picture of us. I'm about to post this on Facebook," I giggled while uploading our photo.

"Yassss! It surely is," Mercedes chimed in.

"We are too cute."

"We really are."

Within minutes of me posting the picture, we were already at eight hundred likes. As I continued to scroll through my news feed, I came across a post from a blogger by the name of *Zee with the Tee*. This chick was hella funny and stayed on top of all of the tea with celebrities, and that's why I was following her. Not only was she dope, but she was also pretty too. The heading read, *Superbowl champ Aaron Young's home was burned to a crisp. Do y'all think her new nigga was involved?* That shit threw me for a loop. Immediately, I got off the book and called Foreign.

"Hello."

"Hey, I just heard about the fire from social media. Are you okay?"

"Yeah. I'm fine. I wasn't in there."

"I'm coming to you. It looks like you need my help."

Foreign exhaled in the phone. "No. You don't have to. I'll be okay."

"I'm not taking no for an answer. Corey and I will be there. Send me your address."

"Okay, I'll send it now," Foreign obliged.

"I'll see you in a few hours."

Then I hung up. The savage in me wasn't taking no for an answer. She was too timid to handle this on her own, and I knew she needed me. Foreign's pride and fear were in the way.

"Who was that and what's going on?" Mercedes asked with great concern in her voice.

"Do you remember my cousin Foreign?"

Mercedes tilted her head to the side in deep thought. "Yeah."

"Well, her house was set on fire and I'm willing to bet that her baby daddy is behind it."

"How do you know that?" she asked.

"He's been threatening to kill her, that's how."

Mercedes had Dre and Sierra's son, Denim, sitting in her lap. That was the name Sierra picked for him before she was tragically killed. "Wow! That's crazy as hell."

"It is because she's pregnant with his baby."

"What's going on, B?" Dre walked into the living room.

"Hey, Dre. How are you?"

"I'm good and you?"

"I can't complain."

Dre leaned down and kissed Mercedes on the forehead. "Bae, I'll be back. I'm about to slide to the hood real quick."

"Okay. Will you be able to pick up Sienna or do I need to get her?" Mercedes asked sweetly.

"I'll get her. Daddy will be back, fat man." Dre kissed his baby boy on the head and left.

When the door closed, I looked at Mercedes and smiled. "Aww! Y'all are so cute together. If anybody would've told me years ago that y'all would be a couple, I wouldn't believe it."

"Me too, but Dre is different from the way he used to be. And I see why Sierra fell in love with him. He makes that shit so easy to do."

"Hell, don't forget crazy-ass Tokee. She cherished the ground that nigga walked on," I added.

"Big facts. That bitch took crazy to another level." Denim fell asleep in Mercedes' arms. "Let me put him to bed. I'll be right back."

A few minutes later, Mercedes returned. "Okay, bitch! Now that my baby is gone to bed, who do we have to kill?"

"This nigga named Domestic."

"His name is a dead giveaway. Who the fuck calls themselves Domestic? A nigga who beats ass. Foreign should've run for the hills when she heard that."

"That's true and sad, but hilarious at the same time." Mercedes was a total fool, but it was funny. "Well, I'm going to have Corey drive me up there to make sure she's okay and get her to come back with us."

"Bitch, I clearly said who do we," Mercedes pointed her finger back and forth between us, "have to kill and you talking about Corey."

"Now, you know damn well he is not letting me go up there without him. And besides, you have to stay here and help your man with y'all kids."

"I know right," Mercedes giggled. "I never thought I would see the day that I took care of kids. But I love these kids like I gave birth to them myself."

"Oh, I know. Do you think you and Dre will have a baby?"

"We have a ready-made family."

"You don't want to have your own baby?"

Mercedes scrunched up her face. "I don't know about that. We have enough going on as is. The timing isn't right."

"Girl, please. You can have a damn baby."

"Can we talk about something else besides my damn ovaries?"

"Sure," I shrugged. "Can you watch the kids while we go to Tampa?"

"Now you know you don't have to ask. Dre and I got the kids. Go and help your cousin."

"Thanks, sis. I appreciate you so much. I'm about to go home and get ready to hit the road." We both stood up and hugged. "I'll keep you posted on the craziness we're about to walk into."

"Be safe, sis."

"Always," I replied and headed for the door.

Corey was sitting on the porch, smoking a blunt and watching the kids play in the yard when I made it home. "I need a favor." I didn't waste any time getting to the point.

He exhaled the smoke through his mouth and nose. "What's that?"

"I need to go to Tampa and help Foreign."

"What happened?" His brow was slightly slanted.

"That crazy ass nigga set her house on fire."

"Is she okay?"

"Yeah. I told her we were coming up. If we don't go and help, I feel like he's going to kill her. Mercedes is going to keep the kids until we get back."

"Okay. When are you trying to leave?"

"As soon as possible. Like the next couple of hours. Do you have something to do?"

"Nah," he nodded, and took another hit of his weed. "I'm glad you squashed that beef with her. At the end of the day, family is all we got."

"That's true," I agreed. "Well, I'm about to go and pack the kids up."

"A'ight. I'll be in there in a few."

Chapter 19

Foreign

"So you're with the CIA, huh? Why you never told me that?"

Maurice was sitting on the edge of the bed, looking at me. "It's not something I'm supposed to disclose to anyone. Not even my family."

"So, why did you bring it up last night?"

"The officer was giving you a hard time, so I had to flex my authority a little bit. You see how easy he gave up that information. That's why I disclosed my job."

"Okay," I smirked. "I won't ask any more questions about it. I've watched enough television shows to know how that works."

Maurice placed his hand on my cheek. "All you need to know is that I will always protect you. As long as I'm around, you will never have to worry about a thing."

"That's so sweet." Maurice always knew what to say to make me feel good.

"I don't know what you're used to, but I'm a real man and I always put my woman and her feelings first."

All I could do was smile and giggle like a teenager talking to her high school crush. "Where have you been all my life?"

"Waiting on you to leave these childish men alone and recognize your worth." Maurice gently stroked the side of my cheek, and sent chills down my spine and into my vagina.

"Why are you like this?" I screamed while clutching my pearls. "You better get out of here and go to work before I make you late."

Maurice smirked and stood up. "Yeah. Let me leave you alone. I have an important meeting to attend in about an hour."

My eyes were on his semi-stiff print in his boxer briefs. "That's not what your body is saying."

"He's easily influenced by you, but I know better," he chuckled. "I'm headed for the shower."

Maurice wasn't bigger than Domestic, but he certainly fucked me better. That nigga was just ruined, crazy, and possessed with a demon dick. If I knew then what I knew now, I would've kept my kitty on ice the night we met. Now, I was pregnant with his child and the bitch was trying to kill me. I didn't have any proof, but I knew he was responsible for that fire. There was only one person that could stop this maniac from fucking with me, and I was about to visit her ass.

After Maurice left for work, I hopped on I-95 and headed north. My foot was heavy on the pedal. There wasn't a single worry on my mind about the state trooper. In no time I was turning into the high-class neighborhood.

Standing in front of the mansion, I took a deep breath and rang the doorbell. My hands trembled. The palms of my hands were sweaty as hell. During my last visit, it wasn't pleasant at all. Right now, that was beside the point because I needed help and I needed it fast. Rubbing my hands against my jeans, I freed my hands from the heavy sweat.

The door swung open, and I was face to face with the maid.

"Hello, how may I help you?"

"I'm here to see Veronica."

The maid raised her brow. Her face was tight like she had been injected multiple times with botox. "And you are?"

"Oh, sorry," I smiled. "I'm Foreign Young. Can you please tell her that it's an emergency about her son, Demerius?"

The sound of his name relaxed those tight ass muscles. "I'll let her know you're here. Come inside."

It wasn't long before I heard the wicked witch's voice. "Margaret, who was at the door."

"She's right here." Margaret pointed in my direction.

Our eyes locked. Based on her facial expression, I was the last person she expected to see standing in her living room. That smile was phony as the weave in her hair. "Mrs. Foreign Young, how may I help you? And don't tell me you were in the neighborhood and decided to stop by. I live too far away for that scenario."

"You're correct about that." It was time to get straight to the point so I could get out of her presence. Evil spirits were hard to shake. "I came by to talk to you about Domestic." Margaret dismissed herself. That was her cue to leave the room.

"Let me guess," she hissed. "He's behaving like that ridiculous name he calls himself?"

"Yes." That comment didn't sit too well with me. It was clear that his behavior came as no surprise.

"Listen, baby, I'm going to tell you like I told Casey, *leave him*. Demerius is not capable of loving anyone besides his child." Veronica eyeballed my stomach. "Is that his baby?"

"Yes."

"Luckily for you, he won't kill you while you're carrying his child."

This conversation was not going as planned. It was like she didn't give a fuck what this psychopath was doing. "Your son is crazy," I snapped. "He set my damn house on fire and I need you to keep him away from me. You're the only person he fears. If you don't do something, I'm going to send him to jail."

Veronica laughed like something was funny. "Baby, I don't care if you send him to jail or prison. That may be the best place for him. He's not my problem. And in case you haven't noticed, we do not have a mother and son relationship. He's estranged to me like a stray dog without its mother."

"Now, I see why he acts the way he does. He has mommy issues from the lack of you being his mother. You're the reason he's incapable of loving a woman."

"Call it what you want, baby. At the end of the day, Demerius is crazy as they come. Therefore, I advise you to set yourself free because I can't help you."

My hands were now on my hips. "You can't or you won't help me?"

"Either is fine with me because I'm *not* doing anything. He's your problem now, not mine. I'm good without the drama he brings."

"The apple didn't fall far from the tree."

"Not at all." Veronica looked down at her watch. "Is that all? I'm about to be late for my manicure and pedicure." She looked over her shoulder. "Margaret," she yelled.

"Don't bother. I'll let myself out."

"Just go home and pray about it. God takes care of fools and babies. It's obvious he's not a baby."

Ignoring that stupid statement, I stepped onto the porch and took a deep breath. "This bitch is crazy too," I mumbled while walking to my car.

On the way out of the driveway, I spotted a car coming into the residence. We made eye contact. It was Domestic, but he was in a different car. "That lying bitch!" I uttered and sped off.

Detective Marshall...

The press stood in ninety-degree weather in front of the precinct. This was one of the many tricks up my sleeves to put a crack in this case. The strong smell of a promotion lingered heavily in the air. My soul smiled on the inside, but my lips were pressed together. This was about to be the most important part of my case.

"Good afternoon. On behalf of the Tampa Precinct, we are holding this press conference in regards to the city's fallen hero, Mr. Aaron Young. He was the quarterback that brought this town a championship after nineteen years. As we all know, he passed away a few months back in a car crash. I would like to say that, as of a few weeks ago, the case has been opened as a homicide. There is a ten-thousand-dollar reward for any tips that lead to an arrest. If anyone was on the Expressway when the accident occurred, you are urged to call us. It doesn't matter how small the tip is, it could be the answers we need. Please, let's help the Young family get answers behind their loved one's murder."

"Detective Marshall, what made you open the case as a homicide?" A female reporter held up a tape recorder.

"At this time I will not be answering any questions pertaining to the case. This is an ongoing investigation, and I cannot reveal any specific details. That's all for now. Thank you for your time."

Smoothly, I stepped away from the podium and went back inside. The sun was beaming, and my face was full of sweat. Using my handkerchief, I wiped the sweat away. Hopefully, I would get some details from the public. There was no doubt in my mind that a lead wasn't about to circulate.

"Back to the drawing board," I sighed. Three hours had passed, and not one single lead came through. I packed my things up to take home. It was about to be an early day for me. Feeling defeated, I walked out of the precinct. I was steps away from my car when I heard a voice behind me.

"Detective Marshall." It was a young black male clutching a phone in his hand. "I have something you might be interested in."

Opening my car door, I threw my items inside and faced the gentleman. "You saw the press conference?"

"Yes." He passed me the phone. "I'm not sure if this will help, but the day of the accident—I spotted a Black Mustang doing at least a hundred miles per hour on the freeway. I recorded it because I love sports cars, and the custom black paint with the loud pipes caught my attention."

The Mustang was hauling ass. *Was it possible that he was responsible for the accident that killed Aaron?* So many thoughts ran through my head. "Can you send me this video?"

"Sure."

"Thanks. Text your name with it. If it leads to an arrest, that money is yours."

"Okay." The young man walked off, and I got in my car.
Immediately, I headed over to the car wash. If anyone recognized this car, it was Tracy.

Foreign...

Seeing Domestic at his mother's house gave me ample time to collect the rest of my things from his house. The necklace Aaron bought me was in the nightstand dresser, and I needed that. I could've done without the clothes, but my jewelry had sentimental value to it. I couldn't leave that behind.
The house was empty like I knew it would be. DP was always missing in action. That was a relief. All I needed was ten minutes, and I was gone forever. Domestic would never see me again. Inside the bedroom, I went straight to my necklace and tossed it into my purse. Then I went into the closet and grabbed the travel bag I left behind. It was less than ten minutes, and I was done.
In a hurry, I rushed out of the room and down the hall. When I got to the steps, my heart hit the floor and shattered into one trillion pieces. It was the devil himself looking at me. I could see my life flash before my eyes, but I refused to go out like that.
"What are you doing in here?" He took a step towards me, and I grabbed the first object within my reach. A vase.
This was a life-or-death situation and I wasn't dying today. He extended his arms. "Wait! Wa—"
Before he could finish his sentence, I smashed the vase over his head. Blood gushed from his skull. Domestic was in a daze as he stumbled backward. I pushed him with all the strength I had in me, and he tumbled down the stairs. The adrenaline rushed through my body. Strength came from everywhere when fear was involved. I grabbed my bag and ran down the stairs. Domestic was still on the floor when I rushed past him, praying he didn't grab my leg on the way out. Now, I was outside and getting into my car. My hands trembled and the keys fell.
When I looked up, I could see Domestic standing at the door. He was shouting something, but I didn't hear shit he was saying. Nor was I trying to. "Dammit! Come on, keys."
Consumed with fear, the keys touched my fingers, and I grabbed them. Just as I started the car and put it in reverse, Domestic reached my door and

pulled it. It was locked. My heart was beating rapidly like it was about to explode. Smashing hard on the gas, I backed out of the driveway fast as hell. "Shit, that was close."

Detective Marshall…

Upon my arrival, Domestic's car wasn't there. That was a good thing since Tracy hated when I showed up and he was present. As usual, Tracy was sitting down behind the counter, popping gum and playing with her nails.

The look of disgust said everything when she made eye contact with me. "What did I tell you about coming here?"

"Relax! He's not here."

"Hello, he does have cameras in here."

"Trust me, I didn't come here to stay. I just need to show you a video and I'm out of your hair."

"Hurry up and show me." Tracy stood up and looked around nervously.

I opened the video and pressed play. "Have you ever seen this car around here?"

"Yeah. It belongs to a guy named Carlos. If I'm not mistaking, I think he's your partner's brother."

"Emilia's brother?"

"Yeah."

A lightbulb went off in my head. "Thanks, Tracy. I'll be in touch with you later. We should be ready to have you out of here in a few days."

"Good. I'm tired of being here."

"Well, quit!"

"That would be too obvious. Just get me in that van so I can disappear."

"Start packing. You'll be out in about three days max."

"Thanks," Tracy smiled.

On my way out the door, I called for backup.

Chapter 20

Foreign

"I'm in the Bay, bitches," Blacque Barbee shouted when she stepped out of her vehicle with her arms raised.

"Oh my God! I can't believe you showed up," I screeched with excitement. If no one was going to help me escape this fool, she was.

"I told you I was coming." Blacque Barbee hugged me. "You see who I brought with me."

"I see," I smiled. "Hey, Corey."

"Hey, Foreign. How are you?" We hugged briefly.

"I'm better now that you guys are here."

"That's what family does," Corey replied.

"Let's go inside. It's hot out here." The sweat started to form underneath my breast.

Maurice was standing near the door when we walked in. He and Corey shook hands. Then he hugged Barbee. "How was the drive?"

"Like driving down the street," Corey chuckled. "I'm used to long-distance."

"That's what's up. Do you want a drink? I have a bottle of Jack Daniel's we can crack open while the ladies chat."

"Hell yeah! I could use a drink."

"Fix me one too. I'm not pregnant," Barbee laughed and looked at me. "No offense, cousin."

"None taken."

Barbee and I sat in the living room, and the men went out to the backyard. Reaching into her bag, she produced a small manila envelope. "Here are your documents as promised."

My smile was bright as the sun on a hot sunny day. Excitement was all over my face. "I swear you are the best. How much do I owe you?"

"Nothing. I got you covered."

"Thank you so much, B. I don't know how I can ever repay for all you've done for me."

"I'm sure I can think of something," Barbee giggled.

"Anything for you."

"Be careful. I'll hold you to that."

"Trust me. I don't mind." I meant every word I said.

Opening up my package, I removed a driver's license, birth certificate, social security card, and a passport. They all looked legit as hell.

"Elite Banks?" I asked with my brow raised and lips tooted. "What kind of name is this?"

Barbee waved her hand and laughed. "Girl, you know you boujee as hell. I had to find something that fits you."

"It's funny, but I can't lie. The name is cute."

"You're welcome. I knew you would love it."

Barbee didn't realize how priceless her gesture was to me. This meant a new start for me and my baby. A life away from Domestic. That peace was priceless within itself. I pressed the documents against the center of my chest and exhaled. "You saved my life."

Barbee took a sip of her drink. "I can truly save your life if you want me to."

Placing the documents beside me, I looked over with curiosity stricken across my face. "What do you mean?"

"I can just kill the nigga and you'll never have to look over your shoulder again." Her tone was firm. There wasn't a smirk or smile in sight.

"You're serious, aren't you?"

"As a heart attack." There was a pregnant pause in the room until Barbee spoke again.

"Foreign, here's the thing. Why should you live your life in fear? This nigga needs to be buried, period!" Blacque Barbee shook her head and sighed. "I'm going to give you a little insight. When you become a mother, your main goal in life is to protect your child. You have to fight with the fangs of a wolf and the claws of a dragon. Don't ever allow anyone or anything to stop you from protecting your baby! And if that means killing the father to stay safe, then so be it. He didn't deserve to live in the first place."

Barbee's words hit me in the chest. It made perfect sense, but I didn't want anyone getting caught up behind my drama. "I get that, but I don't want you to go to prison because of me. Your kids and man would never forgive me for pulling you into my drama."

Leaning forward and clasping her hands together, Barbee exhaled. "You don't know me that well. Trust me when I say, I'm not getting caught. Contrary to your belief cousin, I'm a killer. A cold-blooded one at that. You need to check my résumé. When you were away at college, I was hustling in these streets and sending niggas to meet their makers at the same time. I'm good at what I do. All you have to do is say the word, and I'll body that nigga. Real shit!"

"Damn, I didn't know you were living like that." Her confession took me by surprise.

"I did." Barbee and I both looked up, and saw Maurice standing there holding a glass in his hand. "Your name has come up in a few investigations in the past."

"Oh really?" Barbee smirked.

"Yes. When I worked with the Feds, you were a hot topic. But, we were never able to make the charges stick. I'm glad we couldn't since I know that you and my lady are related."

"That's good to know." Blacque Barbee sat up and folded her hands. "Is my name still ringing in the federal building?"

"No! All of those cases were closed. You have nothing to worry about. And please know that whatever you say in my home is like Vegas. It will never leave this room. I promise you that. And if Domestic comes up dead, I'll cover it up for you."

Barbee smiled. "Foreign, girl, you hit the jackpot with this one. You can never have too many allies. Maurice," she smiled. "I fuck with you the long way. We are blood for life."

"I hope so," he smiled. "Well, since you feel that way, I was hoping that you and Corey would stay here instead of a hotel. Family of Foreign is a family of mine. And from the looks of things, we're about to be bonded for life."

"I'll talk to Corey. I'm sure I can convince him to stay. He doesn't like to be a burden at anyone's house."

"No burden at all. The both of you are welcome to stay."

"Thanks! You can tell him I said it's okay."

"Tell me what's okay?" Corey stepped into the living room, holding his glass of Jack Daniels.

"That we should stay here and not the hotel. Maurice isn't taking no for an answer."

"That's fine. I'm tipsy and don't feel like driving." Corey looked at Maurice with sleepy eyes. "Thanks, bro. You just saved me a ticket and a headache."

"It's all good. We're family now."

"Already," Corey replied.

Domestic...

The A/C blew cold in the Cadillac truck I rented to keep a low profile, but my ass was sweating bullets. Anger pumped through my veins as I watched Tracy having a conversation with Detective Marshall's punk ass. This nigga just keeps popping up at my shit with no problem. He got some shit up his sleeve, and I know that for a fact. I was about to find out too.

Once the punk-ass detective left, I pulled up in front of the entrance and left the truck running. It was a slow day, and it was time to shut it down early.

Tracy smiled when I walked in. "Hey, Bossman. What are you doing here?"

"It's been slow so you can shut it down."

"Cool because my ass is tired. I'm ready to go home, shower, and get in my bed."

"I'll give you a ride so you don't have to wait."

"Okay."

I headed to my office and closed the door. It was my last time in here for a while, and I wasn't leaving my stash behind. Demetri would have enough money for day-to-day operations. Unlocking the safe, I grabbed a duffle bag and filled it with bills.

Tracy was standing by the door with her hands on her hips when I stepped out of my office. "Where are you going with a bag and a new truck?"

"I'm about to take a vacation for about a week, and I need you to be in charge until I get back."

"Where you going?" she quizzed.

"If I tell you, then I'll have to kill you." I laughed and smacked her on the ass. "You gon' give me a sample before I go?"

"As long as you know the terms. This shit is not for free, Domestic."

"Don't I always handle that?"

"You do." Tracy activated the alarm and pushed the door open.

It was only right that I was a gentleman that night, so I opened the passenger door for her. "I like this truck. It's presidential and fits you well."

"I agree." I smirked, closed the door, and went to the driver's side, climbing in.

"So, where are we going?"

"Someplace quiet," I replied while pulling off.

"We could've handled business in the office." Tracy put on her seat belt.

"Nah, I don't need Foreign popping up over here. We have enough shit going on. I don't need that extra drama."

"Trouble in paradise, huh?"

"You can say that. It's all good. I'm going to fix it."

"You better," Tracy nodded. "She's a good woman, and I've never seen you this happy. That woman is doing something right."

"I can admit to that."

"Happy wife, happy life."

Nodding, I continued to drive. Tracy lived twenty minutes from the job—close to a park, so that's where we ended up. The sun was nowhere in sight. Darkness took over the skies, and dim lights were just what I needed to be discreet. Pulling into a parking spot at the far end of the lot, I put the truck in *park* and took a deep breath.

"This will be our last encounter. After tonight, I'm turning over a new leaf. I have to change my life."

"I've never heard this before. You must be serious. The Domestic I know doesn't talk like this." Tracy looked at me, and we locked eyes.

"How well do we really know people?"

"That's true. We only know what people want us to know."

"Now we're on the same page," I nodded. "I've been rocking with this ungrateful bitch from day one. I was there when she needed me. No questions asked. It's crazy how a muthafucka could sit around and act like shit all gravy. I hate that fake and phony shit."

"Me too! Trust me, I know exactly how you feel," Tracy smacked her lips.

"Let me ask you a question."

"Okay."

"Why was Detective Marshall at the wash? What were y'all talking about?"

Tracy's eyes widened in surprise. All I could see was the white. It was obvious it wasn't a question she was expecting. "When?"

"Today."

"Oh. Um. He didn't want anything. Just following up with the same ole questions about the shooting." Tracy lied straight through her teeth.

Frustrated, I opened and closed my fist like I was holding a stress ball. "Why would he ask you follow-up questions when I've already spoken to him? That case isn't open anymore."

Tracy stammered over her words, trying to explain, but I wasn't trying to hear any of that shit. Picking up my phone from the cupholder, I connected it with Bluetooth and pressed play. The sound of her voice was pissing me off. This bitch betrayed me in the worst way, and I was sick of her shit.

"It was you all this time. You've been working with this nigga since I killed Keith about my money."

"You, you killed him," Tracy stuttered.

"Tracy, stop playing with me. You knew that all along."

"I didn't know that—I swear," she pleaded with tears in her eyes.

"Yeah, you did. After all of the shit I've done for you, you'll betray me like this."

"I'm sorry, Domestic, but he threatened to take my kids if I didn't tell him what I knew. I didn't have a choice."

"That's fine because now I have no choice." I was fed up with Tracy's shit. Producing the chrome gun, I aimed it in her direction. "You must think I'm a slow ass nigga like your baby daddy. That nigga didn't threaten you. If he did, you wouldn't be so comfortable in his presence."

"Domestic, please don't do this. Think about my kids." Tracy's bottom lip quivered as she begged for her life.

"You should've thought about your kids." I placed the silencer on the tip. "Now, I'm thinking about my kids. I can't go to prison and be away from them."

"Domestic, please," she begged.

"You were planning on snitching on me and going into witness protection. Tracy, Tracy!" I shook my head. "I thought we were better than that."

Tracy reached for the handle and tried to get out of the truck, but a single bullet to her forehead stopped all of that. *Pew!* Blood spewed from the hole in her head, as her body slumped against the window. Leaning over to the passenger seat, I opened the door and pushed her body out. Tracy's corpse hit the ground with a loud thump. "Now, I gotta go and clean up this mess," I huffed and closed the door.

Chapter 21

Detective Marshall

The Next Day

"Hey, it's Detective Marshall. Can you confirm witness protection transportation for Tracy Miller?"

"Yes. I was just about to call you. She is all set to leave tomorrow morning. Bring her to the safe house on the west side."

"Thank you."

"You're welcome. Is there anything else that I can help you with?" the secretary asked.

"No. That's all. Thank you."

"You're welcome."

Tracy was going to be happy with the good news that I had for her. Living in fear of Domestic was about to be a thing of the past. The quicker I could solve this case, the better. I placed multiple calls to Tracy, but she didn't answer. Once she heard my message, I knew she would call back. In the meantime, I had an arrest to make.

As I walked up the driveway, I was greeted by the infamous Mustang. "Bingo!" I grinned and knocked on the door. The wait wasn't long before it was opened by a young male.

"How can I help you?"

"I'm Detective Marshall, Emilia's partner. May I come in?"

"Sure."

A man shouted. "Carlos, who's at the door."

"Emilia's partner from work." Carlos closed the door.

Mr. Flores walked into the living room. Emilia's death had to be taking on a toll on him. His thick, black hair was disheveled, and the bags underneath his eyes suggested he hadn't slept in days.

"Hello, Mr. Flores. I am so sorry for your loss. Emilia was like my work sister, and we're going to find out who did this to her."

"Thank you." Mr. Flores sat down in the recliner.

"I'm sorry that I had to show up under these circumstances, but I believe that Emilia's death is related to Aaron Young's homicide."

"What do you mean?" Mr. Flores asked.

"I can't go into detail about it all since this is an ongoing investigation. The quicker I solve this case, I'll have the answers you need."

"Is that why you came here?" Carlos asked.

"That's one of the reasons."

"What's the other reason?"

"I'm glad you asked. I need you to come down to the station and answer a few questions about your whereabouts on the day Aaron Young was killed in a car crash."

"What does that have to do with me? I didn't know him. So there is no need for me to go down to the station." Carlos was cocky, and I could smell his guilt from where I was standing.

"You know it actually has a lot to do with you."

"That's where you're wrong at. I was nowhere near his accident. You have the wrong guy."

"Carlos, what is he talking about?" Mr. Flores asked with hesitation in his voice.

"I don't know," Carlos replied.

"Well, according to the video footage at the station, you were in the area. Now, here's what's going to happen. You are going to come down to the station and tell us everything that happened. Including the relationship that you have with Demerius Payne."

Carlos' shift in his body language told me I was close.

"I don't know what you're talking about."

"You're about to find out." I grabbed my phone and placed a call. "You may come inside and apprehend the suspect."

A group of officers stormed into the house and arrested Carlos. While he was being cuffed, he was adamant that we had the wrong guy. "You're arresting me for no reason. I had nothing to do with any of this shit."

Mr. Flores stood up. "Carlos, just go and answer the questions. I'll come down to pick you up."

"That won't be necessary, Mr. Flores. He's going to be there for a while." I turned to my colleague. "Take him in. I have another arrest to make."

It was on to the next one.

Casually, I strolled through the hallway with my hands inside my pockets. Things were coming full circle, and Tracy still hadn't returned my call. She had until the end of the day before I popped up at her place of residence. Stopping in front of the hotel room door, I knocked twice. There was no answer, so I knocked again, but harder that time.

"Who is it?"

"Detective Marshall." The door became ajar, and a woman peeked out. "How can I help you?"

"Mrs. Young?"

"Yes," she replied.

"You are under arrest."

Foreign...

"What time should I expect to see you?"

"I'm wrapping things up at the office right now. Then I'm on the way."

"Okay. We'll be here."

Packing up my clothes felt like a bitter-sweet moment. It was time for me to embark on a new journey, but it felt like I was leaving Aaron behind, although he was gone. The house was filled with so many memories. It was funny how I could see the good and bad times play out in every room as if it were a movie.

"I'm hungry as hell," Barbee whined.

"As you saw already, there is nothing here," I laughed. "There are some food places close by that y'all can go to."

Blacque Barbee stood up. "Let's go. I'm starving."

"Y'all can go. I'm going to stay here and finish up. I want to be finished by the time Maurice gets here."

"Are you sure?"

"Yeah," I smiled. "Just bring me something back. I'm hungry too."

"Okay. I'll call you when I figure out what we're going to eat."

"Sounds like a plan."

Blacque Barbee left the room, and I continued to pack. Alexis and Calvin would come over at a later date and go through Aaron's remaining things. That would give them both the opportunity to keep something that belonged to him. It was only right in my eyes. They loved him just as much as I did.

My phone dinged with a text notification from Barbee. I replied with my order. The thought of food made my stomach growl. Rubbing my stomach, I spoke to my baby. "I know you're hungry. Mommy is very sorry for taking so long to eat."

Just then I heard the door close. I knew it was Maurice, since Barbee was still at the restaurant. Poking my head out of the room door, I shouted downstairs. "Babe, I'm upstairs in the bedroom. Come on up so you can grab my suitcase."

All of my clothes were packed in multiple suitcases and boxes. The hard part was just about over. I could hear Maurice walk into the room. "I am so tired and hungry. I just want to sleep."

When I turned to face Maurice, I was stunned by the face of Domestic instead. My jaw hit the floor hard. "Domestic, what are you doing here?"

"I'm here for you. What do you think?" he smirked.

"I told you that it's over between us."

"That's not an option, Foreign. The two of us belong together forever. What part of that didn't you understand?"

"If you don't leave, I'm going to call the police."

Domestic laughed, but it was evil. "By the time they get here, you'll be dead and I'll be in the wind."

My eyes bounced around the room for my purse. And that was when it hit me. The gun was downstairs inside my purse. That was so dumb on my behalf. I kicked myself for not having it close to me. The phone was closer, so I tried to grab it. Domestic lunged towards me, snatched the phone from my hand, and threw it. "Oh, you trying to call the police on me."

The palm of his hand landed on my right cheek. *Whap!* It was so powerful that I lost my footing and landed on the bed. Domestic leaped on top of me, ignoring my stomach.

"You're going to hurt the baby," I pleaded with fresh tears in my eyes.

Domestic wrapped his hands around my neck. "You think I give a fuck. I heard that wasn't my baby anyway."

"This is your baby and you know that."

"Nah. I don't know shit."

"Domestic, please stop!" It was insane that I had to plead for my life and the one of my unborn child.

"Bitch, you gon' die today."

Domestic's hands grew tighter and tighter around my neck. I tried to fight him off by clawing at his hands. That didn't work. My breathing was getting shallow. I could see tiny red dots flashing before my eyes. Without a doubt, he was trying to kill me. The life that I knew was slipping away at the hands of a man who claimed to love me beyond the earth. It was funny how life worked. All of my defense prep was doing no good at the moment. It was over. I accepted my fate and stopped fighting.

Suddenly, I could breathe again. When I opened my eyes Domestic and Maurice was in a blow-for-blow fight. They were going toe to toe. Maurice hit Domestic in the jaw with a mean left hook, and it sounded like bones cracking. Blood leaked from his mouth. Domestic took a step back and pulled out his gun. I tried to scream, but nothing came out. Maurice raised his foot and kicked the gun out of Domestic's hand. I don't know what type of karate move it was, but that shit caught him off guard. Me too.

The two men locked up with each other and ended up in the corner of my bedroom. Glass shattered as my picture frame hit the floor. I didn't know what to do, so I just stood there. Domestic managed to get loose. He scrambled for the gun, and Maurice gave chase. Everything was happening so fast, and my feet were stuck to the carpet like I was standing in cement. Domestic pointed the gun in my direction, and all I heard was: *Boom!* My eardrums were ringing, and everything in front of me went black. The room was silent.

Chapter 22

Detective Marshall

In my hand, I carried an active arrest warrant. To have it issued wasn't easy, but I got it done. It was time to take out the trash once and for all. I banged on the door three times before I waved my hand in the air. One of my men rammed a battering ram through the front door, knocking it off the hinges.

The house was quiet when I walked in with backup right behind me. As I made my way towards the stairs, Domestic was running down.

"What the fuck is going on in here?"

"Demerius Payne, you are under arrest for the murder of Foreign Young."

"What? I don't know what you're talking about. I'm not Domestic," he shouted.

"And I'm not a detective," I chuckled. "Get him out of here."

Domestic was cuffed, and his rights were read. Back at the station, he was placed in the interrogation room. His head was down on the table when I walked in, but he looked upright as I came in.

"Demerius Payne," I grinned. "You finally killed your pregnant girlfriend. You also killed my partner Emilia, Keith, and Tracy. Your ass will never see the light of day again."

"I ain't do shit."

"That's not what my evidence shows."

"Well, your evidence is wrong," he smiled. "So, I suggest you go back to the drawing board. You're going to be very surprised when you find out who I am."

"I know exactly who you are. A man who is about to go on death row for the death of my partner."

Domestic chuckled and nodded. "If you say so."

"What did you do with Foreign's body?"

"I don't know who that is. I don't know any of those people you are speaking of. As far as I'm concerned, this interview is over because I'm not saying shit until my attorney arrives."

Just like that, the interview was over.

Veronica...

"My son was arrested and I would like to see him now."

"What's his last name?"

"Payne."

"Oh yeah, I see it. He's in the interrogation room."

"Well, take me to him."

"I can't do that."

"You can and you will," I barked.

"Let me handle this." Hugo stepped up to the counter. "My name is Hugo Valentino. You have my son back there and I'm also his legal attorney, so take me to my client."

The desk officer fixed her crooked glasses and stood up quickly. "Yes sir, right this way."

My Louboutin heels clicked against the tile, as we made the short trip down the hall. The room was cold as ice when we stepped inside.

"How are you, son?" I asked.

"I'm fine. Just ready to get out of here," he replied.

The first thing I spotted was the big ass gash on his head. "What happened to your head? Did the cops do that to you?"

"Nah."

"Where is this detective?"

"I'm right here. My name is Detective Marshall. And you are?"

"Veronica Valentino and this is my husband, and my son's attorney—Hugo Valentino. We're here to take him home."

"I'm sorry, but he will not be leaving here. Not now, not ever. He's looking at the death penalty."

"That's where you're wrong at. He's not looking at anything. I suggest you go back to the drawing board and pick up the correct person."

"We have the correct person."

"Let me ask you this, detective. Have you run his fingerprints? Checked his records? If you would've done that, you'll know that this is my son Demetri Payne."

"What?" Detective Marshall scratched his head. "What are you talking about?"

"Demetri is Demerius' twin. You have the wrong person in custody."

"That's impossible." He was clearly in disbelief.

"Let me make this easy for you." I opened the folder and produced two legal documents. Birth certificates. "Here you go. Now, go and verify that information so I can take my son home. And you can go and find Domestic."

Detective Marshall took the documents and left the room.

"What's going on?" I sat down. "What has that brother of yours gotten you into?"

"A bunch of shit. They say he killed another detective, that Foreign girl, and two other people. He came to me and said he needed to go away for a while and asked if I could run the washes for him until things calmed down."

"See, I told you he couldn't be trusted. But no, you feel so obligated to step up and help him. Now, look at what he's dragged you into. He's out there on the run, while you're inside trying to clear your name."

"Your mother is right," Hugo added. "It's time that you stopped covering for him. I get it. You love your brother, but how much does he love you? These are some pretty serious charges you're in here for."

Demetri sighed.

"You know what you have to do."

He was silent. I knew he didn't want to snitch on his twin, but he had no other choice if I had to help.

"Domestic doesn't care that you're locked up and I'll prove that to you." Digging in my purse, I pulled out my phone and called his number. No answer. I called two more times before sending a text message. "I've called him multiple times and he's not answering. He doesn't give a fuck about you. Domestic wants you to take these charges for him."

"Yeah. I see that now."

"That girl came to visit me. She told me Domestic set her house on fire. She wanted my help, but I turned her away in hopes she would have him locked up."

"Well, she's dead now."

"I see."

One hour had passed before Detective Marshall returned to the cold room. There was a look of defeat in his eyes. "Demetri, where is Domestic?"

Demetri shrugged. "I don't know."

"Demetri, what did we just talk about?" It disgusted me that he was sitting there and not saying a damn word. "Tell this man what he needs to know so we can go."

"He can't leave. Although it's been proven he has a twin, we don't know if this is Demerius or not. We need a DNA swab to clear this up."

"Listen, I'm beyond frustrated with this entire mess, so do whatever you need to do to get my son out of here. Demetri, where is your brother?"

Demetri sat there looking stupid before finally opening his mouth. "Utah."

"How is he traveling?" Detective Marshall placed both hands on the table and leaned forward. "And don't lie. You're making this worst on yourself, and I will charge you as an accomplice. So, I advise you to start talking."

"I don't know. He didn't say."

"When was the last time you saw him?"

"A few days ago. He said he was leaving for a while."

"I'll be right back."

Detective Marshall…

"Captain, we have a problem," I shouted while barging into his office unannounced.

"It better be—since you've come in without as much of a knock. What's the problem?"

"Demerius Payne." That was all I could say.

"He's in custody. What's the problem?"

"The problem is—Demerius has a twin, Demetri. I believe that's who we have in custody. He claims that his brother left the state and we can't hold him forever. What should we do?"

"If he's involved or knows the brother's whereabouts, he will eventually reach out to him. We just have to make sure that we're in place so that we can follow them."

"Can you arrange that?"

"I will. Give him an ankle monitor. We need to be able to track his movements."

"Okay."

"He will be required to wear that until we can get a hold of his brother. You have my approval."

"Thanks, Chief."

"You got it."

Chapter 23

Foreign

Kansas City, Mo.

Beep! Beep! Beep!

That was the constant sound that I heard throughout the hospital room. Face up and looking at the ceiling was what I did regularly. The day I was shot was the day my old life was put to rest. With the help of Maurice and his job, they moved me to another state after the incident to keep me safe. Due to complications, I gave birth to my baby early. Daily I prayed because things could've played out differently, and I could be dead.

"Are you ready to go down to the nursery?" Maurice stood on the side of the bed.

"Yes."

Slowly, I scooted to the edge of the bed. Maurice helped me on my feet. "How are you feeling?"

"Better than yesterday." That C-section was no joke. I couldn't laugh or anything. Hell, I could barely breathe.

"Well, you won't be here much longer. You'll be going home soon, and I'll be going out of town on business."

"Who's going to help me?"

"That's a part of the surprise. I reached out to your cousin Blacque Barbee, and she agreed to come here and help you. I hope that will make up for my absence."

"It really would make up for your absence. Thank you."

"Anything for you."

The NICU was quiet. To my surprise, I was the only parent in the room. I made my way over to my baby boy. Being a mother was everything to me. It was something I always wanted.

"Hey, Messiah. It's mommy."

I chose the name Messiah because it means, *anointed one*. My baby was an example of what a miracle was. Messiah Aaron Young was his full name. The results of the paternity test determined that Aaron was the father of my baby. That threw me for a loop because I didn't think that Aaron was a possibility. Somewhere down the line, I miscounted. It hurt because Aaron will never meet his son. What was worst is that I'd spent all that time with Domestic, thinking he was the father. A lot of drama could've been avoided as well. The last day that I saw Domestic, he called it out and I didn't have a clue.

All of my clothes were packed in multiple suitcases and boxes. The hard part was just about over. I could hear Maurice walk into the room. "I am so tired and hungry. I just want to sleep."

When I turned to face Maurice, I was stunned by the face of Domestic instead. My jaw hit the floor hard. "Domestic, what are you doing here?"

"I'm here for you. What do you think?" he smirked.

"I told you that it's over between us."

"That's not an option, Foreign. The two of us belong together forever. What part of that didn't you understand?"

"If you don't leave I'm going to call the police."

Domestic laughed, but it was evil. "By the time they get here, you'll be dead and I'll be in the wind."

My eyes bounced around the room for my purse. And that was when it hit me. The gun was downstairs inside my purse. That was so dumb on my behalf. I kicked myself for not having it close to me. The phone was closer, so I tried to grab it. Domestic lunged towards me, snatched the phone from my hand, and threw it. "Oh, you trying to call the police on me."

The palm of his hand landed on my right cheek. Whap! It was so powerful that I lost my footing and landed on the bed. Domestic leaped on top of me, ignoring my stomach.

"You're going to hurt the baby," I pleaded with fresh tears in my eyes.

Domestic wrapped his hands around my neck. "You think I give a fuck. I heard that wasn't my baby anyway."

"This is your baby and you know that."

"Nah. I don't know shit."

"Domestic, please stop!" It was insane that I had to plead for my life and the one of my unborn child.

"Bitch, you gon' die today."

Domestic's hands grew tighter and tighter around my neck. I tried to fight him off by clawing at his hands. That didn't work. My breathing was getting shallow. I could see tiny red dots flashing before my eyes. Without a doubt, he was trying to kill me. The life that I knew was slipping away at the hands of a man who claimed to love me beyond the earth. It was funny how life worked. All of my defense prep was doing no good at the moment. It was over. I accepted my fate and stopped fighting.

Suddenly, I could breathe again. When I opened my eyes Domestic and Maurice were in a blow-for-blow fight. They were going toe to toe. Maurice hit Domestic in the jaw with a mean left hook, and it sounded like bones cracking. Blood leaked from his mouth. Domestic took a step back and pulled out his gun. I tried to scream, but nothing came out. Maurice raised his foot and kicked the gun out of Domestic's hand. I don't know what type of karate move it was, but that shit caught him off guard. Me too.

The two men locked up with one another and ended up in the corner of my bedroom. Glass shattered as my picture frame hit the floor. I didn't know what to do, so I just stood there. Domestic managed to get loose. He scrambled for the gun and Maurice gave chase. Everything was happening so fast and my feet were stuck to the carpet like I was standing in cement. Domestic pointed the gun in my direction, and all I heard was: Boom! My eardrums were ringing, and everything in front of me went black. The room was silent.

When I finally gained consciousness, Domestic was on the floor—bleeding—and Maurice was carrying me out of the house. I was discombobulated and confused, but I could hear Maurice on the phone.

"Yes. I would like to report gunshots in the area."

The rest was history!

Once I was released from the hospital, Maurice took me back to his four-bedroom home. Everything was updated with stainless steel appliances and marble tile. The room I loved the most was the one he gave me for the nursery. Messiah was going to be in the hospital for at least a few more weeks, so that gave me a little bit of time to prepare. While I was in the hospital, Maurice bought me a wooden rocking chair. It was the cutest thing. Sitting down, I rocked back and forth with a smile on my face. I couldn't wait to bring my baby home.

Maurice walked into the room. "This has got to be your favorite room in the house."

"It is. I love it."

"I'm glad to hear that. Messiah doesn't know this yet, but he is going to love it too."

"Of course he will."

"Do you need anything? I'm about to take a shower."

"No. I'm fine."

"Okay."

My body was in a little pain, but I needed to walk around. I did not want to be this needy person. My ass was too independent for that shit. Careful not to fall, I made my way through the first level of the house and onto the porch. It was nice and sunny out, but the breeze was awesome. It was refreshing compared to the bone-chilling hospital.

Inhaling the fresh air, I closed my eyes and rocked on the swing that was on the porch. This was my second favorite place at the house. The sound of a car passing quickly interrupted my thoughts. It was a silver mid-sized car. Once it was gone, I closed my eyes. Five minutes hadn't passed, and the same car was driving by again. This time it rode past slowly. I couldn't see inside because the tinted windows were extremely dark.

Panic stroked my body, and I rose from the swing. The car pulled into the driveway of a vacant house and parked. The brake lights shut off, but no one emerged from the car. The pain was no longer on my mind as I rushed inside the house and locked the door.

Maurice was coming out of the bathroom when I rushed down the hallway, sweating ad breathing hard. He saw the fear-stricken look on my face and rushed to my aid. "Baby, what's wrong?"

"I just—I just—"

"Slow down and breathe," he instructed tenderly. I did as I was told. "Now, tell me what's wrong?"

"A car keeps riding past the house. What if it's Domestic?"

"Calm down, baby, Domestic is in custody. He can't do anything to you. Nor is he coming here."

I nodded.

Maurice embraced me tightly. "I'm not going to let anyone hurt you or our son. I promise." He then kissed me on top of my head. "I love the both of you."

"I love you too."

Later on that night, Maurice held me all night long. Not once did he let me go. He was a different man. Maurice was compassionate and loving. Someone worth settling down with forever. My needs were always tended to without me having to open my mouth and ask. That was something I wanted. It was something I deserved.

The following morning, I watched Maurice pack a bag for his business trip. It saddened me that he had to leave so soon. Maurice was my protector. I needed him at all times. I felt safe when I was with him. "Why do you have to leave so soon?"

"If it was up to me, you know I would stay. But they need me right now. It will only be for three days."

"That's a long time without my knight in shining armor." My bottom lip was poked out. "I need you."

Maurice laughed. "I know, baby. I'll be back before you know it. Besides, I've enlisted a powerful woman to look after you while I'm away. You're in good hands. I've seen Barbee's track record. You're in good hands."

My cousin was a beast. All I could do was laugh. "You're right about that."

"See, you have nothing to worry about."

"I know. I'm going to miss you."

"Not more than I'm going to miss you." Maurice buckled up his pants.

That man was so fine. I wanted to have sex: stitches and all. "I'm horny. Can I at least get a sample before you go?"

"Baby, that is not safe for you right now. And I would hate to hurt my baby. You know how I get down in the bedroom." He winked seductively.

"You can go slow," I whined.

"When I get back. I promise. You need a few more days at the least."

"Ugh!" I groaned and laid down on the bed. "Why are you doing this to me?"

"Aren't you bleeding?"

"Barely."

"No, thanks. I don't like ketchup on my hot dog," he laughed.

"If you can walk through mud, you can fuck through blood." My ass was horny as hell.

"No. I don't like mud or blood."

"Fine," I replied softly.

Maurice looked at his Rolex, then at me. "Baby, I have to go. My jet leaves in forty-five minutes."

"Okay."

"I love you. I'll be back soon, and we can work on baby number two." He smiled and kissed me passionately. That kiss was everything that I desired through sex as he stroked my pussy into multiple orgasms. Unfortunately, that wasn't happening today.

"I love you too. Be safe."

"Always." Maurice flashed that beautiful smile. "Barbee's flight lands in a few hours. Stay calm until then."

"I will." And just like that—Maurice was gone.

Chapter 24

Blacque Barbee

"Ouuu! Ahhh!" I screamed for the third time. Corey had me bent like a pretzel in the room for the last two hours. "You just fucked me like you'll never see me again."

"Don't I always," he grinned.

"You surely the fuck do," I grinned, giving my baby all of his props.

"Get on top!" Corey released my legs and laid on his back.

"I have to get dressed."

"You can't leave me like this. It's still hard." He held his dick in his hand.

Glancing at the time, I realized I had a few more minutes to burn before I left. Straddling his lap, I eased down onto his thickness. The feeling was euphoric. Straight lip-biting action. Slowly, I rocked back and forth.

Corey pinched my nipples while grunting. "Damn, bae!"

My man was enjoying it, but not enough for me. Grabbing the headboard, I planted my feet into the mattress and bounced up and down.

"Ouuu! Shit!" I moaned.

Sweat protruded from my face and body. A bitch was putting in that work. I had to make sure I left my man satisfied. Corey cheating was the least of my worries. He would be a damn fool to risk losing a bitch like me. Boss bitches like me were hard to come by. I was a rare breed, and there was only one *Blacque Barbee*! And that was a fact.

Corey had the sexiest fuck face that I'd ever seen. His grunts were even sexy. My pussy made squishy sounds with each thrust. These eggs were getting scrambled the right way. If I was to get pregnant, I wouldn't be mad. We didn't use condoms, and I wasn't on birth control. I would have all of Mandingo's babies.

My legs were starting to hurt. A bitch still had Megan Thee Stallion knees, but Corey had me folded up for too long. As soon as I stopped bouncing and attempted to put my knees on the bed, Corey stopped me.

"Bae, what you doing? Keep going."

"My legs hurt."

"I was just about to nut."

Once again I was back on my feet, bouncing and putting my legs to work. Corey matched my energy and thrusts. The intense pleasure of his thumb on my clit made me weak. And a minute or so later, he forced a powerful orgasm from my pussy. It was over from there. If he thought I was staying on my feet, he was crazy.

Then again, I was the crazy one. Corey flipped me onto my back and pinned my thighs to my chest. Aggressively, he drilled me with his eyes closed until he caught his nut.

My eyes were on the clock. I had to be at the airport in less than two hours. Therefore, I needed to be ready in the next thirty minutes. The last thing I needed was for the airport to be super crowded and had to rush. My ass was too cute for that.

After that mind-blowing, crying-to-God sex, I needed a thorough shower. The water was hot just the way I loved it. Corey still knew how to satisfy a girl. There wasn't a dull moment in our sex life. I loved, cherished, and appreciated days and nights like this.

The hot water hit my skin and gave me an instant massage. I just wanted to melt. Using my loofa, I poured some of my favorite body wash—coconut coffee—and scrubbed my body.

As much as I wanted to stay in, I had to make it snappy so I could get to the airport in time. Stepping from the shower, I slipped into my bathrobe. Once I covered my body in the coconut coffee lotion, I slipped into an Adidas tracksuit. I had to be comfortable for my flight.

Corey was sitting downstairs when I walked into the room. "Are you ready?"

"Yes, I am."

"Let's ride." Corey grabbed my Louis Vuitton travel bag and headed towards the door.

It took us twenty minutes to get to the airport. Corey pulled up to arrivals, and parallel-parked. Being the gentleman that he was, he opened the door for me.

"Be safe and make sure you call me when you land."

"I will. Take care of my babies and make sure you face-time me when they go to bed."

"I will." Corey handed me my bag. "I love you."

"I love you more."

The check-in was quick and easy, so was the security check. Once I made it to my area, I shot Foreign a quick text letting her know that I would see her in a couple of hours.

Foreign…

After receiving the text from Barbee, I felt better knowing that she was on the way. In the meantime, I sat in the living room and watched movies on *Lifetime*. From time to time, I would doze off and pick up where I left off. The doorbell chimed. It caught me off guard because I knew Barbee wasn't in town just yet. Unless she was trying to surprise me.

Strolling through the living room, I approached the door and stood on tiptoes. It was an Amazon delivery guy holding a package. I unlocked the door and opened it. That was the moment I wished that I hadn't. All of the feelings in my body went numb.

"Are you happy to see me?" Domestic grinned and barged his way into the house.

I was speechless.

Domestic closed the door and secured the locks. Now, facing me, he touched my skin with his cold hands. "You know it's funny. All of this time I thought you were dead and here you are alive and well."

"You. You were in jail. Wha—What are you doing here?" I stumbled over my words.

"That wasn't me, love. You had my twin brother Demetri arrested for your murder. Do you know that faking your death is a felony? A criminal charge punishable by law."

"Not when you fear for your life," I replied. "What are you doing here?"

"Isn't that obvious? I came to collect my wife and child. Did you honestly think I would let you get away from me that easily?"

"Domestic, I don't belong to you." I took a step back.

Domestic moved closer to me and grabbed me by the back of my neck. "You do belong to me. I made that clear when you gave me some pussy in my office."

His grip on my neck was tight. "Domestic, please don't do this. Don't you think you've hurt me enough?"

"No!" He barked. "But I will if you don't do what I tell you to do." Domestic looked around. "So, you done relocated with the nigga you was fucking while carrying my child?"

I didn't respond.

"Where is he anyway?"

"Um. He went to the store. So, I think you should leave before he comes back. He's a Federal Agent, and I know you don't want to go to prison."

Domestic laughed. "He's not coming back."

"He is," I pleaded.

"He's on the plane right now. I followed him to the airport," Domestic sucked his teeth. "It looks like it's just me and you, baby. I've planned this out carefully. See, I've been watching the two of you for a few days now."

My whole world tumbled down at once. The feeling of me being watched was unnerving. I knew I wasn't crazy or being paranoid. It was Domestic all this time.

"Where is my baby?"

"I—I lost the baby." There was no way I would allow him to see my child. It wasn't happening. I would die first before I did that.

Domestic finally moved his hand. "Stop lying to me and show me my child," he shouted.

"You shot me. What did you think was going to happen?" I snapped.

"Nah. You're lying. He's in here."

"I'll show you." Domestic walked behind me, as I showed him every room in the house. "This was supposed to be his room."

Domestic grabbed me by the waist and pulled me close to him. His breath reeked of alcohol. "I guess we have to make another one."

"No! I'm not."

Domestic pulled out a gun and pressed it against my forehead. "If I said we making a baby, then that's what we're doing."

"Okay. Okay. Just put the gun away, please."

"Take me to y'all bedroom."

My body trembled in fear. Domestic was unpredictable, and I had no idea what his end game was going to be. I just prayed that it didn't end up with me taking my last breath.

Domestic sat down on the bed. "Take off your clothes."

That was the moment I started to cry. "Don't make me do this. I just had a C-section."

"Bitch, don't question me! Just do what the fuck I said."

Trembling, I removed all of my clothes and dropped them on the floor. There I stood naked, in front of a man that I feared. And the last thing I wanted to do was give him my body.

"Come here," he said softly.

My steps were slow.

Domestic traced my cesarean cut. "We have to replace what we lost. Our family." He looked up at me. "Don't you want a family with me? That's what you told me or was that a lie?"

Tears streamed down my face. "No. It wasn't a lie. I wanted that, but then you changed on me. You abused me. You cheated on me. What was I supposed to do? You threatened to kill me."

Domestic kissed my stomach. "I'll die without you. Why would I kill you? That's crazy."

Domestic put his hands between my legs. At one point in time, it excited me. I craved his touch. Now, it made me cringe. The same hands that made me wet had me wanting to throw up. His fingers stroked my clit before making their way inside my tunnel. I just wanted him to stop. Sadly, I was at his mercy.

"You want me and I can tell."

That was the furthest thing from the truth. I wanted him to leave me alone.

"Lay on the bed."

Motionless, I stood in place.

"I'm not going to hurt you." Domestic rose with the gun clutched in his hand. "Don't make me repeat myself."

He didn't have to. I complied.

Domestic took off his clothes and stood between my legs. Clenching my eyes shut, I took a deep breath and prepared myself for what was about to happen. His head penetrated my opening. It was dry, so it hurt going inside. But I wasn't about to complain. That would only make matters worse.

My stomach was in excruciating pain. At times I held my breath. I was certain that I would pass out. Domestic held both of my wrists to the bed while thrusting slowly. He planted kisses on my face. It was hard to not think about it, but I did my best to visit any place besides in this room with a killer.

The minutes felt like hours, but eventually, it all came to an end. Domestic growled and grunted until he was done. Finally, I sighed with relief. The sex was over, but my misery had just begun.

"Clean yourself up and after we take a nap, I want you to pack a bag."

"Why? Where are we going?" I asked.

"Me and you are leaving the country. You know we can't raise a family here. It's too hot in the States. Besides, you and I need a fresh start."

"But our family is here."

"We don't need them. All we need is each other."

"Okay," I agreed.

In the bathroom, I stood in front of the mirror after I washed my lady parts. Just when I thought the horrific ordeal with Domestic was over, reality showed up and slapped me in the face. If I wanted to make it out of this alive, I needed to be smart and play my role.

Domestic was lying down when I walked back into the bedroom. "I'm ready for our nap." The minute he fell asleep, I was getting the fuck out of dodge.

Climbing onto the bed, I laid on my side. Domestic pulled out a pair of handcuffs from the side of the bed. "I'm sorry baby, but I have to cuff you."

"Why?"

"We can't have you running out on me. Now, can we?"

Domestic cuffed my wrists and held me in his arms. There was no way out.

Chapter 25

Foreign

When I woke up, I realized two hours had passed. Blacque Barbee would be arriving at any moment. Domestic wasn't in bed either. "Domestic," I called out. A few seconds later, he emerged.

"How was your nap?" he asked.

"It was good."

"See, I know exactly what you need. And that is why you need me in your life."

The man was delusional as fuck.

Domestic jumped when he heard the doorbell. "Who is that?"

"It's my cousin."

He looked over his shoulder. "Well, ignore the door. She'll go away eventually."

"No. She won't. If I don't answer the door, she'll know that something is wrong and call the police."

Domestic grabbed me by the arm and pulled me from the bed.

"Oww! My stomach," I cried.

"I'm going to uncuff you and if you scream or say anything to alert her, I will kill the both of you. Do you understand?"

"Yes."

Domestic uncuffed me, and we went downstairs. As expected, it was Blacque Barbee. He stood behind the door with his gun pointed at me. "Remember what I said," he mumbled.

Cracking the door open, I made sure I looked pathetic as hell.

"Girl, open this door. I had a long flight and I'm ready to unwind and raid y'all bar. Then we going to the hospital to see my baby later." Barbee tried to move closer, but I stopped her.

"Um. I'm not feeling well. Can you just stay at the hotel tonight and we'll catch up tomorrow?"

"Now, why would I do that? What's wrong with you?"

"I ate some oysters and I'm feeling sick."

"Okay. I'll stay at the hotel. After I get settled, I'll call and check on you."

"Thanks. I would appreciate that."

Barbee walked away, and I closed the door. As soon as I turned around, I was met with Domestic's fist. My body crumbled to the floor. He kneeled and grabbed a fistful of my hair. "Bitch, you lied to me. You telling me that you lost my child, but my child is in the hospital."

Blood dripped from my mouth. "He's in the NICU. I had him early. I'm sorry I didn't tell you."

"Not as sorry as you're about to be."

Domestic stood and kicked me in the stomach. It felt like he kicked every staple out of my cut. I screamed at the top of my lungs. Then he grabbed me by the hair and dragged me up every step.

"Just kill me," I begged. "I can't take this anymore."

Domestic slung me into the room, and I hit my head on the edge of the bed. My shit was banging, and I could see stars. When I looked down, the bottom of my shirt had blood on it. Death crossed my mind. I was scared that I was going to bleed to death.

Blacque Barbee...

I jumped into my rental car and circled the block. The phone rang multiple times before I got an answer. "Hello."

"Maurice, he found her," I shouted.

"What?"

"Yeah. He's in the house. When I got there, she told me to stay at the hotel because she was sick and we'll catch up tomorrow. Then she said she ate oysters. That's our code word when she's in trouble."

"Fuck!" he shouted. "I just landed in Maryland. Where are you now?"

"I'm in the neighborhood."

"Call the police. Also, there is a spare key underneath the flower pot. I left it just in case you needed it."

"Okay. I'm going inside. I'm not waiting on the police. Where do you keep your guns?"

"There's one in the kitchen on top of the refrigerator."

"Okay. Call the police for me."

"I will. Be careful."

"Always."

After we hung up, I circled back to the house. Quickly, I made my way back to the porch and retrieved the key from underneath the flower pot. Once I was inside, I went into the kitchen and grabbed the gun. Loud screaming and shouting could be heard from the lower level.

"Bitch, I'm going to kill you. You know how much I hate a liar and you do it anyway."

If Foreign was responding, I couldn't hear her.

Proceeding with caution, I crept slowly down the hallway. The closer I got, the louder his voice got. "I love you, Foreign, but you couldn't appreciate what a man like me had to offer."

Foreign was on the floor, crying and in the fetal position. Blood was all around her. Domestic raised his foot to kick her, but I made my presence known.

"I wouldn't do that if I was you." The Beretta was clutched in my hand, and my finger on the trigger.

Domestic turned around. "Who the fuck are you?"

"Your worst nightmare if you don't get the fuck out of here. Get away from her!"

Domestic backed up with his hands in the air. "You got it, lil' mama. Ion want no trouble."

Domestic lunged in my direction, and that was all I needed to pop his ass. I fired a shot, and the bullet slammed into his shoulder. This nigga had to be bionic because he kept coming for me. His body collided with mine, and we both crashed into the wall, making a hole. The gun slid across the floor.

At that moment, it was fight or flight. Domestic grabbed me around my neck and squeezed. I fought back and rained multiple blows to his face. This nigga was strong as fuck. He ate those punches. Raising my leg, I introduced my knee to his crotch. That slowed him down and brought him to his knees. Domestic held onto my jacket and took me down with him. Both of us hit the floor.

"You crazy bitch. I'm killing you and your cousin."

"I don't think so."

Domestic climbed on top of me and started choking me. His grip was getting tighter and tighter. Within arm's reach, I spotted a metal lantern. Struggling, I extended my arm so I could reach it. I failed. Something had to give. Sinking my teeth into his wrist, Domestic screamed and released me. That was my chance to grab the lantern. And I did. Using every ounce of strength in my body, I slammed the lantern against his head. Domestic rolled over in pain.

Scrambling across the floor on my hands and knees, I rushed towards the gun. When I looked up, Domestic was coming in my direction at top speed. Easily and with no hesitation, I let off two rounds. *Boc! Boc!* Domestic's body hit the floor.

Dropping the gun, I rushed over to Foreign. She was bleeding profusely and barely conscious. I rubbed her head. "Foreign, you're going to be okay. I can hear the ambulance. Hold on for me. The baby needs you. You have to fight, okay!"

The police and the paramedics walked into the room. We were safe, and it was all over. Foreign and Domestic were both taken to the local hospital. I had a slight headache, but it wasn't anything a little alcohol couldn't cure.

THAT'S NOT IT FOREIGN WILL RETURN WITH BLACQUE BARBEE IN THE SPINOFF: A FETTI GIRL WEDDING

COMING IN NOVEMBER 2021

If you haven't met Blacque Barbee, here's your chance. Go to Amazon to read: *The Fetti Girls*. Books 1 through 3 are available now!!

HERE'S A SAMPLE…

THE FETTI GIRLS: MONEY IS THE MOTIVE

Chapter 1

It was a Friday, and the club was jumping. There were so many hustlers in the spot, I didn't know which one I was walking out with that night. Judging by the way they were gawking at a female, it wouldn't be long before I made up my mind.

I strutted through the crowd wearing a purple satin shirt, gold skinny jeans, and a pair of Jimmy Choo pumps. My hair was in a long, jet-black flat wrap with a Chinese bang. *"Damn right, Blacque Barbee coming through!"* My makeup was on fleek, and so was my body. I was 5'6", weighing a buck sixty, thick in all right places, and I was bowlegged. I knew I was the shit, and so did the hating-ass hos who were posted up, mean-mugging. They were the least of my worries because each and every last one of them knew how my click and I got down. No bitch in her right mind would get out of pocket at any given moment.

When I approached the bar, there was an empty stool, so I took a seat. The bartender looked my way and walked over quickly to take my order. She was a plain-looking chick who could use a makeover, even though she had a cute face. She smiled.

"What can I get you?"

"Let me get a Long Island."

She fixed my drink in sixty seconds flat and handed it to me. "That will be twelve dollars."

Just as I was about to give her a twenty-dollar bill, a voice behind me said, "I got this, Stacey."

I turned around to see who it was, and to my surprise it was a familiar face. I didn't know his name or anything like that, but I saw him around my way a few times. From the look on my face, he knew I was about to say something, so he spoke first.

"The drink is on me."

I gave him a phony smile. "Thanks."

He handed her the money, and based on their conversation, I could tell they definitely knew each other. I was about to walk away, but he stopped me. "Hey, ma, what's your name?"

I was really not in the mood for this lame-ass nigga who thought he was about to get some play because he bought me a twelve-dollar drink.

"Trina," I lied. It was the first club name I could come up with.

"Can I talk to you for a minute?"

I had to get rid of him quickly, fast and in a hurry. "Nah, my dude is looking over here. I have to go." I didn't give him a chance to respond before I took off in the other direction. Chyna, Mercedes, and Nehiya were standing in the cut, waiting on me to return so we could get to the V.I.P. section. We walked upstairs, found a table, and posted up. The D.J. was playing some new, hot rapper.

Just as I was about to get comfortable, I spotted an entourage of niggas off in the corner, and from what I could see they were jocking hard. Of course I played it cool and turned my head as if I had no interest whatsoever. Not even a minute later one of them was out of his seat and heading our way.

"Excuse me, Miss Lady, how you doing?" His speech was slurred.

"I'm okay."

He was an okay sight to look at, with the exception he was completely wasted.

"How about you and your girls come over here with me and my squad and I'll buy y'all a bottle?" He paused. "What y'all drinking on?"

I had no intention on drinking, but I did tell him to get a bottle of Patron. When the waitress returned, she told him the bottle was one-sixty. He pulled out a bankroll of nothing but hundred-dollar bills. From that point I knew he was paid, and he wasn't only flossing with that big-ass Cuban link draped around his neck with a diamond-studded cross and a matching bracelet.

All night long I showed him so much attention by dancing on him, getting his dick hard and telling him anything he wanted to hear.

He whispered in my ear, "Lets get a room."

"I can meet you there instead of riding with you and your crew."

"You don't have to do that. I'm riding solo."

I could tell by the way he responded that he was a fast-talker and was used to talking bitches out of their panties, but little did he know I was on a whole different level from the rest of the bitches he was used to fucking.

I smiled mischievously. "Is that right?"

"Yeah," he replied.

"Okay, let me tell my girls and I'll be right back."

After I put my girls up on game, we broke out like bandits. When we made it downstairs, a voice called out. "Hey, Khalil, are you leaving, man?" I kept walking so I wouldn't be seen.

"A'ight, my nigga, I'll holla at you tomorrow."

Khalil and I walked outside and stopped by the valet booth. He handed the valet guy the ticket while we waited on his car. A few minutes later an all-white Porsche truck with 24-inch rims pulled up and stopped in front of us.

"I see you got some cash, Mr. Khalil," I grinned.

"Come on," he said as he escorted me to the truck. I climbed inside and sat back so I could relax. Club Tornado still had a line of people waiting to get in when we pulled off.

Approximately twenty minutes later we were pulling up to Comfort Inn & Suites. I sat in the truck and waited patiently.

Once we were upstairs, I sat and made small talk while I watched him down two full cups of Hennessey. This dude was really fucked up and taking too long to pass out. My cell phone buzzed; it was Chyna. I texted her back and gave her the room number. When Khalil went into the bathroom, I put the key outside the door and sat down on the bed. When the bathroom door finally opened, he came out wearing a t-shirt and a pair of boxers.

He was ready to fuck.

"Come lay on the bed," I instructed. He did exactly what he was told. I straddled him while kissing him on his neck and chest. He was anxious to get started, but I needed him to relax. I stuck my hand in his boxers and jacked him off slowly. He must have thought he was about to get some head by the way he was pushing my head down.

The door crept open slowly and Chyna slid in like a thief in the night with Mercedes on her heels. Khalil was so lost in the moment he didn't know what hit him, but I did. It was the butt of Chyna's all-black gun. One hit was all it took, thanks to the Visine I dropped in his cup. I jumped up quickly, making a mad dash for his pants while they stripped him of his jewels.

***

Back at the house we all sat on the bed and counted out the money we took. "I can't believe this dumbass nigga was in the club with eight stacks in his pocket."

Nehiya looked at me. "Yeah, Barbee, you picked a good one."

I gave her a devilish grin. "Well, you know how I do. And to top it all off, the fuck-nigga wasn't even strapped."

Mercedes laughed. "Damn, I love a lame-ass nigga."

After the money was counted, I walked into our spare room and removed the huge painting that hung on the wall. I punched in the security code and pulled the lever to open the safe. We had stashed half of a million dollars in less than six months. I guess we could say business was sweet.

Every female had a hustle, whether it was boosting, working a nine-to-five or selling pussy, but not I. Robbing these dope boys was my hustle. It was simple and quick, no education needed. When it came down to it, pussy made a nigga weak, and they fell short every time. I learned this early in the game by an old-school cat named Fox. He used to have me setting up dudes in my younger days. We would take trips out of town twice a month and hit up big-time drug dealers and the local loan sharks.

Fox was a dirty old bastard, and he got just what he deserved, especially after using me for two years. About two summers ago he was found dead in a sleazy roach motel. His throat was slit and he was face down, butt-ass naked, with a dick in his ass. Yes indeed, he had been officially fucked, and that served him right. I could've been a rich bitch right about now, sitting on a mountain if I knew what I knew now.

"Barbee," Chyna yelled, bringing me back from memory lane.

"What?" I yelled back.

"Come get the phone."

"I'm coming." I closed the safe and put everything back in its place before walking into Chyna's room. "Did you answer it?" I was hoping she didn't.

"No, I only made it stop ringing."

She handed me the phone, but I sat it back down after I looked at the screen.

"Who was that?" Nehiya asked.

"Jeff."

"Oh you're not talking to him anymore?" Nehiya folded her arms across her chest.

"I told his ass to stop calling me this late. Shit, it's three in the morning. I don't know what his problem is, but if I answer it, his ass is getting cursed the fuck out, simple as that."

"Well don't answer him." Mercedes stated. "'Cause you know his feelings are easily hurt."

"Fuck his feelings!" I snapped. Not on her, but at the situation. "He already knows what it is. He better man up and get some balls."

"How can he get some when you always cutting them off and handing them back to him?" Mercedes replied.

"You know I don't care anything about that, and you shouldn't, either."

Mercedes sucked her teeth. "Now, you know I'm the last person to give a flying fuck about his feelings. Besides, he's a pussy, anyway. He'd jump off the Eiffel Tower if you told him to, but if he likes it, I love it."

"And you know I love it, right?" I grinned.

"Shit, I don't blame you."

I walked toward the door. "I'm going to bed. I'll see y'all in the morning."

"Good night," they replied.

My eyes were heavy and sleep was near. I walked into my room and switched off the light before jumping into my bed and pulling the comforter over my head.

***

The next morning we were up and at it. The weekends — Saturday, to be exact — were our shopping days. We would spend hours and hours in the mall, going in and out of every store.

"I'm tired as hell," Nehiya complained while strolling behind us. That was to be expected, considering the weather was a scorching 91 degrees. That was one thing about South Florida that drove me crazy: the damn heat index. I swear it was hell on Earth.

"I don't know why. It ain't like you did shit last night," Chyna joked.

"You must be crazy, because I was the driver," Nehiya became defensive.

"How could we forget that? But it's okay, because you have the next lick," Chyna said.

"Oh, baby, you ain't said nothing but a word. I got this."

I couldn't help myself. I had to join in. "Tell them you would lay a nigga down quick. Don't let the shy shit fool you."

"Oh, ok, I see you co-signing that mess," Chyna added.

"Damn right, but tonight we chilling." I knew they wouldn't agree.

"Damn it, Barbee, why?"

"I just want to chill tonight and party. Besides, I want to sit back, observe, and hit a major lick, but that takes research. They are having a grand opening for this new strip club called Flexx in Palm Beach. I know it's going to be a lot of ballers in the building, so I want to take it slow and clean house. I have that Mossberg pump I've been dying to use."

Chyna glanced at me. "You just trigger happy."

"That's not true," I smiled. "I only shoot when necessary." I had to defend myself, although she was a little more than right.

"Now you know you need to quit, Bee, because you get off to that shit."

"Y'all leave her alone. It's not her fault she's a control freak," Nehiya laughed.

"Damn, you too, Nehiya?" I had to express my inner emotions. "I can't deny your accusations because I love being in control, and I can't help it." I was getting caught up in the moment. "I get this rush, like I'm unstoppable like that dude in crank."

"Is that right?" Nehiya asked.

I paused for a second. "I feel like I'm the female Jessie James of my time."

"Girl, you are crazy as hell."

***

I hit the alarm on my brand new Lexus and filled the trunk with our shopping bags. It was still early when we made it back to our middle class neighborhood, which was extremely nice and quiet. We had six bedrooms, four bathrooms, a den, and a swimming pool.

Life for us has not always been this sweet; we had to work hard to get to where we were. We decided at a young age we wanted to have nice cars, expensive clothes and the biggest houses, so we made it happen and never looked back.

Chyna, Mercedes, and I grew up together, thick as thieves. Although Mercedes was not our blood sister, we shared the same bond. We met her in the fourth grade, and by the time we were juniors in high school her parents were killed in a car accident. Mercedes didn't have any immediate family, so my mother and father took her in and treated her as if she was one of their kids.

The transition was easy for the most part, but things got a little rocky after my 16th birthday. I had become this rebellious soul, and all I wanted to do was run the streets. That's what happens when a girl gets her first piece of dick. No one can tell her what to do. I was sneaking out of the house, and one day my father got tired of it and changed the locks on my ass. He wouldn't let me in the house, and I was forced to live in those same streets. One thing I learned quickly was the streets didn't love me back.

After getting kicked out, I went to live with Meat and his mom, but that shit was cut short, and I was back where I started. One late night I was chilling with the neighborhood hustlers and I was approached by Fox. My life changed from that point on. It took two years for me to come to my senses and dip out on that nigga, and just like clockwork I was back with Meat once again – but this time around he had his own place.

Chyna was the child who listened to my parents and didn't give them any problems. After I was kicked out, she wasn't allowed to talk to me. However, she would sneak away and come visit me just to make sure I was okay. If my father knew, he probably would've kicked her ass out, too, for disobeying his rule.

There was never a doubt he loved me because he cried as I stood on the opposite side of the door, begging for him to let me in. I could remember seeing his tear-stained face like it was yesterday.

"Barbee, baby, I cannot let you back in here. You wanted to be an adult so bad, so here's your chance. One day you will realize everything I tried to instill in you was for your own good."

"Daddy, I'm sorry. Please don't kick me out."

He shook his head and cried. "I'm sorry, baby, but you have to learn the hard way. You made a hard bed, and now you have to sleep in it."

Chyna heard the commotion and ran to the door. "Daddy, let her in, please."

He turned to face her. "She can't come here, and I better not catch you talking to her."

"But she's my sister."

"I will not allow her to corrupt you. I've done all I can do for this girl. If I can save one of y'all, I've done my job." My daddy turned to face me. "It's a tough world out there, baby doll, so be careful and remember I love you, no matter what."

My daddy closed the door on me, and I had no choice but to face the world alone.

Nehiya joined the circle when I was out getting money with Fox. She was running the streets and hanging out with the local petty hustlers. I took her up under my wing as a little sister and taught her the game. During her teenage years she spent her time bouncing between different group homes thanks to her mom being an unfit parent and living from pillow to post. One day Nehiya's mom and uncle got into it because she left her home alone on one too many occasions. Completely fed up, he called the police on his sister and Nehiya was removed from the home. To this day she had no relationship with her family.

I remember when I first introduced her to Chyna, she was not having it. She couldn't get over the fact I befriended a complete stranger and brought her into our circle. I could hear her now.

"Why are you bringing that snake around us?" Chyna pouted.

I would always brush off her comment as a form of jealousy, so she eventually let go and the comments stopped.

One thing about my clique, there was no one who could tear us apart, and there was no way we would allow anyone else in our circle, let alone our home. Our plans were all the same: no settling down, getting married, or having kids. Our focus was simple: get money, stay single, and live lavish. Our rules were not to be broken. There were no niggas whatsoever to step foot or sleep in the Pussy Palace, our home. Our motto was written in stone: fuck a nigga and his friends and take them motherfucking ends.

I parked my car in the driveway next to Chyna's Infinity Coupe. We kept our rental car in the garage until we were ready for work. There was no way in hell we were going to make our rides hot.

I popped the trunk. "Chyna, go and open the door."

After unloading the trunk and putting away my clothes, I was extremely tired. All I could do was lay on my king size bed and close my eyes. As soon as I was comfortable, I was rudely interrupted by Chyna.

"Get up!" she demanded.

"What do you want?" I whined. "Why are you in here?"

She sat her 125-pound frame right beside me. "I just got off the phone with Mommy, and she wants us to come over tomorrow for a barbecue."

"Is that all she wanted?" I was prepared for her to tell me we had to go to the store and pick up a few things on the way there.

"No, we don't have to go to the store this time."

I didn't reply. I was hoping she would get the hint and leave me alone, but she didn't. I rolled over. "What now?"

"She said call her."

"Okay."

I rolled back over so I could take a quick nap, and she was still sitting there. "I will call her when I get up." Two minutes had passed, and in walked Mercedes with her loud mouth.

"Black girl, get up," she shouted.

I snapped. "If you don't get your loudmouth-ass out of here, I am going to kill you." She totally ignored me and lay down directly in front of me. I could feel her breath blowing in my face. "I'm glad your breath doesn't stink."

She laughed. "Damn, I was hoping that it did."

"Why can't y'all just leave me alone for a little while?" All I wanted was a nap.

"You know we can't function without you," Mercedes said.

"I know."

It was crazy because I knew it was true. They depended on me like a cancer patient depended on chemo.

I could hear the sound of music playing. I knew it was my phone, and I also knew who the caller was, so I picked it up without hesitation.

"Hey, Amon, what's up?" I sat up with my back against my headboard.

"Just cooling. What you doing?" Amon asked while rolling up a blunt.

"I was trying to take a nap, but you can't get any sleep around here."

"Did y'all go out last night?" he asked.

"Hell yeah, we did."

"Was it smooth?"

"Like a baby's ass."

"I started to call you earlier, but I got tied up."

"Oh, I was out shopping anyway, so you probably wouldn't have gotten an answer."

He laughed, but I didn't catch what was funny. "Why are you laughing?"

"Because you are the only person I know who turns off their phone when they go shopping."

"I have to concentrate," I laughed with him. "Are you going to Club Flex tonight?"

"I thought about going. Are you?"

"Hell yeah," I replied.

"What time you heading out?" he asked.

"Eleven."

"Okay, we'll meet up and go together."

"I'll call you when I get dressed."

I was just about to hang up before he started talking again. "One more thing. Do you know about the cookout tomorrow?"

"Yeah, Mommy called Chyna and told her about it." Amon and I were first cousins, but we were more like sister and brother. Our mothers were sisters.

"Yeah, she called me, too. But I have to go. I have this crazy-ass chick waiting on me. I'll see you later."

"Ok."

I sat my phone down on the bed, stretched my arms out, and yawned.

"What did Amon want?" Mercedes asked while twirling her hair.

"He was trying to see if we were going out tonight."

"Why, is he going?" Chyna asked.

"Yes, ma'am."

I got up to escort Mercedes and Chyna out of my room and lock my door. There was no way I was going out without taking a nap first.

Chapter 2

Amon met us at the Marathon gas station, which was closer to the interstate. He was in his '71 brandy wine donk with 26-inch rims, and in the passenger seat was his best friend Corey. The two of them had been friends for as long as I could remember. I walked up to the car.

"What's up, Amon? It's just the two of y'all?"

"Nah," he replied. "Dame and Mike went inside the gas station."

I glanced at Corey as I watched him checking me out.

"Damn, you wearing the hell out of that leather, girl."

I blushed. "Thanks."

I knew I was looking good, and I never needed validation from a man, but with Corey I made an exception since he was close to the family. I always knew he had a thing for me, but I never wanted to cross that line with any of my cousin's homeboys. That would always cause a problem, no matter how much anyone tried to avoid it; therefore, I kept my distance. Now, don't get me wrong, Corey's a good catch. And the brother is absolutely, positively fine, so whoever locks him in will be one lucky-ass bitch. He was the type to buy a girl anything she wanted and everything she needed, but all of that came with a price to pay. Corey was a street nigga to the depth of his soul, and all he wanted was a female who was fit to be a housewife. I knew those were a pair of stilettos I wasn't willing to walk in, so I turned him down every time. I'm an independent bitch, and I stack my own paper, so I don't need no nigga telling me where to go, when to go, or how to spend it.

"So, when you gon' let me take you out?" Corey smiled.

I had to shut him down quickly because I already knew where he was trying to take this conversation, and this wasn't the place or the time.

"Corey, please. You can't do anything with me."

He sat his cup down on his lap. "What is that suppose to mean?"

"Exactly what it sounds like."

"So, you're saying I can't handle you?" He questioned me like I was speaking a foreign language.

"Bingo." I smiled. "That's exactly what I'm saying."

He looked at me with those bedroom eyes, and I almost forgot who I was talking to for a split second. "That's because you like messing with these lame-ass niggas. You need a real man like me that will tame your ass."

"You must be joking?" I laughed. "I almost thought you were serious for a minute."

"I am, now stop playing with me. I'll take you wherever you want to go."

"Is that right?"

"Hell yeah."

Nothing turned me on more than seeing this nigga beg, but I wouldn't tell him that. I figured Amon would step in and say something, but he didn't. "Okay, the next time you ask me, I will have an answer for you."

I wasn't expecting him to ask me again at that very moment, but he did.

"So, when can I take you out?"

"I will go whenever you're ready to trade places."

He was clearly confused. "What?"

"Whenever you're ready to stop wearing the pants and let me be in control, I will let you take me out."

Amon burst out into laughter. "Why are you giving my round a hard time?"

"Because he's used to these chicks who do whatever he says." I put my hand on my hip to show him I was serious. "I'm a different breed of what you used to. This is where you'll get it at."

Corey sipped his drink, obviously not intimidated by what I just said. "Keep thinking like that and I will show you exactly what I'm talking about."

I didn't respond since I saw Mike and Dame walking up to get in the car.

"What's up, Barbee baby?" Mike asked.

"Waiting on y'all so we can get to this club."

"What's good, B?" Dame said as soon as he was in earshot of me. "You're looking good."

I clearly ignored his comment out of respect for Corey. There was no need to add fuel to the fire while he was sitting there.

"Ready to party."

Corey jumped in without hesitation. "I don't know what for, and I better not catch you talking to anybody." He looked at Dame funny. "Stop talking to these niggas, and y'all can keep your eyes off of that one." He was specifically talking to Dame because Mike never came across as if he wanted to holla.

Corey faced me and pointed his finger in my direction. "Go get in the car, because you pissing me off. Amon, let's ride."

I smiled at Amon. "Hm. Somebody has an attitude. I guess I better walk away."

I walked back to my car, and before I could get all the way in, I could hear Chyna stirring up some shit. "I saw you over there flirting with Corey."

"You are awfully nosey if you saw that from over here."

"Whatever!" Chyna lifted her arm, telling me to talk to the hand.

***

Once we made it to the club, we stepped in like celebrities. We were sharper than a double-edged sword. Of course, I was rocking a black leather mini-skirt with the matching jacket and a pair of Cole Haan thigh-high boots. We strutted through all the crowds with style and grace, and I can't begin to say how many dudes were grabbing at us, trying to get our attention. We didn't stop until we made it to our designated area. Amon signaled for the waitress to come over.

"What can I get you?" she asked with a huge smile on her face.

"Louie VIII."

"Okay, I'll be right back." She walked away with a swish in her hips, just a little more than what she walked over with. Amon's eyes followed her until I broke his stare.

"You like what you see, huh?"

"Damn right."

She was wearing this pink and white referee outfit with booty shorts with a pair of pink and white Jordans. She was a yellow bitch, just the way Amon liked them. I could tell she was checking him out on a sly tip, but she wasn't sure if I was his chick or not.

Club Flex had a nice vibe to it — not the average strip club by far. Little miss high yellow returned quickly and set up our table. Corey fixed me a drink and handed it to me.

I was just about to sit down until I heard my song, *Fuck boi,* banging through the speakers. There was no way I could sit still. I stood up and rapped along with the music while holding my drink in one hand and waving the other in the air. Of course I had to put on a show, so I swung my hips slowly and seductively to the beat. They say men can tell if a woman can fuck by the way she dances. I can do both, and Corey's stares were proof he wanted to find out how true it was.

My girls were right at my side, performing like we were on stage. I was enjoying myself, but at the same time I was scoping out the big spenders, the ones who popped plenty of bottles and threw plenty of bills. I'm not talking about a few dollars here and there or the ones who had the strippers sitting in their laps, having a conversation. All that meant was they were trying to run game because those pockets were weak. I mean the ones making it flood, fuck making it rain. I'm talking about a tsunami. Damn, a hurricane.

My eyes locked in on this dude who was holding a gold bottle of Ace of Spade. He was well dressed and clean cut. I watched discreetly as the waitress handed him several stacks of bills. He put a few bills in her hand and she walked away smiling, he must had given her one hell of a tip. Based on the way he carried himself, I knew he wasn't lame, and he watched his surroundings carefully. That shit didn't matter to me because I loved a challenge. I knew for a fact I could clean his ass out faster than a cat can lick his ass, and his tongue drawn out. Tonight was a regular party night, but I was taking mental notes. Everyone else was making it their business to get fucked up, but not me. My mind stayed on the money, and I wouldn't have it any other way.

Amon yelled over the music, "Are you okay?"

I hollered back, "I'm good, just watching these three cut up like they work here."

When the strip club's theme song came on, *Throw This Money*, I could see the dude I was watching followed directions well. He was doing just that: throwing that money. He stood off in the cut, throwing money on this chick who was giving him a private dance.

Every one of his actions let me know he was cautious. He had his back against the wall to keep a nigga from sneaking up from behind. If anything went south, he would be face-to-face with any man. This dude had my undivided attention, and I'm not talking about just on a getting-money-tip, either. I'm talking about on a take-me-out-and-fuck-me level. He was so smooth and laid back. Let me just say that his swag was sickening, and he knew it, too.

I thought about catching him on the next go-round, but my mind was telling me tonight was the night. Throughout the night I sipped on a cup of Patron. I had to make sure I was alert at all times, and besides, somebody had to watch my girls. Every once in a while I would lock eyes with my target. He would sip from his cup and give me a smile. At that point I knew I had his ass. All I had to do now was wait on the perfect opportunity to make my next move.

The DJ came over the speaker to make the announcement they were about to start their first boxing match. "Welcome to Club Flex's grand opening. Tonight we have something special for the ballers and ballerettes in the building. I don't know about y'all, but watching two naked women fighting makes me a very happy man." He laughed at his own joke. "Now coming to the stage, we have Cocoa and Sparkle."

The two females stepped in the ring wearing thongs and pasties. When the bell rang, the fight began, and they were duking it out. There were titties and ass all over the place. The men were going wild. The things we do as women really doesn't surprise me, but it's so funny to watch the men react. The way they shouted and yelled was as if they were watching a boxing match with Kimbo Slice.

After watching the fight, I rounded up my crew so we could call it a night. One thing you wouldn't catch me doing is closing down a club. I left that for the thots to do. Those are the fly-by-the-nights that sit around until the end and see who they can pick up. They usually end up with the scraps. Real bitches leave the club early and still get what they want. Trust and believe if he want a woman, he will hit that exit door with the woman, ready or not!

On my way out of the club, I went to find Amon. I found him chilling at the table with the referee chick. I glanced at her, and then back to him.

"I'm about to leave."

She must have thought I was his girlfriend, judging by the look on her face. "I guess I'll go," she whispered. I guess my facial expression was one of those I'll-slap-a-bitch looks.

"Nah, you don't have to get up. I'm not his girlfriend." I could sense the relief she felt.

Amon grinned. "Chill out, mama. That's my cousin." He looked at me. "Y'all out?"

"Yeah, you know I can't close the club down." I stood with my hand on my hip.

Amon stood up, then turned his attention to his company. "Sit right here. I'll be right back." She looked like she wanted to say something, but she didn't. "I'm going to walk her outside real quick."

"Okay," she replied.

As soon as we were out of hearing distance, he laughed. "Man, Barbee, you be spookin' these hos." We walked side-by-side.

"I know, and I don't do it on purpose all the time."

"Li'l mama was ready to dip out on a nigga."

Chyna joined in. "Yeah, these hos better recognize." She was pretty tipsy.

"You know you don't have to walk us all the way outside." Persuading him to turn around was a hard task. As we made our way to the exit, I noticed the big spender in front of me. He seemed as though he was waiting for me, but then he noticed Amon. I tried once again to get rid of him. "You can go back. We got this."

He was a tad bit skeptical. "Are you sure?"

"Yes, I'm sure." I loved the way he looked out for me, but right then I was on a mission, and if he didn't turn away, he could blow my chances.

"Are you strapped?" he asked out of curiosity.

I rolled my neck. "Now, you know I stay strapped. Go back and grab your chick. We are good. I promise."

Reluctantly, he stopped in his tracks and let us go. "A'ight. Call me when you get in the car and when you get home." Amon strolled back toward the entrance.

"Okay."

When I finally made it out, I didn't see my target anymore, so I figured he had to be outside. The parking lot was well lit, and I counted about four security guards patrolling the area. That was a surprise. There aren't many clubs with a good security system.

I scoped the lot out, but I didn't see who I was looking for. "Fuck it," I exhaled just a little too loudly.

"What?" Chyna asked.

I was steady, trying to peep the scene. "Nothing," I lied.

"It's something, so quit lying."

"There was a guy I wanted to talk to, but I lost him," I finally confessed.

"Oh."

She wasn't on her game, so that's the type of response I expected to hear from her. But Nehiya and Mercedes were on point. They both replied, "How?"

"I had him in my sight when we were leaving. I was about to get at him, but Amon didn't walk away quick enough. When I finally got him to go back, dude was gone."

Mercedes replied, "No sweat. We'll be back. And if we don't find him, we'll just get a new one."

As soon as she finished her statement, a smoke-gray Challenger pulled up and stopped in front of us.

I hit the alarm on my car and opened the door quickly so I could get to my Berretta. I reached my hand under my seat and drew my weapon. I had my finger on the trigger, ready for anything. Chyna had her Glock 40, Mercedes had her Glock 40, and Nehiyah had a semi-automatic pistol. We were fully loaded and ready to empty our clips on whoever was in the car.

The inside light came on and the passenger window came down. I could tell there was only one person in the car, but I wasn't about to chance that. I was ready, and so were my girls.

I looked a little closer and a little bit harder, and I realized it was a familiar face. A face I was looking for. He stepped out of the car, but he was cautious. Either he knew what time it was or he didn't want to appear as a threat. At that moment I was sure I wasn't in harm's way, and I sat my weapon down.

"How you doing, beautiful? Can I talk to you for a second?"

I acted as if I was uninterested. I didn't want to appear thirsty. "What's up?"

Tall, brown, and sexy introduced himself as Rich and informed me he had his eyes on me all night. The feeling was definitely mutual, but that was for me to know. We spent another five minutes having a shallow conversation. It wasn't deep, just a brief introduction about one another. After we exchanged numbers, he called my cell right away to make sure I wasn't playing games.

"Oh, you didn't believe I gave you the right number?"

Rich had the most gorgeous smile I'd ever seen, despite the fact he had golds in his mouth. "I'm just making sure I'm not wasting my time."

My arms were folded across my chest. "If I didn't want to be bothered, I would've gotten in my car and pulled off on you."

"Oh, really?" he grinned.

"Yes, really."

"Well, I won't hold you up any longer. It's already late, and a woman like you shouldn't be driving this time of the night."

"And what does that mean?"

"It's dangerous out here, that's all I'm saying."

That made me laugh, because he had no idea who he was talking to. "Hell, I am dangerous, so they better be careful. I'm the one they should be worried about."

Rich laughed like I told some sort of joke. "Aw, look at you."

"Yeah, look at me. Don't let the baby face fool you."

"I won't." He flashed those golds again. "Go ahead and go home. I'll call you tomorrow. Drive safe, beautiful."

"I will." I got into my car and pulled off.

Setting Rich up was running through my mind, but I starting to second-guess myself. That was something I never did when it boiled down to getting my money. Mr. Rich had me intrigued, to say the least, and I was curious to find out more about him.

The look on my face must have been a dead giveaway for Mercedes. "I guess we have to find a new target?"

"Why you say that?" I was playing dumb like I didn't know what she was talking about.

"You know what I'm talking about. You out there exchanging numbers and shit." Mercedes sounded big mad.

"Duh, I need to talk to him first."

"Barbee, miss me with the bullshit, okay? I know you like a book, and I know that you feeling the dude."

I brushed her comment off. "Girl, please. I don't even know this dude well enough to like him."

"If you wanna get at the dude, then go 'head. It ain't like we can't find another target."

"Oh, trust and believe that if I want him, I will keep him. If not, we can rob his ass blind, but first I need to do my research and see what he working with."

My intuition was telling me he had that sack, so I was sticking to my guns. It hadn't let me down thus far. My chances at being wrong were slimmer than hitting it big on a Vegas slot machine.

I was so caught up in the moment I almost forgot to call Amon. He didn't answer, so I left him a message.

Once we made it home, I went straight to the shower and made it hot and steamy. My legs wouldn't allow me to be great, so I couldn't take a Moses shower. I had to take a ho bath and call it a night. Due to sleep deprivation I couldn't wait for my head to hit the pillow. I applied lotion to my body quickly and slipped on a sleeping shirt and dived into the bed headfirst. As soon as I closed my eyes, my cell rang.

"What the fuck man!" I mumbled. My mind just knew that it was Amon calling, but I was in for a surprise when I heard the man of the hour on the receiving end. Mr. Rich himself. I caught myself smiling. Normally I wouldn't entertain a conversation this time of the night, but for him I would have to make an exception.

"Did you make it home safe?"

"As a matter of fact, I got in, like, twenty minutes ago."

"That's good to hear. I couldn't let myself go to sleep without knowing you were okay."

My mind quickly responded, *Aw, that's so sweet,* but my mouth said something else. "Are you sure you not calling to make sure I don't have a man at home?"

"Damn, baby, you don't hold no punches. I'm just trying to make sure my future lady didn't get kidnapped."

Did this man just call me his future lady? I thought to myself. *Yes, he did!* I couldn't see his face, but I could hear the smile in his voice.

"I guess I can give you the benefit of the doubt."

"Thanks. I appreciate that," he replied. "I see you're very blunt and outspoken."

That made me giggle a bit. "Oh, baby, you haven't seen or heard nothing yet. If I want to know something, I will ask. For instance, do you live alone?"

"As a matter of fact, I do. Why? Do you want to come over?"

"You sure about that?"

"I can show you better than I can tell you. Maybe you can come over one day and cook a hungry man a meal?"

Based on this conversation, I wasn't dealing with a rookie. Therefore, I knew I would have to play my cards right with him.

"That's a privilege." I caught myself yawning into the phone.

"We'll see about that." He paused for a second. "Well, I can see that you're tired, so I'll give you a call tomorrow so you can get some rest."

"You mean later on today?"

"Oh yeah, my bad, I'll call you later on. Sweet dreams, beautiful."

"Goodnight."

That fine piece of male specimen had me blushing my ass off. I knew I would have sweet dreams.

I tried Amon one more time, and he finally picked up. Afterward, I put my phone on silent because I didn't want any more interruptions.

Sleep found me easily that night as I floated on cloud nine.

Go to Amazon to read: The Fetti Girls. Books 1 through 3 are available now!!

Submission Guideline

Submit the first three chapters of your completed manuscript to ldpsubmissions@gmail.com, subject line: Your book's title. The manuscript must be in a .doc file and sent as an attachment. Document should be in Times New Roman, double spaced and in size 12 font. Also, provide your synopsis and full contact information. If sending multiple submissions, they must each be in a separate email.

Have a story but no way to send it electronically? You can still submit to LDP/Ca$h Presents. Send in the first three chapters, written or typed, of your completed manuscript to:

LDP: Submissions Dept
Po Box 944
Stockbridge, Ga 30281

DO NOT send original manuscript. Must be a duplicate.

Provide your synopsis and a cover letter containing your full contact information.

Thanks for considering LDP and Ca$h Presents.

Coming Soon from Lock Down Publications/Ca$h Presents

BLOOD OF A BOSS **VI**

SHADOWS OF THE GAME II

TRAP BASTARD II

By **Askari**

LOYAL TO THE GAME **IV**

By **T.J. & Jelissa**

IF TRUE SAVAGE **VIII**

MIDNIGHT CARTEL IV

DOPE BOY MAGIC IV

CITY OF KINGZ III

By **Chris Green**

BLAST FOR ME **III**

A SAVAGE DOPEBOY III

CUTTHROAT MAFIA III

DUFFLE BAG CARTEL VII

HEARTLESS GOON VI

By **Ghost**

A HUSTLER'S DECEIT III

KILL ZONE II

BAE BELONGS TO ME III

A DOPE BOY'S QUEEN III

By **Aryanna**

COKE KINGS V

KING OF THE TRAP III

By **T.J. Edwards**

GORILLAZ IN THE BAY V

3X KRAZY III

De'Kari

KINGPIN KILLAZ IV

STREET KINGS III

PAID IN BLOOD III

CARTEL KILLAZ IV

DOPE GODS III

Hood Rich

SINS OF A HUSTLA II

ASAD

RICH $AVAGE II

By Troublesome

YAYO V

Bred In The Game 2

S. Allen

CREAM III

By Yolanda Moore

SON OF A DOPE FIEND III

HEAVEN GOT A GHETTO II

By Renta

LOYALTY AIN'T PROMISED III

By Keith Williams

I'M NOTHING WITHOUT HIS LOVE II

SINS OF A THUG II

TO THE THUG I LOVED BEFORE II

By Monet Dragun

QUIET MONEY IV

EXTENDED CLIP III

THUG LIFE IV

By **Trai'Quan**

THE STREETS MADE ME III

By **Larry D. Wright**

IF YOU CROSS ME ONCE II

By **Anthony Fields**

THE STREETS WILL NEVER CLOSE II

By K'ajji

HARD AND RUTHLESS III

Von Diesel

KILLA KOUNTY II

By Khufu

MOBBED UP III

By King Rio

MONEY GAME II

By Smoove Dolla

Available Now

RESTRAINING ORDER **I & II**

By **CA$H & Coffee**

LOVE KNOWS NO BOUNDARIES **I II & III**

By **Coffee**

RAISED AS A GOON I, II, III & IV

BRED BY THE SLUMS I, II, III

BLAST FOR ME I & II

ROTTEN TO THE CORE I II III

A BRONX TALE I, II, III

DUFFLE BAG CARTEL I II III IV V VI

HEARTLESS GOON I II III IV V

A SAVAGE DOPEBOY I II

DRUG LORDS I II III

CUTTHROAT MAFIA I II

KING OF THE TRENCHES

By **Ghost**

LAY IT DOWN **I & II**

LAST OF A DYING BREED I II

BLOOD STAINS OF A SHOTTA I & II III

By **Jamaica**

LOYAL TO THE GAME I II III

LIFE OF SIN I, II III

By **TJ & Jelissa**

BLOODY COMMAS I & II

SKI MASK CARTEL I II & III

KING OF NEW YORK I II,III IV V

RISE TO POWER I II III

COKE KINGS I II III IV

BORN HEARTLESS I II III IV

KING OF THE TRAP I II

By **T.J. Edwards**

IF LOVING HIM IS WRONG…I & II

LOVE ME EVEN WHEN IT HURTS I II III

By **Jelissa**

WHEN THE STREETS CLAP BACK I & II III

THE HEART OF A SAVAGE I II III

By **Jibril Williams**

A DISTINGUISHED THUG STOLE MY HEART I II & III

LOVE SHOULDN'T HURT I II III IV

RENEGADE BOYS I II III IV

PAID IN KARMA I II III

SAVAGE STORMS I II

AN UNFORESEEN LOVE

By **Meesha**

A GANGSTER'S CODE I &, II III

A GANGSTER'S SYN I II III

THE SAVAGE LIFE I II III

CHAINED TO THE STREETS I II III

BLOOD ON THE MONEY I II III

By J-Blunt

PUSH IT TO THE LIMIT

By **Bre' Hayes**

BLOOD OF A BOSS **I, II, III, IV, V**

SHADOWS OF THE GAME

TRAP BASTARD

By **Askari**

THE STREETS BLEED MURDER **I, II & III**

THE HEART OF A GANGSTA I II& III

By **Jerry Jackson**

CUM FOR ME I II III IV V VI VII

An **LDP Erotica Collaboration**

BRIDE OF A HUSTLA **I II & II**

THE FETTI GIRLS **I, II& III**

CORRUPTED BY A GANGSTA I, II III, IV

BLINDED BY HIS LOVE

THE PRICE YOU PAY FOR LOVE I, II ,III

DOPE GIRL MAGIC I II III

By **Destiny Skai**

WHEN A GOOD GIRL GOES BAD

By **Adrienne**

THE COST OF LOYALTY I II III

By Kweli

A GANGSTER'S REVENGE **I II III & IV**

THE BOSS MAN'S DAUGHTERS I II III IV V

A SAVAGE LOVE **I & II**

BAE BELONGS TO ME I II

A HUSTLER'S DECEIT I, II, III

WHAT BAD BITCHES DO I, II, III

SOUL OF A MONSTER I II III

KILL ZONE

A DOPE BOY'S QUEEN I II

By **Aryanna**

A KINGPIN'S AMBITON

A KINGPIN'S AMBITION **II**

I MURDER FOR THE DOUGH

By **Ambitious**

TRUE SAVAGE I II III IV V VI VII

DOPE BOY MAGIC I, II, III

MIDNIGHT CARTEL I II III

CITY OF KINGZ I II

By **Chris Green**

A DOPEBOY'S PRAYER

By **Eddie "Wolf" Lee**

THE KING CARTEL **I, II & III**

By **Frank Gresham**

THESE NIGGAS AIN'T LOYAL **I, II & III**

By **Nikki Tee**

GANGSTA SHYT **I II &III**

By **CATO**

THE ULTIMATE BETRAYAL

By **Phoenix**

BOSS'N UP **I , II & III**

By **Royal Nicole**

I LOVE YOU TO DEATH

By **Destiny J**

I RIDE FOR MY HITTA

I STILL RIDE FOR MY HITTA

By **Misty Holt**

LOVE & CHASIN' PAPER

By **Qay Crockett**

TO DIE IN VAIN

SINS OF A HUSTLA

By **ASAD**

BROOKLYN HUSTLAZ

By **Boogsy Morina**

BROOKLYN ON LOCK I & II

By **Sonovia**

GANGSTA CITY

By **Teddy Duke**

A DRUG KING AND HIS DIAMOND I & II III

A DOPEMAN'S RICHES

HER MAN, MINE'S TOO I, II

CASH MONEY HO'S

THE WIFEY I USED TO BE I II

By Nicole Goosby

TRAPHOUSE KING **I II & III**

KINGPIN KILLAZ I II III

STREET KINGS I II

PAID IN BLOOD **I II**

CARTEL KILLAZ I II III

DOPE GODS I II

By **Hood Rich**

LIPSTICK KILLAH **I, II, III**

CRIME OF PASSION I II & III

FRIEND OR FOE I II

By **Mimi**

STEADY MOBBN' **I, II, III**

THE STREETS STAINED MY SOUL I II

By **Marcellus Allen**

WHO SHOT YA **I, II, III**

SON OF A DOPE FIEND I II

HEAVEN GOT A GHETTO

Renta

GORILLAZ IN THE BAY **I II III IV**

TEARS OF A GANGSTA I II

3X KRAZY I II

DE'KARI

TRIGGADALE I II III

Elijah R. Freeman

GOD BLESS THE TRAPPERS I, II, III

THESE SCANDALOUS STREETS I, II, III

FEAR MY GANGSTA I, II, III IV, V

THESE STREETS DON'T LOVE NOBODY I, II

BURY ME A G I, II, III, IV, V

A GANGSTA'S EMPIRE I, II, III, IV

THE DOPEMAN'S BODYGAURD I II

THE REALEST KILLAZ I II III

THE LAST OF THE OGS I II III

Tranay Adams

THE STREETS ARE CALLING

Duquie Wilson

MARRIED TO A BOSS I II III

By Destiny Skai & Chris Green

KINGZ OF THE GAME I II III IV V

Playa Ray

SLAUGHTER GANG I II III

RUTHLESS HEART I II III

By Willie Slaughter

FUK SHYT

By Blakk Diamond

DON'T F#CK WITH MY HEART I II

By Linnea

ADDICTED TO THE DRAMA I II III

IN THE ARM OF HIS BOSS II

By Jamila

YAYO I II III IV

A SHOOTER'S AMBITION I II

BRED IN THE GAME

By S. Allen

TRAP GOD I II III

RICH $AVAGE

By Troublesome

FOREVER GANGSTA

GLOCKS ON SATIN SHEETS I II

By Adrian Dulan

TOE TAGZ I II III

LEVELS TO THIS SHYT I II

By Ah'Million

KINGPIN DREAMS I II III

By Paper Boi Rari

CONFESSIONS OF A GANGSTA I II III

By Nicholas Lock

I'M NOTHING WITHOUT HIS LOVE

SINS OF A THUG

TO THE THUG I LOVED BEFORE

By Monet Dragun

CAUGHT UP IN THE LIFE I II III

By Robert Baptiste

NEW TO THE GAME I II III

MONEY, MURDER & MEMORIES I II III

By **Malik D. Rice**

LIFE OF A SAVAGE I II III

A GANGSTA'S QUR'AN I II III

MURDA SEASON I II III

GANGLAND CARTEL I II III

CHI'RAQ GANGSTAS I II III

KILLERS ON ELM STREET I II III

JACK BOYZ N DA BRONX I II III

A DOPEBOY'S DREAM

By **Romell Tukes**

LOYALTY AIN'T PROMISED I II

By Keith Williams

QUIET MONEY I II III

THUG LIFE I II III

EXTENDED CLIP I II

By **Trai'Quan**

THE STREETS MADE ME I II

By **Larry D. Wright**

THE ULTIMATE SACRIFICE I, II, III, IV, V, VI

KHADIFI

IF YOU CROSS ME ONCE

ANGEL I II

IN THE BLINK OF AN EYE

By **Anthony Fields**

THE LIFE OF A HOOD STAR

By Ca$h & Rashia Wilson

THE STREETS WILL NEVER CLOSE

By K'ajji

CREAM I II

By Yolanda Moore

NIGHTMARES OF A HUSTLA I II III

By King Dream

CONCRETE KILLA I II

By Kingpen

HARD AND RUTHLESS I II

MOB TOWN 251

By Von Diesel

GHOST MOB

Stilloan Robinson

MOB TIES I II

By SayNoMore

BODYMORE MURDERLAND I II III

By Delmont Player

FOR THE LOVE OF A BOSS

By C. D. Blue

MOBBED UP I II

By King Rio

KILLA KOUNTY

By Khufu

MONEY GAME II

By Smoove Dolla

BOOKS BY LDP'S CEO, CA$H

TRUST IN NO MAN

TRUST IN NO MAN 2

TRUST IN NO MAN 3

BONDED BY BLOOD

SHORTY GOT A THUG

THUGS CRY

THUGS CRY 2

THUGS CRY 3

TRUST NO BITCH

TRUST NO BITCH 2

TRUST NO BITCH 3

TIL MY CASKET DROPS

RESTRAINING ORDER

RESTRAINING ORDER 2

IN LOVE WITH A CONVICT

LIFE OF A HOOD STAR